THE
PERFECT
BABY

BOOKS BY SAM VICKERY

One Last Second

My Only Child

Save My Daughter

Her Silent Husband

The Guilty Mother

The Child at My Door

The Promise

One More Tomorrow

Keep It Secret

The Things You Cannot See

Where There's Smoke

NOVELLAS

What You Never Knew

THE
PERFECT
BABY

SAM VICKERY

bookouture

Published by Bookouture in 2024

An imprint of Storyfire Ltd.
Carmelite House
50 Victoria Embankment
London EC4Y 0DZ

www.bookouture.com

Storyfire Ltd's authorised representative in the EEA is Hachette Ireland
8 Castlecourt Centre
Castleknock Road
Castleknock
Dublin 15 D15 YF6A
Ireland

ISBN: 978-1-83525-858-3
eBook ISBN: 978-1-83525-857-6

For Rob.
Who may someday listen to this story and smile when he hears
his name.

PROLOGUE

Some people don't believe I'm fit to be a mother. They think that somewhere along the jagged path of my life, I lost that right. That the mistakes I've made should stop me from having a child of my own. Over the past few years, I've had to keep a lot of secrets. I hide who I am. Because some people can't forgive me – even though I have forgiven myself.

But if there's one thing I've learned, it's that being a mother means more than simply rocking a baby to sleep and making sure they know their ABCs. It means being *strong*. Fighting for what you know to be right, even when the whole world tries to sabotage you, throwing out lazy accusations of being unfit... unsafe even.

They couldn't be more wrong about me.

This is what I was born to do, to *be*. To lie to myself and pretend otherwise would be a path to madness, simply intolerable. There's not even a choice. Not really...

I took a deep breath as the lift jolted to a stop, the doors squeaking as they rolled slowly open, offering a glimpse of the busy corridor beyond. I suppressed the urge to push them with my bare hands, tapping my foot to dispel the urge to break into a run. I wouldn't be so careless now. I was too close to the finish line.

Finally they opened fully, and I stepped out into the atrium of the hospital, losing myself in the crowds of patients coming and going, doctors rushing to the café on their break. The sound of the tiny newborn gurgle rose from the plastic bassinet I was wheeling ahead of me, and I looked down, seeing those beautiful green eyes fixed on mine, innocent, questioning almost.

Unable to suppress a smile, I paused, reaching into the crib to lift her gently into my arms. Everything about her brought me the sense of peace I'd been aching to find for so long. If I'd had a shred of doubt over what I was about to do, it would have been wiped out the moment I felt the reassuring weight of her in my arms, smelled her soft downy skin. She was everything. She wasn't mine to take, but that was irrelevant. This was my chance, and I wasn't going to blow it.

I pressed a kiss to her forehead and lowered her gently back into the waiting blanket, tucking it around her tiny body. Then, resuming my place in the crowd, I pushed the bassinet towards the wide glass doors, out into the sunshine.

And after that, everything was simple.

ONE
ELISE

I ran up the concrete slope, a magazine held over my head in lieu of an umbrella, smiling as the elderly woman waiting just inside the community centre pressed the button for the automatic door, letting me rush inside without slowing my pace. 'Thanks,' I said, dropping the magazine on a low table in the lobby, shaking off my thin cotton jacket and running my fingers through my wiry ginger hair. 'It's tipping it down out there!'

She returned the smile, nodding towards the path, where streams of water were running in rivulets, creating a puddle at the bottom of the slope. 'That's good old English summer for you, isn't it? Practically autumn now, and we've had barely a handful of nice days.'

I nodded, though it wasn't true. It had been a beautiful summer and I'd spent every moment I could outside, enjoying the sensation of the hot sun warming my skin, the smell of cut grass and dusty pavements bringing a sense of peace I'd been grateful for. Small pleasures that always made me stop and smile.

The woman, seeming to have a selective memory, continued, clearly getting into her stride. 'I always say August is the new April. Rains every bloody year now.' She lowered herself gingerly onto a chair, pointing to the steamed-up glass door. 'I feel for the kids on their summer holidays, cooped up with nothing to do. They go back to school this week, don't they? August was a complete washout for the poor loves, and now it looks like September will be just the same. It was endless sunshine when *I* was a kid. We lived at the beach in the school holidays. Never bothered with suncream either.'

I glanced at her face, seeing the brown sunspots on her temples, the laughter lines framing her sparkling blue eyes, and got the feeling she'd lived a full, happy life, taking risks, heedless of the consequences. 'I hope you're not heading out in that?' I said, trying to be polite though I was conscious of being late.

'My son's coming to get me. I'll be fine. I'm waterproof, you know.' She flashed another toothy grin, and I couldn't help but smile back.

I turned towards the desk, seeing the sign for the group I'd booked on to directing me to the large hall on the first floor. I'd been nervous before leaving the house, almost on the verge of not coming, but I'd forced my legs to move, telling myself I could just come the once – if I hated the dynamic, I didn't have to do it again. And it *would* be nice to meet some people going through the same experience as I was.

The carpet smelled damp, other people having trodden wet shoes through the halls, and the windows were coated with condensation, making it feel like a winter's day. I wasn't yet ready to let go of the balmy summer we'd enjoyed, still dressed in sandals and a cotton T-shirt, but the old lady was right – it felt like autumn was determined to make an early appearance this year, and now I found myself craving a cosy jumper to hide beneath.

I could hear the low rumble of conversation as I made my way towards the hall, the acoustics terrible. My stomach tightened nervously, my resolve faltering. I heard footsteps behind me and turned to see a middle-aged woman in a floral dress, red in the face as she carried a silver urn, presumably full of hot water. 'Trolley's broken,' she said by way of explanation. 'You here for the surrogacy support group, love?'

I nodded. 'Yes.'

'I'm Sheila. I run it. Go on in then. I'll bring this, and you can have a cuppa and meet everyone. We've got a lovely bunch here. Nice group.'

I walked a little ahead of her, stepping into the hall to find a group of eight women sitting on padded office chairs in a little circle. There was a man who looked around twenty standing awkwardly by a long table beneath the window, organising mugs and plates of biscuits.

'Thanks, Richard. Did you get the milk?' Sheila asked as I waited nearby, feeling self-conscious.

'Right here.' He nodded, then glanced over his shoulder at the group of women, looking like he wanted nothing more than to escape. 'Is that you all sorted then?'

'Yep. Off you go. You're needed on reception.' She turned to me. 'Help yourself to a hot drink and a biscuit, then go and join the others. We'll start in a few minutes.'

I picked up a mug, spooning instant coffee into it, casting furtive glances over my shoulder. Ignoring the biscuits, I turned, making for the one empty seat, on the far side of the circle. Most of the women looked to be around my age, mid thirties, with the exception of Sheila, who was closer to fifty. I wondered if she'd been through it all before, hence her qualification to start up the support group.

I sat down, gripping the handle of my mug tightly. The person to my left was deep in conversation with the pregnant lady on her other side, but the woman to my right smiled shyly as I made myself comfortable, extending a hand out over her swollen abdomen.

I felt a stab of emotion at the sight of it. I had actively

avoided anything to do with pregnancy for so long now, unable to cope with seeing the bloom of a woman's belly, to know that life thrived inside it while mine remained empty – a sterile, useless void. But, I reminded myself, things were different now. I wasn't in the same awful place I'd been before. I could do this. I forced my face into a smile. 'Hi,' I said, returning her handshake.

'I'm Maya. This your first time here?'

I nodded. 'Elise. Yeah. You too?'

She shook her head. 'No, I've been coming a few months now.' She rubbed her belly unconsciously.

'How far along are you?'

'Eight months. It's a little girl.'

I pressed my lips together to stop myself asking how she felt about giving the baby away. I wasn't sure what the etiquette was, how open to be, nor what might be considered offensive.

She saved me from having to ask. 'The intended parents are a lovely couple. They've looked after me so well. This little one is going to have a wonderful life; they're both lawyers, but the mother, Nina, will be taking a year off after the birth. They're in the South of France right now seeing her parents.' She leaned forward, lowering her voice. 'Her dad had a stroke, so they had to leave in a hurry. I wasn't expecting them to be gone so late in the pregnancy, but they're planning to be back for my next midwife appointment.'

'I see.' I noted that she didn't mention her own feelings and wondered how she could separate herself from the baby emotionally like that. It seemed like it came naturally, but I was sure there was more she wasn't saying. Then again, people like her were a different class. Angels, selfless. People like my sister. I glanced up as Sheila came to stand at the head of the group.

'Welcome, everyone! I hope you've had a good week?' She smiled around the circle as a murmur of voices rose, some of the group nodding or shaking their heads.

'I'd forgotten the backache. I'm fucking exhausted,' complained a woman with dark shadows under her eyes and a full, low bump. There were several echoes of agreement around her.

The woman to her left, her own abdomen notably flat, grimaced, then reached out to squeeze her hand. 'I'm so grateful for you, Laura. I wish I could take your pain away,' she added quietly.

Laura grinned nonchalantly, brushing off the comment with a light-hearted remark, but I saw the flash of pain in the other woman's expression and understood exactly what she was feeling. The guilt, that intense longing, wishing there could be some other way, that she had been gifted the opportunity to carry her own child, to have the privilege of feeling the slow roll and kick of the baby inside her and know that *she* had created it.

It had been hard for me to fathom how a group like this might work – the women desperate for a child slotted between others who had volunteered to birth babies for them. It was an environment that bred hurt, invited opportunities for pain, and I found it impossible not to see that now, watching the drawn faces of the hopeful women around the circle.

Sheila turned to look at me. 'We have a new member here today. Would you like to give us a quick introduction, love? Tell us a bit about what brings you here?' She phrased it like an invitation, but I got the distinct impression that it was an expectation.

I bit my top lip, half wanting to get up and leave as all eyes in the room swivelled in my direction, each woman waiting in silence for me to respond.

I stood up, my hands hovering over my flat belly, trying to push aside the shame I felt. 'I'm Elise. I'm here because, well, I've wanted a baby for so long. Being a mum is everything I ever...' My throat seemed to close around the words and I swal-

lowed, breathing in deeply through my nostrils as I dug my
fingernails into my palms.

'My sister, Julia... she's the one who's doing this for me,
but she didn't want to come. She's a pretty private person
– not one for groups. I hope it's okay that I'm here alone?'
I added hurriedly, looking to Sheila, who nodded. 'I
thought it would be good to meet some other women going
through the same journey, have somewhere to ask questions and find out the best way to support my sister. She's
doing this incredible thing for me, but I sometimes feel
this sense of just sheer humiliation... this overwhelming
guilt that I'm taking too much from her. That I don't
deserve it.'

Across the circle, Laura shook her head. 'She wouldn't have
agreed to it without giving it a lot of thought. Does she have kids
of her own?'

I nodded. 'She has two and she always said that's what she
wanted. But she's donated an egg to me... Mine are no good. I
can't—' I broke off, tears filling my eyes, and I suddenly wished I
hadn't come.

From beside me, Maya reached out and took my hand.
'There's no judgement here, Elise. We're all on our own journey
and there isn't a right or wrong.'

Sheila nodded as I sat back down, Maya still holding on to
my hand, as if she thought I might suddenly bolt. 'We can talk
about how best you can support your sister. And how to let go of
that sense of guilt and enjoy becoming a mother. How long
until the baby is due?'

'Three weeks,' I said, my voice uncharacteristically small.

'Not long. I know it's a roller coaster of emotions right now,
but honestly, the moment you have your baby in your arms, all
the worries and fears will fade away and you'll just be grateful
you took a leap of faith. Trust me.' She smiled. 'My son is nineteen now, and if it wasn't for my cousin, I'd have missed out on

what has been the most vital part of my life. Do you have a partner? A husband?'

I shook my head, thinking of the man I'd hoped would be by my side as I raised a family, and wished the question hadn't been asked. It brought up too many emotions. 'He... he wasn't supportive; I had to make a choice to go it alone.'

Maya's hand circled mine tighter. 'My partner isn't in the picture any more either. Their loss,' she said, her eyes twinkling, and I felt an intense liking for her, glad I'd found a friend. It had been a long time since I'd felt close to someone.

Sheila moved on to talk to another woman, who'd been having some trouble with her parents disagreeing with her choice to become a surrogate. I listened, fascinated, wanting to hear every detail. My phone beeped from inside my bag and I fished it out, intending to silence it. Discreetly, I clicked on the message that had flashed up on the screen.

I'll be coming to see you Wednesday at the usual time. I hope you're going to give me good news. I expect you to be on your best behaviour, Elise.

I felt the blood drain from my face, my fingers shaking as they gripped the phone, the primal response always the same whenever I thought of him. The instant urge to get up and launch it from the window, hear the satisfying smash as the screen shattered into a thousand pieces made my heart pound, my mouth turn dry. If only I could do just that.

Maya inclined her head, her expression filled with concern, and I realised she'd seen the message. 'You okay?' she whispered, nodding towards the phone clutched tightly in my palm.

'Yes.' I nodded, forcing myself to meet her eyes. I switched it to silent, dropping it back in my bag and picking up my coffee from the floor, taking a deep sip. She frowned but didn't push it, and I sat back, trying not to show how scared I was. I didn't want to see him ever again, but I had no choice. I would have to face him, whether I liked it or not.

TWO
MAYA

I dashed up the path, one arm cradling the weight of my belly, as the rain pelted down in stinging pellets, frigid against my cheeks, my hood slipping back to allow an icy rivulet of water to trickle down my exposed neck, making a shiver run down my spine.

Fishing around inside my bag, my fingers made contact with my keys and I yanked them out, shoving them into the lock and stepping inside, then slamming the door closed behind me. The one bonus about the flat I rented was that it was on the ground floor, with its own separate entrance – a fact I was grateful for. In my last place, I'd had to navigate the shared hallway, the neighbours rifling through my post on the table, the people who would leave bikes and buggies cluttering up the stairwell. The neighbours here weren't much better – I never went more than a few days without hearing some exaggerated row going on through the paper-thin walls – but at least I had the illusion of privacy. And it was all I could afford.

I shrugged off my coat, hanging it on the hook beside the door, then went to grab a towel from the bathroom to lay beneath it, the water already beginning to drip from the hem, creating a puddle on the floor. I wasn't about to lose my deposit by ruining the laminate. I was fanatical about keeping the place clean and tidy.

Heading into the kitchen to put the kettle on, I felt myself pause then smile, thinking of the group today, the woman who had sat beside me. Elise.

I'd noticed her the moment she'd walked into the room – that wild ginger hair, the way her almond-shaped green eyes had scanned the circle, taking us in one by one. I'd sat frozen, transfixed by her, knowing she would have to sit beside me in the only available seat, wondering what she would be like to talk to. To begin with, she'd made me nervous, but as the hour passed and she opened up about herself a little, I'd relaxed. There had been something in the way she'd looked at me that had made me feel seen. Connected to someone in a way I'd forgotten I knew how to do. She'd been so vulnerable as she stood up to introduce herself, and despite my natural inclination to shut myself away, keep my head down, right in that moment, I'd felt an overwhelming need to make her my friend. To help her.

The water came to the boil and I picked up a tea bag from the canister, dropping it into my mug, picturing her pale face, her curls that looked like they hadn't been brushed in a week. She'd been a breath of fresh air. I'd been going to the group for months, and not one of the women had ever tried to get to know me beyond surface level. To be fair to them, I never gave much away, but they were all so much louder, so confident in their opinions, and I often felt overlooked. But Elise had smiled when I'd reached for her hand. She'd seemed genuinely interested in me – not that I'd told *her* much either. I'd been surprised to discover that I liked her. There had only been one moment when I'd seen her face close off, and that had been after she'd got that text. I had a feeling her story with her ex was far from simple. She'd almost looked afraid.

I picked up my tea, carrying it through to the living room. The rain had stopped now, the sky still grey with the threat of more to come. Sighing, I sank down onto the armchair. The room was dim, oppressive, the bleak weather having sucked all the colour from the world, and as I felt a heavy kick beneath my ribs, the baby rolling slowly from left to right, I felt suddenly claustrophobic; overwhelmed by guilt, the emotion engulfing me, making it hard to breathe. My palm went to my bump, her kick strong against it, almost as if she were trying to communicate with me, and I dropped my hand, not wanting to feel it, to let myself be dragged into the darkness.

Despite feeling glad that I'd met Elise today, now, in the silence of the flat, with only my thoughts for company, I could feel the effort it was taking not to be dragged into the past, those memories I fought tooth and nail to avoid. Having her show me a scrap of warmth, a feeling I'd forgotten existed, had cracked the protective shell I'd donned – a shell that was necessary to keep me safe from myself – letting the dark tendrils of my past seep out. I didn't dare to look back, to remember the terrible events of the past, the awful things I had done. I couldn't risk letting her in – it had been a mistake to allow her to think we could be friends, and yet a part of me knew it was an opportunity I'd regret walking away from. I felt trapped, conflicted, forced into making a choice that had the potential to end badly for one if not both of us.

Yanking myself back up to stand, my hips aching with the effort, I paced to the window, wishing I hadn't let my guard down. I was exhausted, but I knew if I stayed here alone right now, I would find myself reliving the same old pattern. And I couldn't bear it. Not today. I wanted to escape my mind, switch it off. Distract myself until the memories quietened and I could breathe again.

Ignoring the steaming mug of tea on the table, I turned, striding back to the front door and shrugging on my sodden coat once again. I opened the door, stepping out into the cool, damp air. I had no idea where I was heading to. All I knew was that I needed to move, to be out of here. Anything was preferable to my own company.

THREE

ELISE

If there was one benefit to not carrying my own child, it was being able to eat and drink whatever I wanted. In fact, I mused now, I couldn't recall a time in my life when I'd consumed more blue Stilton and filter coffee. I carried the steaming mug and plate of cheese and crackers through the kitchen, into the gorgeous south-facing garden room that looked out over the size-able but overgrown lawn. I should be out there mowing before the rain came again, instead of hiding away indoors, but though the sky was a piercingly bright blue today, I wasn't deceived. I'd been out the front to bring the bins in and it was bitingly cold. Certainly no weather for gardening.

I sat in my favourite armchair, positioned just right so I could look out at the birds as they dived for the fat balls I'd tossed into the long grass, the birdbath in a near constant frenzy of visitors, and bit into a cracker, trying to savour the moment.

It was a silly trick I played on myself. Hoping that these little treats, these small pleasures would make up for the bigger things I was missing out on. It didn't work. Not if I was honest with myself. But it provided a distraction, and I needed as many of those as I could get. Today, though, it wasn't having the desired effect. The coffee tasted burned, the cheese cloying. It stuck in my throat, and I dropped the plate on the side table, feeling a surge of anger well up in my belly.

This room was supposed to be my sanctuary. A calming space to re-centre my mind, dispel the anxious thoughts that visited so frequently. I had made it everything I'd ever dreamed of. The polished oak flooring. The thick leafy green plants. The comfy jewel-coloured suite and brass floor lamps. There was a time when I would have pinched myself to think that I might own a house with a room like this. That I could call this space mine. And yet it was all wrong. Nothing as it should be. Try as I might, I couldn't paste over my pain with fancy rugs and soft ambient lighting. It was a crushing realisation, and it gave me cause to fear that nothing would ever have the desired effect. Nothing would be enough.

I leaned back in the chair, watching as a magpie swooped in on a blackbird at the feeder, scaring it away before pecking at the assorted seeds in the wire mesh with cocky self-assurance. I wished the blackbird would come back, fight his corner, not be bullied into submission, but as I watched him skitter over the fence into the neighbour's garden, I frowned. It was an impossible scenario. He knew his place. And the magpie understood he was king – at least in this little suburban English garden.

Sighing, I leaned forward, pulling my phone from my back pocket and pressing down on the thumbprint recognition. I had avoided looking at my messages since the surrogacy group yesterday. Of all the times for *him* to contact me, it had to have been then, I thought wryly. The woman, Maya, sitting beside me had looked at me with a question in her eyes. I'd been sure I'd seen concern – *pity* – etched across her open face, and I couldn't help but think she'd read what he'd written to me. The idea of strangers knowing anything about him, the obligations I was forced to keep up, made me feel vulnerable, exposed.

I had needed a fresh start. I'd spent far too long living in the pits of hell to want to spend a moment longer in any situation that reminded me of the past, and yet every time I thought I was taking a step forward, I found myself being dragged right back to the place I most wanted to forget.

I reread his message, hating that I couldn't text back and tell him no, he wouldn't ever see me again. I wouldn't keep answering to him. A surge of adrenaline fizzed in my veins as I closed my eyes, pictured blocking his number, not being here when he turned up to meet me. The way he would make that quiet little tut beneath his breath when he realised I'd stood him up, unwilling to let his irritation show. He was always so composed on the surface, but I knew it was a ruse.

I read his message one final time, then pressed delete, relinquishing the fantasy of leaving him waiting on the doorstep. It was a pipe dream. Impossible. I would jump to his demands as I always did, resentment crawling over my skin the whole time. I could never stand him up. But still, it was satisfying to imagine.

I dropped the phone on the arm of the chair, leaning my head back against the cushions, suddenly exhausted. Broken. My gaze travelled to the sideboard across the room, the locked cupboard, the heavy brass key wedged in place, my mind drifting to the contents inside it. If I opened it now, I could lose myself in better memories, from long before my life turned to shit. I could transport myself back to another time, another place. Forget the dread that was building inside my belly in the wake of the text – the anxiety about what he might be planning to say or demand of me.

The key seemed to call to me, and I turned my head away, fighting the urge to dash across the room, hear the click of the lock, empty the contents onto the rug and sink into the memories. A few months ago, I would have given in and done just that. Lost a day – a few days even – to what-ifs. But, I thought, as I watched the magpie chase off another songbird from his territory, I was stronger now. I'd learned to control my instincts, rise above them.

I kept my gaze from travelling back to the sideboard and instead picked up a baby catalogue from the coffee table, flipping to the clothes section. My heart swelled at the sight of the sweet little romper suits and doll-sized outfits. With a rush of determination that I *would* move forward on this new path, leaving the past in the locked cupboard where it belonged, I grabbed a pen to circle everything I still wanted to buy for the fresh start I was fighting for.

FOUR

MAYA

My feet pounded rhythmically against the treadmill, and I increased the speed, noting with a sense of frustration that despite my efforts, I was still considerably slower than I'd been before the pregnancy. Gazing through the full-length windows of the gym, I watched the people milling around six storeys below, strolling in and out of the shops, stopping on benches to eat artisan sandwiches and pots of stir-fry from the pop-up cafés in the square.

My stomach rumbled as I saw a woman plunge her chopsticks into a steaming cardboard carton, and I pressed my hand to my bump, making up my mind to go and get some noodles when I'd finished here. Not that I was sure I'd be able to stomach anything right now. My belly was churning with pent-up anxiety. Since the support group yesterday, I'd been struggling to keep calm. I felt as if meeting Elise, seeing the way she looked at me with such warmth – warmth I didn't deserve – had opened a chasm to the past, and despite my attempts to distract myself from the memories I longed to erase, I couldn't stop them seeping into my dreams, catching me off guard the moment I let myself relax. I'd woken in a cold sweat after a relentless night of hyper-colour nightmares, needing to run, to expel the guilt and tension from my nervous system before it drove me mad, and had come straight here without stopping for breakfast.

'Hey! You aren't going into labour, are you?'

I slowed the machine to a walk, turning to see who'd spoken. A man wearing a T-shirt with the gym's logo emblazoned across the front was standing just behind me, his arms folded across a chest that looked to be the product of either obsession or steroids. The veins in his arms protruded like writhing blue snakes, and I looked back to his face, no longer craving noodles.

'Because,' he continued, his tone matching his furious expression, 'I only had the floors done today. I don't want them ruined with you bursting your waters all over the show!'

'I'm perfectly fine, thank you,' I said primly. 'And I think you'll find it's not only very rude to ask a woman that but also a case for discrimination. I've paid to be here, so I'd appreciate it if you'd go away and let me finish my run.'

His eyebrows shot up, but he turned, muttering something under his breath, leaving me in peace, though I was bristling from his comments.

I sped the machine up, letting my legs work harder, enjoying the burn in my calves, the way the indignation flittered away with every long stride, my focus entirely on putting one foot in front of the other. My hips throbbed and my lungs felt fit to burst, but I didn't want to slow down. It had been so long since I'd moved like this. I had forgotten just how much I loved it, how it used to be the only thing that helped calm my mind. I'd given up my gym membership at Nina and Will's request. They'd been worried that any high-intensity exercise would put the pregnancy in jeopardy, and despite my personal desire to continue doing what I loved, I'd agreed I would stop. As I felt the heavy bulge of the baby's head low in my pelvis, I batted away a wave of guilt that I was breaking that promise. But plenty of women kept their exercise routines going through pregnancy. It was harmless.

I knew it was Nina's fear of miscarriage that fuelled her anxiety, her worry that something would go wrong, and I'd been understanding of that, tried to reassure her in every way I could, even if it meant inconveniencing myself. I'd answered her calls multiple times a day. I'd followed the diet sheet she'd helpfully provided for me. I even wore the clunky watch that monitored my sleep habits so she and Will could sign in to the shared app and see if I was getting enough rest.

As if thinking of Nina had somehow summoned her, my phone lit up in the holder on the treadmill, her name flashing, demanding to be picked up. With a sigh, I hit the stop button, bracing my hands on the rails as I waited for my legs to slow down. I grabbed my towel in one hand, swiping it over my face, then, feeling shaky from the run, answered the call, clambering off the treadmill and lowering myself onto a bench.

'Nina, hi, how are you?' I asked, kicking myself when I heard how breathless I was.

'Oh, Maya, you're so sweet to ask. You must feel so abandoned, what with Will and me leaving you like this. I feel awful about it all – I just don't know what to do!' Her voice was reedy, and I could picture her pacing back and forth.

A man's voice cut in and I knew I was on speaker. So many times I'd thought I was talking to just one of them, only for the other to chime in several minutes into the call, making me feel as if they were trying to catch me out, as if I might say more to one of them. It felt sneaky somehow.

'How are you doing, Maya?' Will asked, his tone gently probing. 'You sound breathless. Is our sweet little baby doing okay?'

I smiled to myself, noting that his concerned comment

wasn't for me but for his daughter. 'I'm fine,' I answered. 'I had to rush from the living room to get the phone, and the baby is compressing my lungs. It's reached the stage where everything is a challenge,' I added, hating that I had to lie but having no intention of telling them what I'd really been doing. I'd heard plenty of women at the surrogacy support group complain of the physical side effects of their pregnancies. I'd been lucky – my hips were beginning to ache now I was near the end, but it was still manageable. I hadn't even had the legendary morning sickness everyone had warned me about. It had almost been as if my body knew not to push me too far. That just undertaking the pregnancy was a challenge enough for me to get through.

'Oh, you should rest, darling!' Nina cooed.

'I will. And the baby's doing fine. Still counting the kicks.'

'Still ten a day?' she asked, anxiety pricking through her words.

I laughed. 'More like thirty! She thinks my womb is an assault course. How's your dad? Is he still in hospital?'

'Yes, and it's been a nightmare trying to organise what's going to happen next. Hardly any of the carers we contacted speak English, and you know Mum never really bothered getting to grips with the language, so that's a massive issue. She's adamant she won't let him be put in a nursing home, but she can't take on his care herself. The hospital said he can't stay there much longer. Quite frankly, it's a ridiculous situation! I think they're all expecting us to move down here and become live-in carers for him, but of course that's not an option. We have our work, and more importantly, we need to get back to you.'

'It sounds so hard. I'm sorry you're going through it,' I replied.

Will broke in again. 'Maya, have you had any twinges? Any signs of labour? Because we can come back – we'll just tell the hospital they'll have to sort it.'

'Will!' Nina exclaimed, and I heard her whisper something I couldn't make out. 'You *know* they'll put him in a care home!' she said, sounding desolate.

'It's fine,' I said, interrupting before they could fall out. 'I don't think she's coming any time soon. I feel great; I haven't had a single sign.'

'Good,' they said, their voices overlapping as they both seemed to sigh. 'But you'll let us know, won't you?' Will pushed. 'If anything changes? The first indication you get?'

'I promise. I'll call right away.'

'Oh, damn!' Nina exclaimed. 'The nurse is just outside the door – we have to go. Take care, Maya, and put your feet up. I'll call this evening.'

'And don't forget to eat those dates we sent over,' Will added. 'They'll soften your cervix; make for an easier labour. It's been proven. But only a few every day. We don't want to miss the big event!'

'Right.' I winced, holding the phone a little way from my ear. I said goodbye before they could drag it out any longer, then dropped it on the bench, feeling mentally drained.

Since finding out I was pregnant, I hadn't gone more than a day or two without seeing them. Humouring their fears, letting them paw my belly, even allowing them to rest their heads on my bare skin and read to the baby, Will's hot breath making my belly button damp; having to swallow down my natural instinct to shove him away, to remind myself that this was all part of what I'd signed up to. This trip to France was the first time I'd had to myself in months, and I realised with a sense of guilt that I was enjoying it.

I looked across at the treadmill, a surge of excitement welling up inside me. I stood, taking a step back towards it, then paused as the solid, hard ball of the baby's head sank lower, wedging itself in position, letting gravity do its work. Had the running forced her down? Or would it have happened anyway?

Feeling conflicted, I looked between the treadmill and the door, then, with a resigned sigh, I picked up my belongings and turned away. I was doing this for Will and Nina. They deserved to be home in time for the birth of their baby. What *I* wanted didn't matter. This was my penance, and I would do well to remember it.

FIVE

ELISE

'It's fucking freezing in here, Julia,' I said, pulling my long cardigan closer round my body and gesturing to the little oil-filled radiator in the corner. 'Doesn't that work?'

Julia raised an eyebrow, looking up from a stack of papers on her lap. 'Is it cold? I'm so hot these days,' she replied, her hand going automatically to her sizeable belly as it always did when she was reminded of the baby. 'This little one is like a constant hot-water bottle. You can plug it in, though, if you like,' she offered.

I shook my head. 'No, I'll be fine. Don't want you overheating, do we? And I'm not surprised you're hot. I don't think I ever saw a more glorious bump in all my life.' I walked away from the French windows and leaned down to touch her firm belly. There was a squirming flurry of limbs, reassuringly hard against the palm of my hand, and I smiled, picturing the tiny baby beneath. 'Not long now,' I whispered.

Julia looped her hand around my wrist, easing it back. 'I'm not comfortable... I'll just get some water. Do you want some?' She stood without waiting for an answer, going to pour a drink from a jug filled with iced water and lemon slices on the sideboard.

I frowned. 'You didn't have to get up. I could have done that,' I said, feeling annoyed that even now she still insisted on being so damn independent. I would have loved nothing more than to fetch her drinks, cook her dinner, rub her swollen feet even. Anything to feel like I was a part of the pregnancy, helping, making a difference, contributing in however small a way. But my every offer was rebuffed, and lately, with a tone of clipped impatience from her. It frustrated me no end, especially when I could see her struggling.

She took a long drink of water and remained standing by the sideboard, leaning back, her hand on the base of her spine.

'How are the family?' I asked. 'Kids okay?'

'They're fine.'

'And Ben?'

'He's fine too.'

I pursed my lips, waiting for her to offer up more, but she remained silent, and I got the feeling she'd rather be taking an afternoon nap than seeing me. She stifled a yawn, and I offered a sympathetic smile. 'You look done in.'

I walked over to her, reaching out to rub her back, and she stepped away. 'I'm really not keen on being touched, Elise. I know you're only trying to help, but I just feel very claustrophobic right now. I need you to back off.'

'I was only going to rub your shoulders. You're obviously aching.'

'I'm fine. And I don't want a massage. Thank you,' she said, that familiar clipped tone making yet another appearance. 'I'll be glad when the baby comes,' she muttered. 'I've really had enough of this.'

I stared at her, unsure what to say, and she shook her head, holding up a hand in front of her face, her index finger pressing

into the inner corner of her eyebrow as if she could rub the
tension from it.

'Sorry,' she said at last, looking up at me. She took a deep
breath. 'I'm sorry. That was unfair. I'm just tired – I didn't
mean to snap at you.'

'It's fine.'

I paced back to the French windows, looking out over the
manicured lawn, the rose bushes bare and spindly, having been
cut back in preparation for the autumn. It was a little early for
my liking – I'd have kept them blooming until the last petal
dropped. What was the point of rushing towards a season that
was long enough as it was? There were so few joys in this world,
why cut them short when you found one?

From this angle, I could just make out the upstairs window
where Julia's two children shared a playroom. Phoebe was
sitting on the sill, a doll in her arms as she fed it from a toy
bottle, and I smiled, trying to catch her eye, though she didn't
look down. Those kids were always cooped up indoors. It was a
shame when they had such a big garden they could be running
wild in. I tried not to mention those kinds of thoughts to Julia,
knowing how sensitive she was about her parenting, but secretly
I planned to raise my son very differently, immersing him in
nature at every opportunity. The thought of how soon I'd be
able to dive in and show my little baby all the wonders of the
world made a frisson of excitement rush over me, and I clasped
my hands together beneath my chin, buzzing with pent-up
energy.

Julia cleared her throat. 'Come and sit down, Elise. Tell me
how you've been. Do you have any news for me?'

I stared at Phoebe for a moment longer, then sighed,
wandering over to sit in my usual seat – a comfy armchair with
jade-green velvet upholstery. I leaned back against it. 'Did you
speak to the midwife? You know they're having staff shortages

again. You have to let them know in advance if you're planning a water birth – I told you that, didn't I?'

'Yes, you said. And I'm still not sure what I'll do. I'll decide when the time comes.'

I twisted my mouth, wondering why she didn't ask my opinion on the matter. I was perfectly aware that the birth itself was hers alone to plan and experience, and yet I was the one who'd spent every evening reading books on childbirth. I knew the statistics on how many epidurals ended in C-sections because of the baby going into distress. I knew that even *in utero*, the baby was absorbing the external environment, and that stress in the mother at this early stage could result in ADHD and anxiety disorders in the future. If it'd been me having the baby, I would have wanted everything calm. Dim lighting. Quiet voices. A warm, soothing pool. A peaceful entry into the world. It irritated me that Julia was so lackadaisical in making any sort of plan. I was certain she'd yet to even skim-read the books I had sent over.

I took a breath, reminding myself of how generous she was being, what she was giving up for me. It wasn't fair for me to dictate how she did any of it. But I was finding it so much harder than I'd expected to relinquish control and step back. It was *my* child in there, *my* son who would bear the conse-quences of her decisions.

She walked over, handing me a glass of iced water, and I took it, forcing myself to smile, to be kind. This was just her way. She'd always been the polar opposite of me. Secretive. Keeping the people she loved at arm's length. It was why I knew she'd be fine when it came to handing the baby over. She was able to detach herself in a way I could never have been capable of. The reality was, if the tables were turned and it had been Julia who couldn't have a child, as much as I would want to help, I just wouldn't be able to do it. It would destroy me. But Julia was different.

She sat down opposite me, placing her glass on the table and folding her hands across her belly. 'So, what have you been doing this week?'

I shrugged. I didn't want to tell her about the surrogacy group, I realised. I knew what she'd say. That it wasn't appropriate for me to be going there. She'd ask too many questions and it would open up a whole can of worms. She'd always been a closed book. She wouldn't understand my need to meet others in the same boat as us. She saw it as a family matter, not something to brag about in company. 'I made a new friend,' I said, thinking of Maya, the woman who'd sat beside me. 'I went to a group.'

'Oh?'

'Just a craft thing. Pottery painting. I met a nice woman there and we hit it off.'

'That's great, Elise. Will you go back?'

I nodded, thinking of the way I'd felt supported in a way I couldn't remember. It had been so long since I'd let anyone new into my life. Too long since I'd been able to trust in anyone. It would be nice to be close to someone again.

'Yes,' I said, sipping my drink as I looked over the rim of the glass, my eyes meeting hers. I thought of Maya's bump. The child growing inside her. 'I think I will.'

The rain pelted against the window, relentless and angry as it hammered at the glass, and I suddenly remembered there had been a leak in the loft last time there'd been a few weeks of weather like this. It seemed so long ago now, and while I'd meant to get someone out to fix it back then, life had got in the way, and now I was sure it was only a matter of time before I heard the unwelcome trickle of water seeping in through the cracks, splashing onto the floor.

I sighed, unable to summon the energy to do anything about

it. I hated this kind of thing. Workmen, deliveries, organising the big jobs around the house – of which there seemed to be so many – it all felt so overwhelming. The more the to-do list grew, the more I chose not to see. As had become my habit, I turned on the radio, drowning out the sound and pretending it didn't matter. Let the Elise of next week deal with it. It was only water after all.

I poured boiling water over my tea bag and breathed in the familiar smell of mint as the steam rose from my favourite mug. It had been a gift from a man – and a time – I tried not to think about. We'd never bought expensive gifts, preferring things that would either have some meaning to them or make each other laugh. The mug had been both. In a nod to our first night spent at his flat, where we'd ordered a takeaway and watched *Red Dwarf*, it was printed with the quote *Everybody's dead, Dave*, along with a picture of Holly, the spaceship's computer. It was a line he'd used on me many times over the years when I'd asked too many questions. 'What? Your mum *and* your sister both got stuck in traffic and won't make it to dinner?'

'Yes, Dave. Everybody's dead, Dave.'

'So you're telling me that Tesco was out of beef *and* chicken? *Really?*'

'Yes, Dave. Everybody's dead, Dave.'

It was silly. But it was one of those little in-jokes we'd shared that made us uniquely us. It made me sick to remember that now – given everything that happened later. I stirred the tea, squeezing the flavour from the fragrant bag, and picked up the mug. I really should let it go. Replace it with something without so many conflicting emotions attached. But I could never seem to bring myself to throw it in the bin.

I was drained after my visit to Julia this afternoon. Lately, I'd come away from every interaction with her feeling completely exhausted. It was like trying to get blood from a stone, just to be tossed the smallest scrap of information. I couldn't imagine any of the other women from the surrogacy group having these issues. They understood that the key to success was clear and open communication. But then perhaps I was expecting too much. This was Julia after all.

I took a seat at the kitchen table, pulling my laptop across and flipping it open, navigating to the calendar, where her midwife appointments were recorded. She had a scan tomorrow afternoon, I saw now. It annoyed me that she hadn't had the courtesy to mention it. I sat back, frowning. I would have given anything to be there. I knew Maya and the other surrogates included their intended parents in every single appointment, made sure they were there at every discussion, every scan. And yet not Julia. Was it that she didn't want me around? It was her way, I knew. Private, matter-of-fact. She'd been unemotional about her previous pregnancies too; Ben had even mentioned to me that she'd never shown any excitement, treating the appointments as a burden to be endured. But in her stoicism, she neglected to realise how left out *I* would feel at not being invited. And when she was doing so much for me, it felt churlish to complain.

I wondered if Ben would be there at the scan. I didn't think so. He had donated the sperm, something that he'd seemed only too happy to offer, though I couldn't help but wonder how he might feel after the birth. If he'd suddenly lay claim to the baby that carried his genes. There was so much uncertainty involved, so much fear that things would go wrong. That Julia would take one look at the baby and realise she had made the wrong choice. Or that Ben would change his mind about relinquishing his rights. But I didn't think so. He'd told me in no uncertain terms that he'd only really wanted one child. Ethan had been a surprise, and he swore he was glad he'd come along, but he certainly didn't want a third. I liked Ben. He and Julia had been together a long time, *years*, and he was definitely the yin to her yang. Light-hearted, carefree, funny. I hoped the baby would inherit some of those characteristics.

I shut the laptop, cupping my cold hands around my mug as the sound of dripping came from somewhere upstairs, that leak tormenting me, trying to force me into action, though I refused to budge. I had to make a decision over what to do about the scan. Should I just turn up at the hospital? Act bright and breezy and make out she'd mentioned it? Should I call first? Or, I thought, leaning back in my chair, my fingers squeezing the thick ceramic handle, should I leave her to it? Let her go and see *my* son wriggling around on the screen, have the growth scan she hadn't even mentioned she'd been offered, be given all the information without me present to have a say, an opinion on the fate of my baby? Should I let her take my role and play mummy to my child because I was too afraid of making things awkward? And if I let her push me out now, where would it stop?

SIX

MAYA

I shuffled in my seat, adjusting my position, trying to keep the leg cramps at bay though I knew it would only be a matter of time before I'd have to get up and stretch. My hips felt as if they were too loose, the joints too lubricated, opening in preparation for the impending birth. They were a constant source of discomfort lately, and despite my rebellion at the gym, I was regretting pushing my body so hard now. The group was gathered, hot drinks clasped in swollen hands, biscuit crumbs landing on laps, and I craned my head past the chatting women to watch the door. She hadn't come. It was nearly time to start, and she hadn't come.

I'd spent all morning playing the scene over in my head, thinking of how best to approach the situation with Elise. I'd never been good at making friends. I watched how easily other women slotted into social situations. How they seemed so natural when they invited each other out for a coffee or a walk along the river. I tried to emulate their breezy tones, their ability to be warm yet not desperate, but judging from the flat responses I got, I fell short of the mark. I could never seem to get that balance right, and I'd heard whispers behind my back that I was cold, or, conversely, clingy. It had been a long time since I'd even tried to strike up more than a fleeting acquaintance with anyone.

But since meeting Elise the other day, I'd been thinking about her a lot. There had been something in her eyes – a haunted look she tried to hide – that made me feel we might be more similar than she realised. I wanted to spend more time with her. Invite her for lunch, a coffee, but the thought of doing it sent waves of anxious nausea through my belly and made me feel like a four-year-old on the first day of school. I'd worried myself sick all morning about what I would say, how she might respond, and now she wasn't even here. I felt deflated and shaky, clasping the custard cream between my fingers, too queasy to bite into it.

'Well, ladies!' Sheila announced cheerfully, taking her seat. 'How are we all?'

There were a few shouts, raucous laughter from the more confident members of the group, and Sheila smiled warmly across the circle. 'I see we have a new addition joining us today. Congratulations, Marina. What have you named your beautiful baby boy?'

My gaze travelled across to where Marina sat opposite me, the baby bundled in a crocheted blanket against her shoulder. She'd been coming to the group for more than six months, though Shantell, the woman who had carried her son, had only joined in once, shyly telling us that surrogacy was something she'd dreamed of doing since her teens. This had been the third time she'd acted as a surrogate, and she'd kept in touch with all the families she'd helped create. Marina had chosen her based on that information, on the knowledge that this woman knew exactly what she was offering and had gone through with it twice before. That she loved the magic of pregnancy but had no desire to raise more children herself – she already had four of her own, all teens now.

'His name is Alfred,' Marina said, looking down at his sleeping face.

'Lovely. It suits him. And how are you getting on? Was the birth a smooth process for you all?'

She shrugged. 'Shantell had a fast labour, and he came in less than three hours. She didn't want to feed him after and asked me to take him that day. I don't think she felt strong enough to hold him for very long just then... too afraid of what she might feel.'

There was a murmur of agreement around the circle.

'I get that,' Sheila said. 'And what about you, Marina? How did you feel getting to go home with your son after all those months of waiting?' There was a smile on her lips, a look of expectation, as if she thought Marina would say it was everything she'd hoped for and more. But when Marina looked up, I saw her face was twisted, anguish written on her features as a fat tear rolled down her angular cheek.

'Since the beginning,' she said softly, 'everyone has asked how *I'm* doing. And how *Shantell* was doing. As if *we* were the people who mattered in this.' She shook her head. 'Do you know what we didn't ask? How *he* would feel.' She chewed her lower lip, and I felt my insides tighten, the biscuit turning damp against my fingers. 'I wanted this so much... It was a kind of madness – that need to be a mother. I couldn't think of anything but the moment he would be placed in my arms. But it was abstract... a fantasy. I didn't grasp the reality of what I was doing. What we were *both* doing.'

'What do you mean?' asked Claire, the pregnant woman sitting beside her, and I didn't miss how her hands had tightened involuntarily over her own belly.

Marina shook her head, her forehead creasing. 'Do you think he *cares* that he was grown from my egg, my husband's sperm? That Shantell was a gestational surrogate, not his biological mother? Of course not. To him, Shantell is everything he knows. He grew inside her body. Her blood sustained him, helped him grow and develop. It was *her* heartbeat that soothed him to sleep. *Her* voice he heard night and day. He felt her emotions as he came into this world, and his every instinct was to be with her, in *her* arms, not mine.' She ran a finger along the baby's cheek, swallowing, then looked back up, her eyes meeting mine.

'Before I held him, I watched him root against her chest. He knew her smell, knew he was exactly where he was supposed to be. It was pure instinct. The most natural thing in the world. And then I took him from her... ripped him from his mother's arms...'

She closed her eyes, and I saw the tears streaming from them, dripping down her cheeks, dropping onto the baby-blue woollen blanket. She swiped at them angrily, as if she didn't have the right to her pain, as if she was filled with self-disgust for letting herself break down.

'He never rooted like that for me. He pushed me away... he cried... screamed. He wanted *her*. He doesn't care what we agreed, the deal we made – only what he *feels*. And I see now it was wrong, so very wrong, to play God with his life, to trade him like his feelings didn't matter. He doesn't belong with me, but he *can't* belong with her. And he's the one who will have to suffer that loss, grieve for what should have been. He'll wear those scars his whole life. *I* did that to him. I put my wants over his needs, and I hate that he's hurting.'

She shook her head, her lips pressing into a tight line as she looked back to Sheila. 'I'm not saying I don't want him. That I can't love him. But it's nothing like what I expected. There's trauma involved. Pain that can't be erased. I have to do my best to atone for my choices.'

An uncomfortable silence had spread through the circle. Sheila cleared her throat. 'Be gentle with yourself, Marina. It's a time of huge transitions and big emotions – for all of you. No path to parenthood is without its challenges. There's birth trauma. Adoption trauma. The path through life is peppered with broken paving stones and jagged edges.' She sighed. 'Don't for a moment think I'm discounting how you feel, love. But you're sleep-deprived. You're a new mum. And as hard as it is right now, it *will* get easier for both of you, and that baby is going to be so loved. You'll both be fine.'

There was a murmur of agreement, then Sara began talking about feeling guilty for not sticking to the food plan her intended parents had asked of her, her inability to avoid cakes and sugary treats as they were the only things that didn't trigger her morning sickness. The confession brought a few laughs and the mood was lightened somewhat, but I looked at Marina and found her staring back at me, a shudder working through me as I realised she'd struck a nerve.

There was a bang by the door and I looked up, a shocked smile spreading across my face as Elise came in, her wet umbrella dripping over the wooden flooring as she shrugged off her coat. 'Hi, everyone! Sorry I'm late,' she said, her energy smashing through the black cloud Marina's confession had created. 'Okay if I join you?'

'Of course,' Sheila said, gesturing to the empty chair beside me. I'd put my bag on it when people were taking their seats, hoping to save it for Elise, and moved it to between my feet when everyone had settled down.

'Hi,' I whispered as she slid in beside me.

She smiled warmly, and I felt my nerves jangle, a rush of confidence chasing through my veins. I wouldn't leave here without extending the invite to coffee and getting her number. I'd been too lonely for too long to pass up the opportunity of friendship now.

My thoughts turned dark as they forced me to acknowledge the reason for that... the fact that as much as I might want a friend, I didn't deserve one. That Elise might regret ever having spoken to me if she learned the truth about my past. But then she reached over, touching my shoulder, and whispered that she liked my dress. And all my reservations were shoved beneath the surface. *Why shouldn't I be selfish?* I thought, suppressing a secret smile.

Just this once.

SEVEN

ELISE

I checked my phone, relieved to see there were no messages waiting to surprise me, then slid it back in my bag, waving as one by one the women left the hall.

'Bye, ladies. See you next session,' Sheila called over to me and Maya before she wheeled the trolley laden with biscuit tins and used coffee cups out the door.

'See you later,' I called after her, standing up and stretching.

It had been a bit awkward when towards the end of the session, one of the other women had suggested I invite Julia along next time so she could share her feelings about the journey we were embarking on together. I hadn't admitted that I'd neglected to tell her about the group, knowing she would find it odd that I was attending. That she might even try and put a stop to it. I'd given a half-hearted response, relieved when I'd been interrupted by Maya asking a question about eating dates to soften the cervix in the run-up to labour. She'd given me a sideways smile and I'd got the distinct impression she'd picked up on my discomfort and was trying to save me from the situation. I grinned at her now as she zipped her raincoat over her bump, and her face lit up.

'What are you up to this afternoon?' she asked, her words coming in a rush, her voice breathless. 'Do you have to go into work or something? I never asked what you do... Only I'm going to pop into the café down the road for some lunch and wondered if you might like to join me? No worries if you have plans. I just thought it would be nice to have the company and—'

'I don't work,' I cut in. 'I... I lost my job a while back and I haven't yet found anything to replace it.' I stepped forward, placing my hand on her forearm – tightly folded across her rain-coat. 'I'd love to join you. I'm starving actually.'

'Oh, wow, okay, great,' she breathed, looking surprised and pleased.

I watched as she slid her cross-body bag over her head, clearly flustered, unable to meet my eye for a moment, and wondered if it was something I'd done that had made her so skit-tish or if she was always like this. I followed her to the door, picking up my umbrella as I passed, hoping the weather had settled a bit by now.

'What did you do before?' she asked, looking at me through her lashes. 'For work, I mean?'

'It wasn't a job, more—' I broke off, realising I'd been about to say it had been a vocation, relieved I'd stopped myself just in time. It was best left in the past. If she knew the kind of things I'd been occupied with this past year and a half, she'd never want to speak to me again, let alone invite me for lunch. And I wanted to go with her, I realised. I wanted to understand from her perspective what being a surrogate meant, why someone would choose to go down this path. It wasn't the kind of thing I could talk about with Julia.

Maya was looking at me expectantly as we made our way to the main entrance, past the group of OAPs waiting to head into the line-dancing class. I shook my head and smiled. 'It was a long time ago,' I said as we stepped out into a light drizzle, the sky grey and heavy, the pavements dotted with wide puddles, pedestrians with hoods up and heads down. 'Do *you* work?' I asked, turning the spotlight on her.

'No. I used to. I was quite the career woman, believe it or not,' she said, her cheeks flushing. 'I managed a big team of people. Worked seventy hours a week.' She saw me raise an eyebrow and smiled. 'I loved it,' she admitted. 'I never wanted to stop.'

'So why did you?'

She shrugged, slowing her pace to let a woman with a double buggy pass, and I sensed there were things she wasn't prepared to share right now. 'I went through a bit of a tough time a few years back... fell into a dark place, and where work had once been my escape, my passion, I found I couldn't perform any more. I lost the spark for it.' She gave a heavy sigh. 'It was my own company, you see.'

She glanced at me shyly and said the name of an organic skincare company I'd heard of – used probably – nodding to confirm I hadn't misheard. 'If I could have coasted for a bit, got my head back in the right space, maybe I could have held on to it. But when it's *your* baby, *your* passion that feeds the rest of the team, it doesn't work that way.'

I kept pace with her as she walked, her eyes trained on the street ahead.

'I got us in a mess, made some stupid decisions and ended up being forced to sell at a major loss. I had to sell my house, my car, *everything*, just to survive.'

'Wow. I'm so sorry, Maya. That must've been difficult.'

She twisted her mouth. 'It just wasn't meant to be mine. It's a bitter pill to swallow, but it's the truth. I didn't have the grit to keep going through tough times. I couldn't separate my personal life from my work. The woman who bought the company turned it around, and now they're doing so well. It doesn't belong to me any more, but still, I like seeing what it became, even if it was despite me in the end.'

I didn't know what to say. She was so hard on herself, but I sensed there was a lot more to the story than she was giving me.

'You know what you're capable of now though. It's no small thing to start up a company and get a range of products to become a household name. And maybe, once the baby comes, you can try something new. You must have learned so much from that first business. It shouldn't go to waste.'

She shook her head. 'No. That chapter is over. I can't go back to it.' She was resolutely silent for a moment, and we walked side by side, an uncomfortable energy filling the space between us.

She stopped suddenly, turning to face me. 'Do you ever feel like who you were, you know, in your past, is someone you can't relate to any more? Like you're looking back on a completely different person?'

'Actually, yes...' I nodded slowly, my eyes meeting hers. 'I do.'

'That's what I feel like. I can't go back to that life. Will and Nina have been so generous with making sure I have time to rest, covering my expenses. They were relieved when I agreed not to work during the pregnancy, and if it weren't for them, I'd have had no other choice. We all have bills to pay, don't we? I suppose once this is over, I'll have to do something, but I don't know what it will be. I don't want to think of it yet.'

I frowned, wondering what could have happened to make her lose her self-belief.

'This way,' she said, crossing the road and pointing to a cosy-looking café on the corner.

I followed her inside, a blast of heat hitting me, forcing me to strip off my coat and jumper immediately. Maya did the same, and we squeezed between the tables, taking one by a window on the far side.

'So, you're enjoying the time to yourself then?' I said, picking up on her last comment. 'You seem to take it all in your stride,' I added. 'The pregnancy, the whole surrogacy thing.'

'I wouldn't say enjoying it... but it's been a different pace and perhaps that's what I needed. To be honest with you, up until this past week, I haven't had a lot of time to myself. The intended parents are pretty full-on. Not that I blame them,' she added hurriedly. 'But it's been nice to have them out of my hair for a while.'

I looked at her, trying to read her. She hadn't shared much in the group, other than light-hearted comments and questions. She never seemed to voice any concerns about her attachment to the baby, how she would feel when the time came to hand her over to Nina, and it made me uneasy somehow. There was a coldness to the way she talked about it, making it sound very transactional. It was something I couldn't get to grips with. A few of the other women had been tearful today, sharing their fears, their worries that they would no longer be welcome to stay in the child's life after the intended parents took them away, and that felt far more of a human response. Maya was different, and it made me curious to learn more.

'I don't really know anything about your story,' I said as she picked up the plastic-covered menu and glanced at the options. 'What made you choose to do this? I assumed you had your own kids already, but now, hearing that you used to work seventy-hour weeks, I'm not so sure.'

She shook her head, looking up from the menu. 'No, I don't have any children. Although I suppose if you want to be technical, this one is biologically mine – I donated an egg because... well, I shouldn't share this, but Nina was born without a womb. And we had to use a sperm donor because Will's sperm weren't up to the job.'

I raised an eyebrow, unable to disguise my shock. I'd assumed she was acting as an incubator to Will and Nina's embryo. That she was able to distance herself from the baby she was carrying because, despite everything, it wasn't her own child. But to hear that it *was* her baby she was carrying, planning to give away... it was something I couldn't even begin to understand. It made my stomach tense, nausea building inside me, and I suddenly realised how much of a hypocrite it made me to be judging her now, when I would soon be the beneficiary of the very same generosity.

'You think I'm going to regret it.' Her eyes were trained on my face, seeing far more from my expression than I'd hoped to give away.

'I'm sorry. It's just... how do you know that you won't? This is your first baby. How can you possibly grasp the enormity of what you're agreeing to?'

Maya looked down at her belly, pursing her lips. 'Does it matter? How *I* feel about it, I mean? Isn't it sometimes the right thing to do? To offer something selfless for someone who deserves it?'

'Why don't *you* deserve it?' I asked softly.

As she lifted her face, I saw a fleeting expression – anger, or was it regret? – and I wondered if she wasn't as cold as she portrayed. Or if she really could just separate herself from the baby growing inside her.

'What about you?' she asked, leaning back in her chair, clearly keen to change the subject. 'Are you feeling excited about the birth? Your little one is due the same week as mine.'

I hid a frown, picking up on her use of the word *mine*, and nodded. 'It doesn't feel real to me yet. I want it so much, and there's such a lot that can go wrong between now and then. I can't let myself give in completely to the hope that it will all be okay – not until he's in my arms and I'm walking out of the hospital with him.' I looked out of the window, realising I was glad to have someone to admit this to. I wished I'd met Maya sooner. 'I feel like I've been holding my breath ever since I found out Julia was pregnant, like I can't relax.'

'Because you're afraid she might change her mind?'

I thought of Julia's refusal to include me in the recent appointments, her cold, offhand responses to my questions of late. 'I don't know. It's never going to be a straightforward situation, is it? There are just too many factors involved, too many big emotions... I'm being silly, but it's how I feel.'

'I can understand that. But you'll have your son in your arms before you know it.'

'I'd hoped for a girl.' I froze, wondering what on earth had prompted me to admit that out loud. It wasn't the kind of thing you were supposed to say, especially not to a woman who was practically a stranger. 'Sorry,' I faltered, 'that sounded like I'm not grateful. I just meant, I pictured a little girl when we started this process. It was what I dreamed of. That special mother– daughter connection. But I know I'll have that with a boy too. It's just not what I envisioned.'

She stared at me, and I wondered if it was the first time she was considering the relationship between herself and the baby in her womb in that way. The little girl who would share her features, inherit her quirks. She opened her mouth as if to say something, then stood so suddenly I wondered if she might just rush out and leave me sitting here alone. 'Sorry,' she said, bumping against the table as she tried to get out of the tight space. 'I need to pop to the loo. Baby bouncing on my bladder.'

She rushed off before I could explain my comment further – not that there was any way to make it better – and I watched her go, wondering what motivated her, because so far, it wasn't making sense to me.

EIGHT

MAYA

I stood over the sink in the narrow toilet cubicle, the smell of Harpic wafting from the drain, making my stomach churn, sweat breaking out across my shoulder blades. My reflection stared back at me, my eyes intense as I told myself to stay calm. I couldn't mess this up. There was a vulnerability to Elise that made me want to protect her, and I could see that given the right circumstances, I could convince her to open up to me. I wasn't sure if I even wanted that, but I had an opportunity here, one that I might never have got the chance to explore had she not walked into my life, and I was sure she was the key to my future. It was as if her arrival had unlocked something I'd buried, a part of me I'd pretended was dead, and given me a fragment of hope that something might change – that I didn't have to keep living with my head in the sand, wretched and self-loathing.

Elise wasn't the type of person who could hide her feelings. Not like me. I could read her like a book, and that was going to make this all the more easy to navigate. I met my gaze in the mirror and gave a determined nod, pinching my cheeks to bring some colour back, before stepping out into the busy café.

Elise looked up from her phone as I slid into my seat, breaking into a smile as if she was relieved to see me.

'Sorry,' I said, patting my belly with a smile. 'I don't get a lot of warning when I need to go. One roly-poly and it's game over for my bladder.'

'Must be hard,' she replied with a wan smile, and I wondered if I was putting my foot in it again, reminding her that though she would soon have a baby in her arms, she wasn't carrying him herself. Surely every flippant comment about the trials of pregnancy would hurt? I couldn't seem to stop myself from saying the wrong thing when I was around her. Thankfully she didn't seem compelled to point out my lack of tact.

'Sorry for the delay – we're so busy today! What can I get you ladies?'

I looked up to see a harried-looking waitress standing beside the table, notepad in hand. Elise pointed at the menu, asking for what she wanted, and I nodded. 'Make that two of everything, please. Elise, you read my mind! I'm starving.'

It was a bonding tactic I'd read about in my twenties: order the same food, point out your similarities rather than your differences. A fast track to making friends. I hadn't pulled it off in my personal life, but somehow it had worked well in my company. I'd been a good boss to those women, finding common ground, understanding that they'd work harder, be more committed to the company if they liked me as a person. It had been something that hadn't come naturally after a lonely childhood, and at the time, I'd been grateful for the professional line I'd been able to draw in the sand as their employer, never quite becoming true friends with my staff. But perhaps it was time to dust off some of those old tricks now.

I waited for Elise to break the silence, but she was staring out of the window, a distracted look in her eye, and I realised it was going to be down to me to step out of my comfort zone. I fiddled with the salt shaker, trying to think of something to say, the silence stretching on too long. I glanced around the café, watching the other customers, trying to pick up on something to point out, some funny quip to get us back on track. If the awkwardness continued much longer, I would ruin this, mess up any chance of her agreeing to come out with me again. But just as I opened my mouth to speak, the waitress reappeared bearing a tray of food and drinks.

Elise seemed to snap out of her trance. I wished I knew exactly what she'd been thinking about. What I wouldn't give to step inside her mind for a while.

'This looks amazing. Thank you,' she said, taking a mug of creamy hot chocolate and sipping it. I waited for the waitress to dash off to another customer, then smiled at Elise as she placed her mug on the table.

'So,' I said, dipping my fork into my steaming plate of pasta, 'are your family supportive about the baby? Have they got any other grandchildren?'

She shook her head and, seeing a flash of something that looked like hurt in her eyes, I hoped I hadn't said the wrong thing again. 'I'll be honest,' she replied, fiddling with a sachet of mayonnaise from the bowl in the middle of the table. 'I haven't actually discussed it with them. They aren't in my life – haven't been in a long time.'

'Oh... and your sister? Julia? Doesn't she see them either?'

Elise shook her head. 'They went travelling when I was eighteen and they haven't been back since. They never wanted to be parents really. Just did it because that was what everyone else was doing. But they resented it. The ties. The cost. The intrusion on their lives.' She dropped the mayonnaise, unopened, picking up her fork and stabbing a piece of pasta on its tip. 'I feel like the years they spent parenting were just a chapter to them, something they had to press pause on their *real* lives for. The moment they got the chance, they escaped. I won't be like that. I don't believe you ever stop being a mother. I think once you have a child, you carry them with you for the rest of your life.'

Her eyes glistened and I looked down at my plate, my heart thudding in my chest. Swallowing, I slid my hand across the table, covering hers. 'It's strange,' I said softly. 'You and I had very similar starts in life. My parents were workaholics – I suppose I must have inherited that trait from them – but they never should have had me. They outsourced everything. I had a nanny from birth, went to a nursery attached to a private girls' school from age two, and boarded there from seven. I barely knew either of them – I still don't,' I added, realising how it might sound. 'I see them at big events; they bring me out to show off their success.'

I gave a wry laugh. 'When I was killing it in my business, they told everyone. It was the first time they seemed to even notice me, and it made me work harder, be even better so they wouldn't lose interest. Since I sold the business, they've been too busy to see me, for the most part. And they don't know about this either,' I admitted, looking down at my belly, knowing how deeply they'd disapprove. They would accuse me of giving up on my dreams, of letting myself down, wasting my intelligence. I wouldn't know how to begin to explain to them how I'd ended up here. I'd never been able to confide in them.

'I'm sorry,' Elise said, and I could see she really meant it. I never opened up to anyone, and now I wished I hadn't. I felt suddenly exposed, as if I wanted to claw the information back, to protect myself.

'Boarding must have been hard at that age,' she prompted. 'Did you make close friends there?'

I thought about the way the girls had competed, stamping on each other to get to the top. It hadn't been a nurturing experience; it had been ruthless, something my parents had been aware and encouraging of, claiming I needed to fight to become the best. I'd been thrown into a situation where I had two options: become a victim, or gather my strength and be bullish, undefeatable. I couldn't remember ever making a conscious choice, but I'd taken the latter path, and even now I believed it was the lesser of two evils. I'd witnessed what had happened to the girls who couldn't hold their heads above water. They'd been drowned, slowly and painfully, every single day of their formative years.

I'd changed a lot since my childhood, but the experience of being dumped by my parents time and again, of having to prove myself in order to be accepted, had shaped me in ways I could never escape.

'Friends?' I repeated, fiddling with my fork. 'A few,' I lied, feeling like I'd bared enough of my soul for one day. 'It was another lifetime. I didn't keep in touch. Life keeps moving, doesn't it?'

I scooped up a mouthful of pasta and chewed slowly, watching Elise, hoping more than anything that everything might be about to change.

NINE
ELISE

I slipped my coat back on, feeling full and sleepy after the massive meal I'd consumed. I'd eaten far more than usual as I tried to fill the uncomfortable silences that peppered the lunch. Maya had a strange ability to make me feel she was overly keen to be liked, and yet at the same time she was cagey, hard to talk to. Her eye contact was just that little bit too intense, her smile too wide as she nodded along to whatever I said, but when it came to sharing anything about herself, she became stiff. Since I was unwilling – unable – to delve into my own secrets, it had made for a difficult start.

And yet notwithstanding the pauses in conversation, it was clear that she was a good listener, always watching. She seemed to know all about the lives of the women in the group. It made me uneasy to realise just how much she'd absorbed, like a sponge, while sitting there serenely sipping her tea. I couldn't help but wonder how much she knew – or thought she knew – about me.

Despite that initial awkwardness, her stories had gradually given her more confidence, filling the lulls and saving me from having to fabricate my personal life, and when she'd found her stride after the waitress had replaced our pasta bowls with hunks of chocolate fudge cake, I'd been grateful to her for dispelling the stilted energy that had lingered after our surrogacy revelations. I laughed now as she finished telling me about Sheila's girlish crush on Richard, the young man I'd seen organising the drinks table on my first day. He was less than half her age, if that, but Maya insisted that there was a flirtation between the two of them, which I vowed to look out for in future. I grinned, thinking of the red lipstick she'd been wearing today and wondering if there was something to it.

Pushing open the café door and heading outside, I was thankful to find that the rain had stopped, the air mild and fresh.

'I should let you go; I have to call Nina at three,' Maya said, and she smiled with genuine warmth, as if she'd forgotten for a moment to be self-conscious. There were glimpses of someone interesting under all the layers of awkwardness, and despite the bumpy start, I realised there was something I really liked about her.

I stepped forward, giving her a brief hug, the curve of her belly pressing against my coat. 'Thanks for the invite. I enjoyed it. Let's—'

I broke off as a couple walked round the corner, heads bowed in conversation, almost colliding with us.

'Julia, Ben!' I exclaimed, seeing the shock on Julia's face as she stopped abruptly. I grinned at the sight of her round belly, a feeling of deep maternal love spreading through me as I thought of my baby boy nestled safe inside. I couldn't wait to hold him in my arms.

Ben smiled warmly. He and I had hit it off from day one, sharing a light-hearted playfulness that seemed to irritate Julia, though secretly I thought she was being irrational. Just another case of her trying to keep everything in separate little cubicles, not wanting me to have a friendship with her husband because he was *hers* and she didn't like to think I might create a bond with him.

I reached out to touch his arm. 'New jacket? Suits you,' I said.

'Thanks.' He gave a smile that wrinkled his nose, and Julia cleared her throat.

'Is this a friend of yours, Elise?' she asked. Her tone was cold, and I hated that she was coming across so rudely. It was embarrassing to have Maya see the chill that had worked its way between us lately.

Maya stepped forward, holding out a hand. 'I'm Maya. Elise and I met at the—'

'At the craft group I told you about,' I interrupted, flashing a warning look in Maya's direction, hoping she'd play along, not ask questions... not yet.

She frowned, and I continued to talk. 'How was the scan? Is everything okay? He's not measuring big, is he?'

Julia folded her arms and took a pointed look at her watch, a gesture that rankled no end. She knew she'd been caught out. Knew I'd discovered that she'd gone ahead without me. I could see just how much she was beginning to resent having to answer to me. Our relationship had always been an imbalance of power – she got to be the one asking questions, demanding action, and I, the younger, more amiable party, had to jump to her orders. Was that what this was? That she didn't like the thought of having to involve me, include me in what she deemed *her* business? Whatever the case, it was too important to back down, let her cut me out now. We were bound together, and as suffocating as she might be finding it, it was no less challenging for me. I would have done anything to be the one carrying that baby right now. *Anything.* I felt a wave of emotion building, making my throat tight, my chest swell painfully, and I blinked, determined not to give in to tears as I waited for her to throw me a crumb.

Ben's eyes were trained on my face, and I felt the spark of energy between us that had been there since the first moment we met. It was an unspoken agreement that neither of us ever mentioned it, and despite the magnetic pull, the awareness that in another life, he would have tried something with me – and I might have let him – I had no intention of crossing the line with him. His eyes met mine and held my gaze a second too long; then, seeming not to notice the tension between me and his wife, he grinned. 'All's well. It looks like he's going to be on the big side, but nothing Julia can't handle,' he said, smiling at her. 'Not long to wait.' His eyes found mine again, and though it hurt to realise she'd taken him to the scan rather than me, I was grateful to him for being so open now.

Julia cleared her throat. 'Sorry, Elise, but we really have to go. I have a packed afternoon. I'll see you in a few days, and you can catch me up on everything you've been doing then, okay?'

She didn't wait for an answer as she strode on, leaving Ben behind in her hurry. He leaned in, brushing a kiss on my cheek, his mouth twisting mischievously as he pulled back. 'See you, Elise.' He winked, then jogged up the street to catch up with Julia. I watched him reach her. She swiped his hand away as he tried to grab hers, her face angry as he said something I couldn't hear.

'Wow,' Maya whispered, and I turned back to face her, having almost forgotten she was there. 'What was all that about?'

'Oh, the craft group thing?' I said, relieved she had kept her questions to herself until now. 'I never mentioned this in the group because I didn't want to offend anyone, but Julia has this idea that it's really tacky to air your business in public. She'd hate it if she thought I was telling her secrets to strangers. I should have said something... I know when I spoke about it this morning I kind of made it sound like she might come to a session one day, but I didn't want any of you to think I was

doing something wrong in sharing *my* side of the story – you
know, to say that I should respect her wishes and not come any
more.'

Maya shook her head. 'Don't be silly – you aren't telling us
her secrets; you're sharing your own side of the experience, and
nobody has the right to say you can't do that.' She bit her lower
lip, and I could see there was more she wanted to say.

'Go on.' I nodded.

She frowned. 'I was just really shocked by the way she was
with you then. You should be at those scans. You should be able
to ask your questions directly to the sonographer and be
included in any discussions taking place. I've been going to the
support group a long time now, and I've never heard of anyone
being treated so... well, *coldly* by their surrogate. I mean, I know
she's your sister, and maybe that's why it isn't quite a professional arrangement as such, but still... Were things fractious
between you before she got pregnant?' Her voice was cautious,
as if she was fighting between curiosity and shyness, and I
respected her for having the guts to ask the question.

I sighed. 'We've had our moments,' I answered softly.
'There've been times when I've really thought she hated me...
times when one or both of us haven't been able to see the other's
point of view. You know how sisters can be – the best of friends
one minute and mortal enemies the next. But she knows what
this means to me. I can't have her pull the rug from beneath my
feet now. It's almost time for the birth. What if she tries to back
out? What if...' I shook my head, meeting Maya's eyes. 'Do you
ever think about it? About keeping the baby?'

She made a sound of derision, as if the question was so
ridiculous it didn't warrant an answer, and stepped back, her
eyes darkening. 'Of course I don't. She's not mine to keep; she's
theirs. I'm just the incubator.' She gave an awkward laugh that
sounded fake and did nothing to break the tense mood my question had created.

I opened my mouth to say more, but she was already backing away. 'I have to rush off, but today's been lovely. See you at the next session, okay?'

She turned, heading in the opposite direction from Julia and Ben, and I leaned back against the café wall, my heart pounding, sure that something was going to go terribly wrong.

TEN

MAYA

I lugged the heavy bag through the front door, regretting my decision to pop into the shops after my lunch with Elise. The few things I'd picked up had seemed manageable in the moment, but when I'd arrived back at my flat to find someone had parked in my allocated spot, I'd had no choice but to drive round for fifteen minutes, finally finding a space three roads away. According to the brightly coloured posters pasted onto the bus stops and lamp posts, there was some kind of autumn festival taking place at the local park today, which would explain why my usually quiet street looked like a scene from Woodstock.

The straps were cutting into my shoulder now, the four-pack of sparkling water, along with the limes I'd been craving, weighing heavily as I finally made it to the kitchen, dropping the canvas bag unceremoniously onto the counter. I ripped open the plastic packaging, cracking open a bottle and drinking deeply, sighing with satisfaction despite the water being a bit on the warm side. I'd been so thirsty since getting pregnant. And now that I was home, I was glad I'd made the effort.

As I picked up the remaining bottles, sliding them into the

fridge for later, my phone began to ring. Slipping it from my pocket, I walked through to the living room, desperate to sit down and rest. I slumped onto the sofa with a grunt and frowned at the screen, not recognising the number, then answered, wondering if it was one of the midwives. They often called from their mobile phones.

'Hello?' I said breathlessly.

'Maya, are you okay?'

'Who's this?' I leaned back, allowing my legs to stretch out on the carpet, wiggling my hips against the dull ache that never seemed to let up these days.

'You sound like you've been running. It's Jo. Did you delete my number?'

I froze, wishing I'd had the foresight not to answer, too chicken to hang up now she'd heard me. 'I... I got a new phone and a lot of my contacts weren't transferred over,' I lied. 'It's been two years since we spoke, so...'

I left the words hanging, wondering why on earth she'd be calling now, feeling an uneasy sense of dread building within me. There had been a time when we'd been inseparable. Her, me... Harry. It had been a foregone conclusion that it would never change. And yet in one night it had all come crashing down around us, and when I'd told her I could no longer have her in my life if she kept Harry in hers, she'd picked him. I still couldn't get over that, even now. Even if it had been all my fault.

'I wanted to speak to you,' she said, her voice bringing back a thousand suppressed memories. 'I miss you all the time. You were my best friend, Maya.' She made a familiar sound and I could picture her lighting a cigarette, the way she held it like a fifties pin-up, her blonde hair falling in trained waves around her cherubic face – a face that hid a thousand sins. 'Can we meet?'

A fleeting rush of longing filled me, and for half a second, I wanted to say yes. To share what I'd been through since we parted ways. Tell her about the surrogacy and make her see that everything had changed. *I* had changed. I was different now. Selfless. When she heard what I'd chosen to do, the sacrifices I'd made, she'd be amazed at how far I'd come. But it was impossible. I couldn't see *her* without inviting *him* back into my life. And the thought of that made me sick to my stomach. I would die before I let it happen.

I opened my mouth, struggling to find the words to answer, then pressed my lips together, summoned my courage and ended the call, blocking her number from my phone. I sat in the quiet of my living room, hearing the tick of the clock, the pounding of my heart, squeezing the phone tight against my palm as I tried to hold back the past but found I couldn't. I was drowning in guilt, just as I had been then, as fresh and raw as when it all happened. I had come so far, tried to become a completely different person, but it made no fucking difference. I could never escape what Harry and I had done.

ELEVEN

I woke with a gasp, trying to scramble up to a sitting position, and was instantly rewarded with a sharp, stabbing pain that radiated from my pelvis to my left foot. Leaning back against the pillows, I tried to catch my breath, feeling suffocated by the weight of the baby pressing against my lungs. I stared at the ceiling, the deafening drumroll of my own heartbeat pounding in my ears, an explosion of fireworks marring my vision, and waited impatiently for control of my faculties.

Cradling my bump, trying to move slowly so as not to induce another spasm of pain, I eased myself up to sit on the edge of the mattress, feeling shaken and alert. The nightmare had been too real – the faces, the screaming, that desperate need to undo my mistakes and make it all go away. I hadn't dreamed of Harry in a long time. I'd trained myself not to. Any thought of him was met with a brick wall, iron doors slamming in my mind, preventing his name from ever touching my lips. I'd loved him with all my heart, given him so much of myself, and now I couldn't even bear to picture his face.

I hadn't seen him in almost two years. The last conversation we'd had changed everything, destroyed the person I'd thought I was in an instant.

I shook myself, determined not to fall into old habits. I couldn't change it. Thinking of Harry was the last thing I needed to be doing right now, when I was just about to give birth. I needed to keep my focus on that. On the good thing I was doing for Nina and Will.

I stood slowly, hearing the crack and pop of my joints railing against the motion, then stretched my spine before going downstairs to make a cup of tea. My phone was on the counter, plugged into the charger, and I glanced at it, seeing two missed calls from Nina. With a sigh, I stepped back, knowing I should return her call and yet struggling to summon the energy to do it.

Since my lunch with Elise yesterday, I had been thinking of how strange her sister's behaviour had been, how she seemed almost secretive when it came to sharing the things she *should* be sharing with Elise. I hadn't wanted to mention it to Elise for fear of upsetting her, but there was an energy radiating from Julia that had made me wonder if she *was* in fact having doubts about their agreement. I knew how much Elise wanted this – she'd confided as much to me, though sometimes I couldn't help but feel there was a certain amount of judgement in the questions she asked me, the little comments she made. If it weren't for the fact she was going through the same thing herself, I'd be forced to wonder if she considered surrogacy something to be ashamed of. Almost as if she couldn't relate to a woman who could hand over the baby she'd been connected to for nine months.

Her knack of making me feel under the microscope, combined with Marina's emotional outpouring at the group, had unsettled me, I realised. Brought the things I had taken for granted into question. Was I doing the right thing? It had seemed so black and white all those months ago. To give up the baby I had nurtured with my own body, enabling another woman to experience motherhood... to create a family. It seemed like the most selfless act in the world. But now I was starting to see it wasn't nearly so black and white as that. I hadn't wanted to let anyone else affect the way I felt, and yet I found myself thinking – *overthinking* – worrying about the tiny baby growing inside me. Did *she* see me as her mother? Would I be breaking her heart by handing her over to another woman? Had I let myself be swept up in something I might live to regret?

Nina's name flashed up on the phone screen again. I couldn't put my finger on what had changed, why I felt the need to have some space from her all of a sudden, but I found myself unable to answer, backing away from the phone as if she might see me ignoring her call. She and Will would be leaving France to come home any day now, as soon as they'd figured out the care arrangements for her father. We would go back to our previous routines, just as it had been before. Daily visits. Will reading fairy tales to my bare belly as I pretended not to mind. Nina with me for every scan, every midwife appointment, which would only become more frequent as we reached my due date. She'd continue asking all the questions while I sat mute, somehow not a part of the thing that was happening to my body. They would come home and I would put my fears, these silly last-minute doubts, aside. But for now, I wanted some time just to be alone. Time to think.

There was a loud knock at the front door, and I glanced through the kitchen window, seeing a Royal Mail van at the kerb.

'Morning! Just the one for you today, love,' the postwoman said, handing over a package with a wide smile, and I wondered where Ted, my usual postie, was.

'Thanks,' I replied, taking it from her.

'Look at you! You look ready to pop! Any day now, is it?'

'Yes, in the next week or so.'

'You won't know what's hit you. I've got three myself. Newborns are a dream, but they're full-on. Do you know what you're having?'

'A girl... a daughter,' I said, the word alien on my tongue. It felt wrong to say. Misleading.

Any time in the previous months that anyone had asked about the baby, I'd told them the truth: that I was just the surrogate, that she wasn't really mine. I'd always imagined they'd gone quiet because they were in awe of what I was doing. But what if I'd been wrong? What if when they'd said they didn't know how I could do it, they weren't intending their words to be a compliment but a judgement? Because what kind of a woman gives away her own flesh and blood?

The postwoman grinned, making a joke about explosive newborn poos, and I nodded along, smiling. I knew I should admit the truth, but instead I found myself wrapping my arms around my bump, even as from behind me in the kitchen, I heard the sound of my ringtone bursting to life again.

TWELVE

ELISE

Tomorrow. 2 p.m. Don't try and mess me around. Nick.

I reread the text message, trying to practise keeping calm as the words jumped before my eyes – to remind myself that soon he would be out of my life for good and I would no longer have to leap through his flaming hoops. The way he thought he could command me, make me his little puppet, was *his* issue, *his* power trip, I told myself now. Nick's character flaws were the reason he derived such pleasure from having me at his mercy. It was nothing to do with me at all really. I could have been anyone; I just happened to have fallen into his web. Admittedly, the struggle to break free had been harder than I'd ever envisioned. But I didn't need to rise to his petty baiting. I knew something he didn't, and that knowledge would give me the upper hand tomorrow. I just had to keep my cool, remind myself that he didn't control me... not any more.

I took a deep breath, annoyed that it hadn't worked, that the fear and anxiety his name always summoned was no less intense, despite my trying to stay rational. I turned my phone to silent, dropped it on the living-room carpet beside me and, after a moment to steel myself, resumed what I'd been doing before the message came through, needing the distraction of keeping busy.

Picking up the clipboard, I scanned through the list, handwritten in different-coloured pens, coded for the various categories. Feeding was blue. Changing was red. Clothing was purple. Toys green. I had never been as organised as I was now, and I smiled, running the end of the biro down the column, making certain they were all ticked off. Of all the experiences I'd lost out on this past nine months, nesting wasn't one of them.

There was only one bullet point left unchecked, and as I ripped open the plastic packaging of the parcel that had arrived today, letting the two slings fall onto my folded legs on the carpet, I gave a contented sigh, reaching for the orange pen to mark it completed. I hadn't been able to choose between the hooded backpack-style carrier or the more lightweight ring sling that fitted over one shoulder and kept the baby cuddled close to the chest, so I'd ordered both, and seeing them now, I was glad. I picked up the floaty black muslin material and felt tears come to my eyes as I pictured securing my baby into the folds of it, carrying him so close I could lean down and kiss him whenever I wanted. I couldn't wait.

Leaning back against the base of the sofa, I hugged the material to me, fighting with myself to stay in the state of euphoria, not to give in to the fears that were plucking away at my nerves, the dread that it would all come to nothing, that Julia would cut me out of her life and shatter my hopes in the process. That Nick would somehow discover what I had planned and make it his mission to destroy it... to destroy me.

But I couldn't think like that. I had to keep pushing forward, keep my mind on the end goal. Losing focus wasn't an option. There were too many black holes for me to stumble into, lose myself in. It would be fine. I would get through the visit with Nick, I'd let Julia have her moment to simmer in her hormones, and I would concentrate on the fact that everything was prepared and waiting for the new arrival. It was the only thing I'd been able to control, and I was ready. I just had to keep trusting that it would all work out. That nothing would go wrong. It was the only choice I had.

THIRTEEN
MAYA

Then

'Maya! Open the fucking door!'

The sound of Harry's fist pounding against the wood sent a tremor of excitement through me as I sat in the dim glow of lamplight in the bedroom, a glass of whisky clasped between my shaking fingers. I'd conned him into leaving the house when I got back from work this evening, and while he was off on a wild goose chase to Jo's, I'd called the emergency locksmith, who'd left me with a new set of keys I'd put to use right away.

It was almost midnight now, and I could picture him out there, desperate to be let back into the home we'd created together all those years ago. The way he would go to pieces when he realised what I'd done – when he understood that it was too late to change my mind. He would panic. I'd expected no less. Prepared myself for this very eventuality. If I gave him the opportunity, he would do his best to try and talk me round, but there was no point. My decision was made.

This night, this moment had haunted me for so long now. Kept me from my sleep, driven me half mad with fear and worry as I refused to accept the truth that was right in front of my face. I'd wanted there to be another option, but this past year it had dawned on me just how much I was pretending to be someone I wasn't in order to cushion the blow for him. I'd barely recognised the person I had let myself become.

If the women I employed could see through the walls of our home, witness the person I was when there was nobody watching, they'd be horrified. I'd hidden the truth, the dark thoughts that plagued me, from everyone. Even Harry. But it couldn't go on. I had to follow my gut and put myself first, even if it hurt him... even if it killed him.

The knocking grew more aggressive and I took a sip of the whisky, coughing as it hit the back of my throat. I'd never been much of a drinker. Steeling my nerves, I grabbed the black bin bag from beside me and stood, opening it, moving to the dresser and tossing the bottle of aftershave in first, never wanting to smell it again. It would only hurt. Remind me of the person I'd fallen in love with. There was no point thinking of the past now. We'd both changed too much to ever go back.

I opened his drawers, grabbing handfuls of clothes, underwear, ties that hadn't seen the light of day in months. I flung open the wardrobe doors and took hold of the few suits hanging up, jamming them into the bag, the pounding on the front door growing louder still, his shouts more furious. The neighbours would hear every word. It was humiliating, I didn't want them prying into my business, but there was no point worrying about them now. I had to push on with my plan.

A knot curled around my insides, an undercurrent of fear. I couldn't help but wonder what would happen if he managed to get inside. What I might be forced to do. I hoped it wouldn't come to that.

I opened his bedside cabinet and took out a stack of paperbacks, then froze as I saw something glinting in the lamplight that made anger swell up inside me. I stared at it, shaking my

head. He didn't deserve me. He wasn't good enough for me. If
I'd had any doubts, seeing this would only have cemented my
resolve. I wasn't even shocked. He wouldn't learn until someone
taught him a lesson, and I realised now that it had to be me.

In a blaze of fury, I yanked the drawer off the runners,
tipping the remaining contents onto the bed. There was a small
black velvet pouch among the pile of papers and trinkets, and I
recognised it as one he'd gifted me once, what felt like a lifetime
ago. There had been a long velvet box containing a diamond
necklace inside. I loosened the drawstring and pulled out a
wedge of cash, at least five hundred pounds. I had no idea
where he'd got it from, but the fact that he'd taken such pains to
hide it made me sure he'd known it was wrong. There should be
no secrets in a relationship. I caught my reflection in the mirror,
seeing the flash of guilt cloud my features. Nobody was perfect.

'Maya!' Harry yelled again. 'Let me talk to you! You're not
thinking straight. I'm worried about you!'

I choked back a laugh and picked up my tumbler, downing
the rest of the whisky in one gulp. It slid down more smoothly
this time.

'At least let me pack a bag if you won't let me stay!' he
called. 'I need to get my stuff!' His voice was frantic as he
yelled, hoarse and dry, and I wondered if he really believed I
was that stupid. I wasn't letting him over the threshold of this
house ever again.

After slamming my glass back on the cabinet, I heaved the
bin bag onto the mattress, roughly tied the top, then went to the
window, opening it wide. 'Here,' I yelled, dropping it out onto
the path. 'Take your stuff and leave!'

He stepped back from the door, his eyes meeting mine, and
I saw the question in them, the desperate plea for me to change
my mind and let him in so that he could try and talk me down
from the choice he never wanted me to make. He must have
known this was on my mind... that I was teetering on the edge,

weighing up when to jump. He had to have seen the possibility. I set my jaw, shaking my head, and his eyes widened, clearly shocked that I wasn't backing down, as I had so many times before. I was done yielding to his wants, suppressing my own feelings. My own desires.

'Maya,' he said softly, 'please don't do this. It will end badly. You *know* it will. Just let me in for a minute, and then I'll go.'

'No, Harry.'

'You don't know what you're doing!' he yelled. 'Don't force me into a situation I don't want to be in. You know you're being rash. You can't just do this, not unless you're willing to face the consequences.'

'Harry, *stop*. Walk away. It's too late for this conversation. I have no choice.' My voice was calm, and I realised I had never felt so sure about anything.

His eyes grew wide, and I felt a smug satisfaction as I recognised the fear in them, the blood draining from his face. His hands were shaking, I noted. *Good*. He'd pushed me too far. *Made* me do this. I smiled, feeling free, reckless. 'Goodbye, Harry.'

He opened his mouth to speak, and I slammed the window closed, unwilling to give him the opportunity to respond. I stood behind the glass, waiting for the knocking to resume, but a few moments later, he turned and walked away, not bothering to even glance at the bin bag jammed full of his stuff, leaving it where it lay. He jogged down the street and I forced myself not to care, not to worry about what he would do next.

Harry wasn't my problem any more.

FOURTEEN

Now

'Nina,' I said, tucking my phone under my ear as I stepped past a group of girls to riffle through the racks of jogging bottoms, trying to find something that would fit. I'd accidentally tumble-dried my maternity jeans, and when I'd pulled them on this morning, I'd felt like a sausage squeezed too tight in its casing. Not wanting to buy another pair so close to the finish line, I'd thrown on a stretchy summer dress, bundled a jumper over the top and come out to buy something warmer that could see me through the next few weeks. Despite it being early September, it felt like summer was well and truly over, and I wasn't prepared to freeze hoping the sun might make a final appearance before autumn arrived.

I pulled a plain black pair from a hanger, frowning when I saw the sequinned slogan *Party Girl* emblazoned across the rear. 'Sorry I missed your call earlier,' I said, knowing she'd have been worried when I didn't get back to her right away. I had revelled in the peace, the freedom, but I knew I couldn't push it too far. She'd panic, and who knew what she'd do then? 'How's your dad doing?' I asked.

'Never mind my dad,' she replied, her tone curt. 'I want to know what's going on with you. We seem to be struggling to stay in touch. Are you hiding something, Maya? Is something wrong with her?'

I flinched, shoving the trousers roughly back onto the rack, noting her worries were entirely about the baby, that *my* health hadn't even crossed her mind. I wondered if that was how Julia, Elise's sister, was feeling. Fed up of answering questions that were never about her, as if she was just a vessel, her struggles inconsequential, unimportant. I made up my mind to gently remind Elise to treat her sister with more care, just in case. It couldn't hurt. 'No, nothing's wrong, Nina. The baby is doing fine. I'm just really tired. It's the last trimester now and I'm napping a lot. I don't have much energy.'

'Should we speak to someone about that? I mean, is it normal? Or is it a sign that you're not eating properly? If you don't get the right nutrients, it will affect the baby, you know. And of course we want you to feel your best,' she added, as if she had suddenly realised how she was coming across.

'The midwife checked me yesterday. She said all was well and I'm not low on iron. I'm fine. This is all normal.'

There was a beat of silence. 'I'd hoped you would videocall me during your midwife appointment. I had some questions of my own.'

'Sorry, I didn't think. I assumed you'd be busy with your parents.' The truth was, I'd been glad to have the opportunity to discuss some of my own concerns, my worries about the birth, without Nina standing over me telling me about *deep breathing through the surges* and going on about all the negative conse-quences of every single pain-relief option available. She was vehemently opposed to me having pethidine or an epidural and had even tried to dissuade me from using the gas and air in case it impacted the baby's development. I understood how fright-ened she was of something going wrong, but as mouldable as I'd been so far, I had to draw a line somewhere.

Now she gave a heavy sigh. 'Are you sure you won't consider a planned C-section? If it were me—'

'No,' I said, cutting her off. I'd heard the argument from both of them before. They were convinced it was the safer option, but as far as I could see, major surgery was never the safer option, especially not for the mother... the *surrogate*, I reminded myself. I wanted to be able to recover fully, quickly, not to have a scar reminding me of what I'd done for the rest of my life.

'Okay,' she said softly. 'Look, Maya, Will and I have been talking and we think it might be possible for me to come home and leave him here to help my mum. It's all taking so much longer than we expected, and the idea of not being there for the birth is just unthinkable.'

I shook my head. 'The midwife said I'm not quite ready yet. She thinks I might go late.' I heard the words leave my mouth and wondered why I'd said them. It wasn't true. She'd said the baby was head down and engaged. That it could be any day now, especially as I'd felt her head drop lower than ever in my pelvis. And I wasn't about to tell Nina, but I'd been having Braxton Hicks contractions with increasing regu-larity. 'You stay and help your parents,' I said, keeping my tone light, reassuring. 'I have another appointment with the midwife next week, and if she says things are looking closer then, I'll tell you right away and you can jump on the first flight back. Will doesn't speak French, does he? So you're needed there.'

There was a pause as she hesitated, and I realised I was biting down on my lower lip, tense as I waited for her to answer. 'You're sure?' she said finally. 'You really think it won't be this week?'

'I can't promise, but I'm pretty sure she's staying put for now.'

'Okay.' She sighed. 'I'll hold off for now. You're right that Will wouldn't be much use here without being able to communicate properly. But I want to be included in that appointment next week. Make sure you videocall me so I can speak to the midwife, okay?'

I gripped the phone tightly, wanting to argue, to tell her that as much as she wanted to be included, I had the right to a bit of privacy, reassurance in what might well be the last appointment before I gave birth. I couldn't say what I needed to with her there. But I would cross that bridge later. 'Of course,' I agreed, turning to walk out of the shop and hurriedly ending the call.

I shoved my phone back in my bag, feeling drained and irritated. Not a single question about how I was doing. Not one suggestion of how she could support me. How much she appreciated what I was doing for her and Will. It was all about her needs, her wants, and I didn't know if was my hormones or my tiredness, but I was feeling more than a little fed up with it all. I glanced along the row of shops, wondering which one to try next, then froze, seeing Elise's fiery red hair and pale face coming out of a doorway a few shops away.

'Elise!' I called, happy to see her. I wondered if it was too soon to invite her for lunch again, or a coffee perhaps. She looked worn out as she turned, her smile tighter than usual, less natural as I waddled towards her.

'Oh, hi, Maya. You okay?'

'Other than the fact that I've run out of clothes that fit, and everything I find in the shops seems to be for someone half my age. I suddenly feel very old,' I joked. I waited for her to laugh, to make some quip in return, but she only nodded, glancing over her shoulder, clearly distracted.

'Sorry to hear that. I can't stop – I'm late for—' She broke off, glancing at her watch, seeming to forget what she'd been about to say. When she looked back up, she appeared surprised to see me still standing there. 'Bye then, Maya. I'll see you soon, okay? Good luck with your shopping.'

She turned, jogging down the street towards the car park, leaving me staring after her, an uneasy feeling in the pit of my belly. Admittedly, I didn't know her well yet, but still, even *I* could see that she wasn't herself. She'd looked worried. Frightened even, her eyes that little bit too wide, her mannerisms jittery.

Before I could talk myself out of it, I found my feet moving in the direction of the car park too, somehow travelling quicker than I had in days, despite the pressure on my hips, the way I had to waddle like a hurrying duck to get there. I scanned every car that passed me on the main road, discounting them until I saw Elise's pale face behind the wheel of a blue Mercedes. I was momentarily surprised at how nice her car was. It looked new, expensive, and I realised it wasn't what I'd expected her to drive. Rushing forward, I turned into the car park, reaching my own battered Honda and jamming my key into the lock.

I was being ridiculous. She was already gone, and besides, what exactly was I hoping to achieve? But even as my logical mind tried to talk me into stopping, *thinking*, I found myself in the driver's seat, manoeuvring out of the space and into the road, following the direction I'd seen her turn. I drummed my fingers on the steering wheel, scanning the road ahead, a relieved breath hissing through my teeth as I spotted her at the junction, indicating left as she waited at the traffic lights. She disappeared around the corner, and I put my foot down on the accelerator, crossing the lights a second after they turned red. It wasn't reckless, I reasoned, not really. The cars at the lights to the right hadn't even started moving. I was fine.

I took another deep breath, overtaking a learner driver and a bicycle, being careful to leave enough space, to prove to myself I was still in control. Spotting Elise's car a few ahead of mine, I let myself breathe out, forcing my shoulders to relax as I trailed her, more cautious now. I couldn't risk being seen. I wouldn't know how to explain myself if she realised I was following her. I held back just enough to keep a few cars between us as we meandered through the nicer side of town, and I realised that just like her car, this wasn't what I'd been expecting either. The houses here were all big, detached, expensive, several with iron-barred gates and keycodes, manicured lawns peeking out from behind them.

She turned into one to the right, a large Victorian detached house with a gravel driveway. The garden was overgrown, a little wilder than the surrounding neighbours', and there was something friendlier, less imposing about the oak gates, which had been left wide open, the sparse hedge in lieu of a solid brick wall. I pulled up on the kerb opposite, slightly behind the gate, where I was at just the right angle to see the front door through the spindly branches of the hedge. Was this *really* her house, or was she visiting a relative or friend?

I watched as she used the key fob to lock the car, then let herself in through the front door without knocking. I kept my gaze fixed on the window of what I assumed was a sitting room, hoping to catch a glimpse of her, but when she didn't appear, I sighed, leaning back against my seat in frustration. What the hell was I even doing here? I could ruin everything if she saw me. Any hope of a friendship would be gone. She'd think I was deranged.

Pulling myself together, and squashing my curiosity about how she could afford a place like this when she didn't work, I reached to turn the key in the ignition. My fingers paused as another car, far less fancy that the one Elise had driven, pulled up on the drive behind her Mercedes, blocking her in. A man climbed out, a hard expression clouding what might otherwise have been a good-looking face. I suddenly remembered the text I'd read over her shoulder that first day at the group. The way she'd shoved her phone back in her bag, the blood draining from her already pale face; how she'd retreated into herself for a moment, her smile when I'd asked if she was okay entirely too bright, too false. I'd wondered what had caused her to look so afraid. Was it *him*? I stared, heedless of being discreet. He looked to be in his late thirties. Was this her ex? And if it was, why was she meeting him? She'd looked so afraid just now... so unlike the bubbly, confident woman I'd known so far.

I watched as he slammed the car door, walking up the driveway and pressing his finger on the bell. There was a long wait, and I wondered if she was just going to leave him standing there. His expression darkened, and as he banged on the door with his fist, I found myself squeezing the steering wheel, tension fizzing through me. Was my friend in danger? Should I go over there? Call the police?

The door swung open, her expression as she laid eyes on the man a mixture of recognition, resignation and something that looked like fear. Elise had seemed so strong, so sure of herself every time we'd spoken, but the woman who stepped meekly back now to let this cocksure man cross her threshold was someone I had yet to encounter.

I ducked as she cast a glance behind him, as if looking for someone who might save her, and when I looked back up, the door had closed. I watched the sitting room again, hungry for more, to find out why she was so rattled, why she would let him in if he'd hurt her in the past, but the room remained frustratingly empty.

I jumped as a loud knock sounded at the passenger window and turned to see an old man peering in. 'Yes?' I asked, rolling the window down.

'Are you lost? Only I couldn't help but notice you sitting there. Need directions?'

I shook my head, and he leaned in through the window, nodding towards my belly. 'Not in labour, are you? I was there for the birth of all six of mine. My wife insisted on it. Taught me a lot about the world, about what you lasses go through, I can tell you!'

'Oh... no, I'm not. I'm fine. I'm heading off now.'

He frowned. 'You're sure?'

'I am. Thanks for your concern,' I said, gesturing for him to step back.

With an air of reluctance, he did, though I was sure he'd have loved nothing more than to regale me with tales of child-birth – the last thing I needed in the run-up to the big day. With a last regretful look at Elise's window, I turned the car around and headed home, hoping I wouldn't regret not doing more.

FIFTEEN
ELISE

He was in my house and I couldn't fucking stand it. I watched his trained eyes raking over every room as was his habit, taking everything in, judging me without ever saying a word. Every time I allowed him to come here, it made my blood boil, but it was far preferable to meeting on his turf, his sterile, cold decor giving me chills and making me feel trapped. I could never get over the fear that he'd secretly bolt the door and creep up behind me, and I would be his prisoner once again. That he'd misunderstand something I'd said, or produce some imaginary misinformation, and use it to exert his power over me. So this was the lesser of two evils, but still, I couldn't bear it.

The smell of his aftershave was familiar enough to ignite some primal self-protective response in me, raising my hackles and making me feel constantly on edge – he always wore so much of it. I couldn't help but wonder if it was on purpose, to goad me, stop me from erasing the presence he maintained in my life. The spicy smell would linger for hours after he left, even with the doors and windows flung wide.

I looked at him now, silently reminding myself that I would

only have to put up with him a little while longer. If I could just keep my cool, everything would be okay. Other than Julia, he was the only person left in my life who knew my secrets, my past, and that gave him an advantage over me I would never give another person. Once he was out of my life, I'd finally be free. The nightmare that had been my life this past few years would come to an end and I could forget I'd ever laid eyes on this man who seemed to feel he owned me.

I saw his sneer as he took in the polished wooden counter-top, the expensive bespoke kitchen I'd treated myself to, and knew he was jealous – didn't think a woman like me should get to live like this.

He saw me watching him and feigned a smile. 'You not going to offer me a coffee?' he asked, taking a seat on a bar stool and nodding towards the espresso machine on the counter.

I didn't bother to respond, yet despite my longing to tell him no, I walked around the counter and flicked the switch, pulling a cup from the cupboard.

He smiled, though it didn't reach his eyes. 'I would have expected you to make more of an effort with your outfit, since you knew I was coming.'

I pressed my tongue up over my top teeth, my lips pursing as I concentrated on making the coffee, refusing to let myself get angry. It was what he wanted. I wouldn't give him the satisfaction of rising to it. He'd always been like that, pushing my buttons, reminding me of things I wanted to forget, trying to make me react first so he could feel vindicated, absolved of responsibility when he retaliated.

'What would you *like* me to wear, Nick?' I asked, my attempt at a breezy tone coming out far curter than I wanted.

'A nice dress. Maybe brush your hair. Show some pride in your appearance.'

The coffee machine started up noisily and I turned away

from him, my hand shaking as I reached for his espresso, placing it in front of him. He picked it up without a word of thanks.

'What have you been up to since I was last here, Elise?'

I folded my arms, regarding him, hoping he'd spill the coffee down his pristine white shirt. He was a good-looking man, in a preppy, buttoned-up sort of way, and he knew it, which only served to make him all the more unpleasant. I shrugged, not wanting to tell him anything, yet knowing I would have to if I wanted him to leave. He would never back down. Never had.

'Have you applied for a job yet?' he asked, and I shook my head.

'You know I don't plan to do that.'

'You should. I noticed you were late home Friday evening. Why was that?'

I glared at him, irritated that he'd obviously been checking up on me. He had no right! I could picture him out there in the dark, lurking in his car. Had he been watching the whole time? The thought made my stomach lurch as I wondered what he'd seen.

'You know as well as I do that what time I get home is none of your business. Not any more. I'm free to come and go as I please. Remember?'

He stared at me, and I held his gaze, anger fizzing in my belly. 'I bet you can't stand that you don't get to keep tabs on me now. Is that why you're still trying to get me to stick to your schedule?'

His smug smile faded in an instant. 'Why don't you want me keeping tabs on you, Elise?' he asked, his cold, probing tone making me freeze, a deer caught in headlights.

I'd gone too far, said too much, driven by my need to assert myself, show him he didn't own me. That despite what he might believe, he wasn't my master.

'What exactly are you trying to hide?'

'I'm not hiding anything.' I forced my body to move as casually as I could manage, turning towards the sink, my back to him, regretting having spoken up. It was never a good idea. I just had to get through this visit, play nice, make him think he'd won. 'I made some new friends,' I said, hearing the tremor behind my words. I poured myself a glass of tap water, glugging half of it back in one go, then turned to face him with a bright smile. 'I went for lunch with a woman on Monday. She's nice.'

'Really? And what do the two of you have in common?'

'Oh, I don't know. This and that. We made small talk. It's *something*, isn't it? Better than being cooped up in here on my own.'

He took a sip of his coffee, staring at me over the rim of the cup, then put it down fastidiously on a coaster. 'Does she know about your past? Who you really are? The truth?'

'My past is my business.'

'Is that fair?'

'It's my choice. And that's the end of it.'

He shook his head. 'We both know that your track record of making choices isn't always rational.'

'Any mistakes I've made, I've paid for a thousand-fold. You've made sure of that, haven't you? Karma really paid me back the day they dropped you into my life.'

He gave a smirk that set my spine tingling again, then stood. I felt my back press against the counter, my instinctive desire to create as much space as possible between him and me flaring brightly. My gaze flicked briefly towards the knife block, and as I glanced back at his face, I knew he'd seen the thought cross my mind, could read my fears as if I'd screamed them out loud.

He pursed his lips, regarding me coolly, then with a nod turned for the door. 'Call if anything changes. And tell your friend the truth, Elise. You can't build a friendship on lies.'

He walked out without another word, and I listened for the

sound of his car starting up, driving away, flooded with relief that once again I'd made it through a conversation with him without harm, longing for the day I could finally break the last few chains he had holding me and escape his narcissistic, self-righteous scrutiny for good.

SIXTEEN

MAYA

Then

Water cascaded over the edge of the bedside table as the glass I'd knocked over in the dark rolled to the carpet. I reached again for the shrilly ringing phone, smacking my wrist against the wood and swearing beneath my breath as my hand finally closed on it. Swiping blindly, I tucked it beneath my chin, clasping my hand around my throbbing wrist bone. I'd been in the deepest sleep I'd had for weeks, a dreamless, coma-like oblivion. The ringing had pierced the reprieve, seemingly endlessly, and I didn't know how long it had gone on before it had succeeded in rousing me.

After Harry had stopped trying to break down my door and finally left, a fortnight ago, I'd felt strangely numb. After months of planning, dreaming of the moment when I could finally watch him go, the reality, once the adrenaline had died down, had left me feeling unexpectedly empty. And despite having dreamed up all the ways I was going to make the most of him being gone, I'd yet to do anything but pace the silent house, scared of what would come next. Last night had been the first

proper rest I'd had in as long as I could remember, and I hated
that I'd been dragged from it when I needed it so much.

My tongue stuck to the roof of my mouth and I swallowed,
wishing I hadn't knocked my water over. 'Yeah?' My voice was
thick with sleep as I hitched myself up on one elbow, my heart
pounding at the shock of the unwelcome wake-up call.
Glancing at the digital clock on my dresser, I saw it was just
gone 3 a.m. My heart sank. Only one person would call at this
time.

As if in confirmation, I heard the familiar voice in my ear.
'Maya...'

'I don't want to speak to you, Harry. I've made that crystal
fucking clear.' I pulled the phone from my ear, squinting into
the glaring screen as I tried to cut him off.

'I've done something. Something bad...'

I heard the words reverberate down the line, and though
every part of me wanted to press the red button and block his
number once and for all, there was something in the way he
spoke that put me on edge.

Slowly, I raised the phone back to my ear. 'What have you
done?' My tone was impatient, like a schoolteacher at the end of
her rope, and I didn't have the energy to care that I reminded
myself of my mother in this moment.

'It was *your* fault. I never would have... You drove me to
this, Maya. Remember that. They would be alive if you hadn't
done what you did. If you had just backed down and let me...'
He broke off, an angry grunt in the back of his throat.

I pushed against the mattress, sitting bolt upright, the hairs
on my arms and the back of my neck rising, a chill sweeping
down my spine.

'What the hell are you talking about? What did you do,
Harry?'

'*You* did this, Maya! Remember that. You're the reason
they're dead!'

I shook my head, my hand turning slick as I tried to keep hold of the phone. My heart was pounding so fast I thought I might pass out. Through the throbbing pulse in my ears, I could hear the way his breathing had turned jagged, panicked gasps, unable to suck in enough oxygen. In the background was the unmistakable frantically high-pitched sound of a siren growing increasingly louder. His breath quickened, and I pictured his face, the way his brown eyes would be wide with fear. How he would look to me to be saved – *always* to me. The long-standing habit of needing to protect him enveloped me, but I forced it aside, sick with terror, wanting answers from him.

'Harry, tell me!' I screamed, my fingernails embedding themselves in the pliable silicone phone case. 'What have you done?'

He gave a harsh bark of laughter. 'I warned you, Maya. You should never have kicked me out. You should have let me talk to you. Now look... look what you've done!'

The sirens became deafening. The line went dead, and I knew I'd made a choice that would haunt me for the rest of my life.

SEVENTEEN

ELISE

Now

The sun was glaringly bright in the sky, already sinking low, forcing me to squint through the windscreen as I drove up Julia's street, my eyes scanning her driveway. Her car was missing, and the sight of the empty space where I'd hoped to see it instantly fed the suspicion I'd been battling to suppress. On Thursday evenings, her children always went to Ben's parents for dinner straight from school. It had been the routine for the past five months at least – a chance for her to catch up at home and rest a bit. But she wasn't here now, and I couldn't help but wonder if the reason for that was another appointment that she'd kept from me. There'd been nothing in her calendar, no blocked-out sessions when I'd checked this morning, but maybe that was intentional on her part.

Driving onwards, I found myself heading on autopilot through the winding streets towards town. Her GP surgery was on the high street, and I approached it as slowly as I could get away with, aware of the impatient line of traffic building behind me. My stomach was tense as I stared through the windscreen at the entrance to the surgery, unsure whether I wanted to see her coming out in order to prove my suspicions right, or to leave the question unanswered so that I might talk myself out of the fears I'd been plagued with of late.

If she'd done it again, if she'd kept another appointment from me, it would bring a whole host of unwelcome questions to the forefront of my mind. It would validate the uneasy feeling I'd been trying to suppress, the one that screamed that Julia was actively trying to distance herself from me. That she wasn't just tired and hormonal but purposely trying to withhold information about my baby, along with the plans for his future. The thought was unbearable. The idea that after all this time, after all my planning and dreaming, it could fall apart... I couldn't let that happen. I wouldn't.

The door to the surgery opened and I watched, eagle-eyed, as a man walked out, chiding myself for my paranoia, trying to talk some sense into my overactive imagination. I'd been through a lot over the past few years... a hell of a lot. It was hardly a surprise that I was still feeling the consequences of those experiences now. Seeing danger where there was none. Questioning everything too deeply. I had to remember that not everyone lived on a knife edge like I did. Not everyone saw the world the same way as me.

I pictured Nick's smug expression, recalling the way he'd tried to dominate my space, my home yesterday – how he always wanted to make me feel small, unworthy of his time – and reminded myself that just because I'd been unlucky enough to find myself in a situation with him I had yet to escape from, I shouldn't tar everyone else with the same brush. Julia wasn't the type to cut people out of her life. She wouldn't do that to me. We'd had our issues, our disagreements, but ultimately she was a good person. And if I wasn't able to rein in my anxiety, *I* could be the reason this all failed. I had to calm down.

The car behind me beeped loudly, and I realised I had

slowed to barely more than a crawl. Reluctantly I moved forward, passing the surgery. Julia wasn't in there. She wouldn't let me down. I was overreacting.

I took a steadying breath. It was only to be expected at this stage in the process, with so much at stake. I would go home, call her and arrange to go over tomorrow. I had to give her space, respect the fact that as much as I wanted to be involved every step of the way, my insistence on forcing myself into situations where I knew I wasn't welcome would only make everything worse. I had to be patient, reasonable, though it was easier said than done.

I gritted my teeth, watching in my rear-view mirror as the man stopped to hold open the surgery door. As he did so, a pregnant woman walked out, her dark hair shining, her coat familiar. Stamping on the brakes, I craned my head round to look out the back window, the car behind me breaking into a volley of frustrated beeps again. The woman turned, her attention drawn by the noise, and I saw her face as clear as day. *Julia!* It was her.

I looked back to the road, desperately searching for a parking space, half tempted to just leave the car right where it was, blocking the traffic, while I ran after her, all my resolutions to be less intense vanishing in a puff of smoke. But every space was full and the driver behind me was getting out of his car now, his big frame and furious expression making me take stock of what I was doing. I couldn't stop here. I had to keep moving. I could circle the block and try and find her. Make it seem like a casual encounter. I had to speak to her, to know what was going on. Was it normal to have so many appointments if nothing was wrong? Was she hiding something from me?

The angry driver rapped on my window, gesturing for me to roll it down, and I shook my head, putting the car back in gear and driving on, not even caring when he yelled a stream of profanities after me. I saw him stomping back to his own car as I turned the corner.

I followed the road round, my fingertips tapping impatiently on the wheel as cars, bikes and pedestrians seemed to work against me, darting in front of me, oblivious to my state of urgency. My gaze scanned the side of the road for her parked car, hoping to catch a glimpse of her, but there was nothing. I couldn't see her anywhere. With a groan of frustration, I realised I'd lost her.

I saw a space at the side of the road a little further up and pulled into it, catching my breath as I realised my hands were shaking. What did this mean? She was going behind my back, keeping secrets, and that, as much as I wanted to explain it away, wasn't right. Wasn't fair on me. Not after all we'd discussed. The dreams she'd let me believe in. Would she really be so cruel?

I pulled out my phone, my shaking fingers finding her name, pressing hard on the call button, holding it to my ear as it rang and rang. No answer. Her voicemail clicked in, and I hesitated. This was a conversation we needed to have face to face. It wasn't something that could be said in a message. I would have to go back to her house and wait for her to turn up and give me the answers I deserved. I'd been brushing this under the carpet for too long. I had to know what the hell she was doing before I lost my mind.

EIGHTEEN

The house still looked quiet, the driveway conspicuously empty as I pulled up across the road from it, turning the engine off and climbing out regardless. My palms were sweating despite the cool breeze that rushed down the back of my neck, and I steeled myself for an uncomfortable conversation as I headed up the path to the front door, pressing my finger hard against the bell. I didn't know what I was going to say to Julia, how I was going to express my fears, get her to see the situation from my point of view. Now that I was here, I wondered if I was making a mistake, but before I had a chance to second-guess myself, the door opened and Ben stood there dressed in blue jeans and a loose white T-shirt, his feet bare.

He broke into a confused grin. 'Elise, hi,' he said, his eyes crinkling as they met mine. 'You're not expecting to see Jules, are you? She's not here tonight.'

'Not here?' I shook my head, hoping he'd fill in the blanks. Ben could always be relied on to give more information than he should. Something I'd heard Julia berating him for in the past when she didn't know I was listening.

'Did you go round the back? I had my headphones on,' he

explained, lifting the expensive-looking set from around his neck and dropping them on the table just inside the hallway. 'She's been so forgetful lately. I bet she forgot you were coming.'

'When's she going to be back?' I asked.

'Tomorrow.' He shrugged apologetically, as if it was his fault. 'My mum offered to keep the kids overnight, but they weren't keen to be away from Jules – they're both being super clingy at the moment, what with the pregnancy taking all her time and energy. So as a compromise, Mum offered to babysit and put Julia up in the spare room. She's going to run her a bath, put the kids to bed – pamper her a bit.'

'Couldn't *you* have done that here?'

He wrinkled his nose. 'To be honest, the break will do us good. I needed a night to catch up on a few things.' He pressed his lips together, as if reminding himself not to share all the details Julia would want to keep between the two of them, but it was enough for me to feel the tension behind his words, to know there were things they'd been at odds about lately. I couldn't help but wonder how much of that was down to me.

'Oh... I really needed to talk to her.' I realised I was picking at my cuticles and gripped my hands together to stop the anxious habit I thought I'd managed to break. I hated the feel of the rough skin, the reminder of a time when my hands had been in a constant state of bleeding, cracked and stinging and yet still I'd continued to work away at them. I was in a better place now. I wouldn't do that to myself.

'I can call her?' he offered. 'Tell her it's an emergency?' He reached out, touching my shoulder in a way that looked almost brotherly, but I could feel the energy pulsing through him. It was inappropriate – Julia would have a fit if she could see us interacting this way. But I didn't brush him away.

'Thanks, but no,' I said, sure that dragging her away from her chance of a break would be the worst thing I could do right now.

'Okay... if you're sure?' He waited for me to nod, then took a deep breath. 'I should go back in. I'm not supposed to be... well...' He broke off and I shook my head, confused.

'What?'

He gave a heavy sigh. 'Julia's asked me not to talk to you so much. She thinks I'm crossing a line.'

'What do you mean?'

'She's seen us... on the driveway.'

He didn't need to say more. I hadn't realised she'd been aware of the chats we shared out there. It was silly. Harmless. And I couldn't help it if we bumped into each other on my way to see her sometimes, or if he happened to be out there when I left. Did she really expect me to ignore him because she felt uncomfortable at how friendly we were? A fizz of indignation pulsed through me at the thought of her at the window, watching me, *judging* me. She knew how small my life was right now. How something as insignificant as a bit of friendly banter with someone like Ben, who always seemed to look for the positives in life, could brighten my spirits. Why did she want to take that from me, unless out of spite? Jealousy? She just *had* to be in control, didn't she? We were all just her pawns to play as she liked!

I stared up at Ben, our eyes locked, a thousand unspoken words passing between us. I could feel the heat pulsing in the space between our bodies. It had been so long since I'd been looked at the way he looked at me. So long since a man had wanted me, needed me... God, I missed that.

I swallowed, breaking the stare as I glanced over my shoulder. 'I should go then,' I said softly. 'No need to tell her I was here. I'll call her tomorrow and arrange a time to come back. Let her enjoy her time at your mum's in peace.'

He nodded. 'Thanks, El.' He looked as if he was going to say something else but instead closed the door silently, and I pressed my hands to my face, my heart racing.

Pulling myself together, I took a deep breath, then walked back down the path, crossing the street towards where I'd parked the car. Hearing the sudden bang of a door slamming behind me, I turned, seeing Ben running barefoot across the road in my direction.

'Elise!'

He looked over his shoulder, then grabbed my arm, pulling me into a narrow alleyway that led to a block of garages behind the neighbouring houses. 'You *know* why she doesn't want me talking to you,' he said, his voice low and urgent. 'And she's right.'

I stared at him, hurt, confused. 'Is this about the baby?'

He frowned. 'She's been more... emotional lately, and yes, the baby might be a factor, but...' He shook his head. 'She told me what you did, Elise. I know it was wrong; she shouldn't have said anything, but it just came out when we were talking, and—'

'What do you mean, *what I did*?'

'Elise...'

My heart seemed to stutter in my chest. I couldn't believe it was true, but then the way he was looking at me made me certain that he was referring to something I didn't want anyone knowing. 'What I tell Julia is in confidence! She had no right to share my personal secrets with you – she should never have told you!'

He pressed a finger to my lips, pulling me further into the alley with his other hand and pressing me back against the wall. 'You're right. She shouldn't have told me,' he said, his head bending low over mine, his voice husky. 'And if I were you, I'd be livid that she broke your trust. But honestly, El, what you did... what she told me...' He pressed his forehead against mine, and I felt butterflies rise in my belly, the heat of his skin sending goose pimples over my body. 'I think you're incredible,' he whispered. 'So fucking strong.'

I pushed against his chest, though the effort was half-hearted. 'I'm not. I'm broken. I'm the furthest thing from strong.'

'No.' He shook his head. 'You're amazing.' He gave a sigh, the corner of his mouth curving in a smile. 'You aren't like any other woman I've ever met.'

I looked up at him, unsure whether to run or to hold my head high and agree with him. There were so many people who thought otherwise. He was the first person who'd said anything to this effect, the first who'd heard my secret and not looked at me in disgust, revulsion. Here he stood, accepting me in my entirety – something I hadn't believed anyone could do. Even Julia, though she tried to hide it, didn't understand. I could see it every time we talked. She put herself in a different category from me. And yet here was her husband giving me something I hadn't known how much I needed.

I found myself leaning closer into his minty breath, the spicy aftershave on his neck. 'You really think that?' I asked, my words barely more than a whisper.

'I would have done the same. I mean it.'

Our eyes locked again, and this time I saw the intention in his. This was wrong. He was Julia's husband. But we shared a secret now... Would one more really hurt?

His hand cupped my cheek, then slid beneath my hair, holding the back of my neck, and as he pulled me closer, I found my arguments fading away, his lips urgent as they met mine, his tongue pressing into my mouth – hot, needing. His hips pressed me harder against the wall, and I found I didn't care that it was wrong.

The cocktail of emotions I'd been feeling at Julia's coldness, her inability to see anything from my point of view, was too fresh in my mind, and as Ben's fingers slid beneath my top, finding bare skin, my body suddenly felt as though it had come back to life after a long hibernation. I arched back, gasping as he lifted me up against the wall, my legs wrapping round his waist as if I could keep him with me. A sudden image of the two of us walking with our baby in a pram by the river filled my mind, but I shook it away. It had to be just me. There was no other choice. No way to circumnavigate that fact.

He drew back, looking at me with a question in his eyes, and I heard the sound of his fly zipping open. I nodded, logic and reason no longer playing a role in my choices, gasping as he pulled my underwear to one side, sliding inside me as if we were meant to fit, letting him take me away from all my fears, my worries. He groaned against my ear, the pent-up tension we'd shared finally coming to an explosive conclusion, and I made a silent promise to myself that it was just this once. Never again. And Julia would never know.

NINETEEN

MAYA

The takeaway hot chocolate was burning my fingers through the flimsy cardboard, and I swapped the cup back and forth between my palms, trying to look relaxed as I waited out the front of the community centre. I'd got here twenty minutes early, hoping to have a moment alone with Elise, a chance to make sure she was okay before the rest of the women arrived, but with only five minutes to spare, there'd been no sign of her and I was feeling anxious. I pulled out my phone as a couple of familiar faces approached, pretending to take a call as I turned my back on them.

Since driving away from her the other day after watching that angry-looking man going into her house, I'd not stopped thinking about it, wondering if she'd been in danger. She'd seemed so strange when I'd bumped into her in town, when she'd made her excuses and rushed off – as if she were afraid of being late, not just out of a sense of manners but from genuine fear of the consequences. I'd sent a text, casually asking if she wanted to go for breakfast, or a walk in the park maybe, but when she hadn't replied, my mind had begun spinning, taking me to those dark places I could never seem to avoid.

I wondered if anyone else was this way. I had always been an overthinker, but I was sure it had only been since Harry that I had lost the off switch in my mind. A set of circumstances that would be ordinary to any other person could become the trigger for an ocean of despair, anxiety, guilt – and in the case of Elise, it was a state I knew I wouldn't escape until I had all the answers. It had taken all my strength not to drive back there and find some excuse to knock on her door and check on her. The only thing that had stopped me was the little voice in my head screaming that I would lose any chance of her friendship if I didn't pull myself together. Selfishly, I had let that thought sway me, but the decision had kept me up at night.

I glanced behind me, seeing that the two women from the group had disappeared inside, and yet there was still no sign of Elise. I set the undrunk hot chocolate down on top of the wall, the smell making my stomach churn uncomfortably, and was about to go inside when my phone began to ring with an unknown number. For a moment, I wondered if it might be Elise, calling from a secret burner phone or something, desperate for my help, but then, as I glanced up, I saw her jogging across the road, waving, her smile bright and wide as she called my name.

'Maya! I thought I was going to be late again. You just get here?' she asked breathlessly as she unbuttoned her red trench coat and ran her fingers through her wild mane of ginger curls.

'I was just heading inside. Here.' I picked up the cup, handing it to her. She looked at it without taking it. 'I got myself a hot chocolate,' I explained, 'but turns out the smell is making me nauseous. You want it?'

'Oh, uh, thanks,' she said, eyeing it almost suspiciously before taking hold of the cup. 'We'd better get in there.'

She pushed open the door, holding it open for me, and I dropped my phone back in my bag, relief flooding through me that she looked so well. For the first time in days, I felt my chest expand fully, some of the tension that had been spasming in my shoulders and neck loosening a little.

'Sorry I didn't reply to your message,' Elise said as we walked down the corridor. 'Sometimes I find all this technology overwhelming – I just turn everything off for a little while. I need the silence, you know? I only saw you'd sent it just now when I was getting ready to come here. I'd have liked to meet up though. Maybe we can go for lunch again this afternoon?'

'That would be nice.' I nodded, trying not to show just how pleased I was.

When we reached the hall, I went to make a peppermint tea, noting that as she sat down, she slid the takeaway cup beneath her seat without taking a sip. Was it as simple as her not liking hot chocolate but wanting to be polite? She'd ordered one at the café, so that couldn't be the issue. So, I thought, stirring the tea bag in the mug of hot water, was it that she didn't trust me enough to take a drink from me?

'Welcome, ladies!' Sheila said, standing up and grinning around the circle, her red lipstick a few shades too bright for her complexion. 'I'm glad to have made it here without getting soaked today. Looks like we're in for a couple of days of sunshine.'

'Best make the most of them,' Claire chimed in. 'The long grey winter will set in before you know it.'

Lauren, a young woman who seemed to be taking pregnancy in her stride, stretched out her skinny legs, crossing them at the ankles and unzipping the polyester bomber jacket covering her tidy bump. 'I for one am going to have this baby and then take myself and my sister off for a luxury holiday at an all-inclusive resort in the Caribbean. The intended parents have already paid for it,' she said, wiggling her feet, my eyes drawn to her battered yellow trainers. 'I'm travelling business class too,' she added, leaning further back in her chair, displaying her belly, small and compact. I was certain she'd escape without so much as a stretch mark.

'Is that ethical?'

I paused on the way over to my seat, my mug steaming, as Lauren looked up to see who'd spoken. Elise was staring at her, her eyes intense as she waited for a response. 'For them to pay for your trip? That's not legal, is it? I mean, it's a bit more than paying for a taxi to hospital or funding your maternity wardrobe. It hardly counts as a reasonable expense, does it?'

Lauren gave a casual shrug, though her mouth looked tight as she answered. 'It's just their way of saying thank you.'

'Really?' Elise was folding her arms now, and Sheila opened her mouth as if to interject, but Elise continued, her tone accusatory, 'Because it sounds like compensation. Like an exchange – your baby for a holiday in the sun.'

I flinched, silently slipping into my seat. If someone had directed that remark at me, I'd be devastated – livid, actually, if I was honest – but Lauren looked completely unfazed.

'It's not my baby. It's theirs. And why *shouldn't* I get a treat after giving up the best part of a year so they can become parents?'

'So you're comfortable with that? You don't feel like they're making you offers you can't refuse? Because you can, you know. They might have money, but they don't have the power to rent your womb. What else have they offered you? What other rewards have they promised?'

A flash of anger crossed Lauren's usually laid-back features, her pretty blue eyes narrowing, a blotch of red spreading across her freckled neck. 'What the fuck are you trying to say? That I'm some sort of victim? Let me tell you something, mate – I know what it's like to be a victim, and this isn't it.' She let her eyes rake over Elise from head to toe, making a point of taking in the expensive coat and bag, the bohemian dress that looked like it was made of silk, its expert design obvious without even seeing the label. 'Do you think because I'm from a council estate I'm too dense to make up my own mind? That because I don't have money I let myself be bought by the highest bidder? Is that it?' She glared across the circle. 'I've been through a hell of a lot of shit in my life, love. I've had an education in things you will never be able to wrap your pretty little head around. Just because I can't afford the things you have doesn't mean you have the right to judge me. I'm not being used. I'm being treated well by these people.'

'Of course you are. Because they *want* something from you.' Elise's expression was set, and I admired her gall to keep going, despite Lauren's convincing speech.

'Yeah. Something I'm more than happy to give.' Lauren shook her head, playing with the zip on her jacket, pulling it up and down over her bump, and for the first time I saw a different side to her, a lost little girl who'd been put on the spot and didn't like it. Maybe there *was* something to what Elise was saying. Was it possible that for all her easy-going banter, Lauren had been manipulated into making this choice? She was so young.

She turned her gaze to the woman sitting to her left and said in a low tone, 'For God's sake, this was a decent group before *she* started coming. Why does she have to make it so awkward?'

Sheila cleared her throat, chiming in before Elise could respond, though I could tell she was itching to say more. 'It's only natural that we all have fears, strong feelings, concern for one another. It's a life-changing journey, one that none of you should take lightly. But perhaps we can all take a moment to think about how our words might land, and how what we say can make others feel? We're all experiencing a lot of emotions; let's stick together as we work through them, okay?' she said softly.

There was a murmur of agreement around the circle, and Lauren pulled a half-empty packet of Maltesers from her pocket, popping them one by one into her mouth and crunching loudly. She stood up. 'Actually, Sheila, I'm not feeling it today. I'm going to head off.'

'You don't have to do that,' Elise said. 'I'm not trying to be judgemental. I'm sorry I hurt your feelings. I can be' – she shrugged – 'blunt at times.'

'Yeah, fine, whatever.' Lauren picked up her shoulder bag, giving a half-hearted wave as she left.

Sheila bit her lower lip, looking uncomfortable, then took a breath and clapped her hands together. 'Right, so let's go around the circle and have a catch-up, shall we?' she said, taking her seat and smiling a little too brightly.

Despite the awkwardness of Lauren leaving, I was glad she'd gone. The rest of the session would have been unbearably uncomfortable had she stayed, the tension between her and Elise preventing anyone from moving forward.

I placed a hand on my bump as the baby made a slow roll to the left, her foot digging under my ribcage as she started up a rhythmic kicking. One by one, the women shared their news, their worries, and I found myself starting to relax, the anxious energy that had lingered relentlessly over the past few days finally dissipating, leaving me feeling tired and ready for a nap. I looked up as I heard Sheila ask, 'And what about you, Elise? Are you feeling up to sharing with us today?'

Elise gave a slow nod, and I felt my exhaustion evaporate, sitting up straighter, keen to hear what she had to say.

She glanced down at her lap, looking suddenly vulnerable, unlike the strong, outspoken woman I'd learned to recognise. 'I don't know how much to share,' she said softly. 'It feels like when I say anything, I'm opening myself up to my fears being realised. Like voicing them out loud will somehow make them true.'

'We've all had fears, love,' Sheila said softly. 'And I think that's a feeling we've all experienced at some point in this journey. But it might help to talk. You might find you're not as alone in this as you believe right now.'

'I'm scared.' The words were soft but filled with a pain that made my chest tighten, my eyes stinging with the effort not to cry. My hormones weren't helping.

'I need this... I can't stand the thought that it might all fall apart. But... there are people who wouldn't agree with what I'm doing. People who would stop me if they knew.'

Her eyes met mine, just for a second, and I saw in them a level of fear that had my mind racing once more. The man... that visit.

I found myself speaking before I knew I was planning to. 'Did you ever try to get pregnant? Was there ever a man in your life? Someone you would have wanted to do this with?'

This time she didn't meet my eyes. 'There was someone...' She took a deep breath. 'Another life... But things don't always turn out as you plan, do they? People can take your dreams from you. Destroy the vision of the future you'd hoped to create.'

I opened my mouth to ask if she was in danger, if she was running from something, but she continued to speak.

'My sister is neglecting to keep me in the loop. There have been appointments she's gone to without me. I know what she's like – she's so organised. So matter-of-fact about these things. She's not the type to get emotional, not like me... Sometimes I think she doesn't see anything wrong with what she's doing. But it hurts. And it scares me... I've not been myself lately. I've acted out of fear, made silly decisions.' She linked her fingers together and I saw her picking at her cuticle, the skin already raw and bleeding, as if she'd been doing it a lot lately.

'You need to sit her down and tell her what you're feeling. Some women just don't get it. I'm guilty of it myself,' Laura said, and I noted that for once she was here without Sarah, her intended parent. It was clearly giving her an opportunity to be more open than she might otherwise have been. 'I'm tired, grumpy, trying to look after my own family, and quite honestly, yes, I'm aware that the parents want to be involved, but sometimes my skin crawls with the need to be by myself, to not have them breathing down my neck at every opportunity.'

She looked apologetically at the two women who were intended mothers sitting opposite her.

'Sorry to say it in front of you, but it's the truth. This isn't a walk in the park. It can be bloody draining, and I think you guys can get so wrapped up in your excitement that you forget we're not machines.' I found myself nodding silently, her words resonating deeply. 'But,' she continued, 'it doesn't mean I'm having doubts. I'm just in survival mode right now. I'm getting by, but when it comes to the big day, they'll be getting their baby. And I'll be getting a full night's sleep without back pain,' she added with a wry laugh.

'Nah, you'll be cursing your tits for swelling up like balloons, and changing your pad so it doesn't leak through your underwear,' someone said, laughing.

'I'd forgotten that part.' Laura frowned. 'My point is, Elise, it's perfectly natural for you to feel frightened, but at the same time, your sister is doing a massive thing and she's just bloody tired. Give her some space, and be patient. You're on the home stretch now, and in a few weeks' time, this will all seem like a distant dream.'

'She's right,' Sheila added. 'I remember that fear so well – even after I had my son in my arms, I kept thinking it was all going to go wrong. It took about six months before I really believed he was mine, that someone wasn't going to bang on the door and demand I give him back to his *real* mother. I felt like an imposter, like I'd stolen him.'

'But that went away? That feeling that he wasn't yours? Did you love him like you would have had you birthed him yourself?' Elise's voice was quiet, but her desperation to hear the answer was clear as she worked away at her skin.

I reached over, taking her hand, afraid that she was going to draw blood if she didn't stop.

'I won't lie. It wasn't the sudden, all-consuming maternal love I'd read about. It took time to develop that bond, but once I felt it, that was it for me. I would have run into a burning building for that boy. I still would, and he's almost twenty.' Sheila laughed.

I felt Elise's hand soften in mine at the words, and she turned her face to me, offering a smile. 'Thanks,' she whispered as the conversation continued around us.

'What for?'

'Being here. Seeing me. It means a lot.'

'It's nothing,' I said, though her words filled me with pride at having made a difference. 'I get why you'd feel afraid. Sometimes I wonder if I'm making the worst mistake of my life.'

I felt her freeze as she looked down at my belly and shook my head quickly. 'But then,' I said, 'I remind myself why I went into this, how wonderful Nina and Will are and how loved this little baby is going to be. And that fear goes away.'

Elise looked at me, an eyebrow half raised as if she didn't quite believe me, then squeezed my hand, nodding. I took a sip of my tea, feeling the hot liquid scorch my tongue, wishing it could burn away the lie.

TWENTY

I stood at my bedroom window leaning out into the night, breathing in the cool, damp air until my lungs were so full they felt as if they might burst. I'd slept fitfully for a few hours, the baby kicking me hard in the ribs every time I lay down, my dreams taking me to places I longed to escape, gripping me in their claws and refusing to let me up for air until I was close to passing out. Three times I'd woken with a scream lodged in my throat, half out of bed before I was fully conscious. I'd finally given up at just gone 2 a.m. My mind was too busy to sleep now anyway.

Every time I closed my eyes, I saw Elise. The house she lived in. The boyfriend who might be hurting her. The immense sense of responsibility I felt at knowing she might be going through something she couldn't extricate herself from. I had an overwhelming desire to see her again.

She'd accompanied me to lunch after the surrogacy group, and though she'd asked after me and the baby, made small talk about the other women, including Sheila's increasingly comical attempts to get Richard's attention – today she'd been wearing a black leather waist trainer over a bright red low-cut top – it hadn't escaped my attention that she wasn't herself. Something was weighing on her mind. Something big. And I couldn't pretend not to notice. As much as I didn't want to admit it, I knew that I had to help her.

The baby stretched out a leg, her tiny foot pressing so hard against my belly I could trace the outline of it through my nightie. It was a comfort having her with me. It had been a long time since I'd felt like I wasn't alone. I closed my eyes, picturing another lifetime. The busy days filled with purpose, the shouts and laughs of my team in that thriving office. The good times when I'd come home after a fulfilling day at work to find Harry waiting for me, and we'd made dinner together, only managing to eat half of it before passion overcame us and we raced up the stairs to the bedroom, tearing each other's clothes off, eating the cold leftovers in bed hours later while watching a movie. The house we'd shared had had the potential to be something so special. A family home, bursting with love.

I turned away from the window, slamming it closed, annoyed with myself for having succumbed to the pointless fantasy. Casting my gaze around the cramped bedroom, the tiny living room beyond, I reminded myself of the reason I was here now. Why I had deserved to lose it all. And why I was obligated to help Elise.

I glanced at my phone and saw I had a voicemail; turning on speakerphone to listen to it, I yanked on a pair of leggings and an oversized jumper that only just stretched across my belly, and slipped my feet into a pair of fleece-lined boots. I could never seem to get warm lately.

Will's voice filled the room. 'Maya, we haven't had an update today. We're not at all happy with the level of contact from you since we had to leave, and we both agree that you're being unfair. We deserve to be kept informed on the progress of our daughter. We've been speaking, and we think that since you aren't working and don't have any other responsibilities to take care of, it would be best if we get you over here. I know you aren't allowed to fly, but you can catch the Eurostar to Paris and we'll send a car to bring you down to Nice from there. I'm sure we can arrange for you to do the journey over a couple of days if you feel you can't manage it in one go, but it's beautiful here and we want to be able to keep an eye on you and resume our bonding sessions with our child. She really needs to be hearing our voices daily. I'm sure you agree.' He cleared his throat, and I heard a woman's voice in the background saying something I couldn't catch.

'The hospitals here are more than adequate,' he continued. 'In fact, there's a lovely private one close to Nina's family home and we've already asked them to give you the once-over when you arrive. I'll wait to hear back from you, and we can get started on the arrangements as soon as possible.'

The line went dead, and I stood with my arms folded tight around myself, completely stunned that he thought he could command me to drop everything and take on two days of travel so that he could read a bloody storybook to my belly. An uneasy sense of dread spread through my veins as I realised there was no way I would agree to it. The thought of being in a foreign country, where I didn't speak the language, at the mercy of Will and Nina – needing to ask their permission for every little thing – was terrifying. And it was *exactly* what they both wanted. They would never even stop to imagine that I wouldn't want to go. They'd expect me to agree, to jump at the chance. I wondered how they would react if I dared to tell them no...

I picked up the phone from the mattress, switching it to silent and shoving it into a drawer, out of sight but not quite out of mind. Then, looking at the clock, seeing it was coming up for 3 a.m., I picked up my car keys and headed out into the night. If

I was going to go, it had to be now. And I knew I wouldn't rest until I did this.

Elise's house was cast in darkness as I pulled up, her blue Mercedes sitting unaccompanied on the driveway, the car that had belonged to the man absent – a fact I was relieved about. I turned off the engine, opening the door as quietly as I dared, scanning up and down the street and finding it deserted. There were cameras and alarm systems on several of the neighbouring houses, but not Elise's.

I began to jog across the road but quickly slowed to a walk as the baby's head pressed down against my bladder, making me wish there was a toilet I could duck into. Elise's drive was covered in gravel, and I skirted around it, knowing my footsteps would be deafening in the silence of the night, padding across the overgrown weed-filled lawn instead to peer in the front window. I had an overwhelming sense that I was doing something wrong, stupid even. But I was here now. There was no turning back. If I went home now, I knew I would wish I'd seen this through.

I walked slowly and purposefully around the house, reaching a side gate and gritting my teeth as it let out a low squeak when I pushed it open. Holding my breath, listening for sounds of movement, a light being switched on, I froze, waiting. When nothing came, I propped the gate open with a rock and made my way to the back of the house. I had no plan, no real idea of what I was hoping to see. Some voice in the far recesses of my mind was trying to get my attention, to tell me that whatever I was intending would look unhinged... If she knew who I really was... if she found me here – she would never speak to me again.

Ignoring the voice of reason, I reached forward, trying the back door handle, surprised when it yielded like butter. I closed my eyes briefly, knowing I should turn back, but instead found myself stepping inside, pushing the door softly closed behind me.

I looked around, my eyes adjusting to the darkness. I was in a large garden room: Victorian-style white-framed windows, polished wooden floors, huge leafy green plants in oversized ceramic pots glazed in blue and green and red. I could picture her here. Looking out over the garden, her feet up on the comfortable jewel-coloured sofa.

I ran my hand over a smooth oak sideboard, scanning the back wall, the only one not made of glass, where pictures hung in a variety of frames. None of them were of her; none gave a clue as to the life she'd led up until now. They were all landscapes: rolling hills, wide-open sandy beaches with azure skies. Escapes... places to lose yourself for ever.

I slid open one of the drawers in the sideboard, finding packets of seeds, a gardening trowel and a pair of muddy gloves. Closing it, I squatted to open the little cupboard. A lidded plastic tub filled the space, and though I knew I shouldn't touch it, should close the door now and leave this place, respect her privacy, I found myself sliding it slowly and carefully onto the floor. It made a dull thud as it landed, and I bit down on my lip, listening hard, hearing nothing but the hum of the boiler, some wooden wind chimes clanking together somewhere in the distance.

Easing off the lid, I tried to compartmentalise what I was doing, reason that it was necessary. I looked down, swallowing a ball of emotion that had wedged itself deep inside my throat, and stared at the contents, my breath coming in short, sharp bursts as I was hit by a thousand flashbacks from a time I wished I could erase. My fingers stretched out, but before I could touch a thing, I yanked my trembling hand back and pressed it to my mouth. I had hoped I'd been wrong; that it had been my overactive imagination, triggered by stress, or perhaps the cocktail of pregnancy hormones confusing my reality. My head began to spin as I felt a sob work its way free, and I gasped, forcing myself to breathe deeper, *slower*. I had to pull myself together. For the baby if not for myself.

Pressing the lid back on and heaving the box back to its hiding spot, I stood, walking slowly through the darkness of the house, looking into each room. I slipped my feet out of my boots, climbing the carpeted stairs with silent footsteps, and pushed open one door after another. I paused as I saw the shape of a person sleeping in a bed beneath a huge window, the curtains wide open, the moonlight casting an ethereal glow over the unmoving form. Watching from the doorway, I wished more than anything that I could convince myself to turn around. But I had to see her... had to look at her.

I stepped over the threshold of her bedroom and walked to the side of the bed, hardly daring to breathe. Her wild, beautiful hair was spread over her pillow, her blonde eyelashes, devoid of mascara now, glinting in the pearlescent light.

I'd wanted so much to be wrong. The instant she'd walked into the surrogacy group, I'd known who she was, and I'd been terrified that she would take one look at me and recognise me too. My face had been all over the news back then. I'd been so afraid she would remember me, hate me, tell everyone the truth, shattering the illusion of the person I'd tried so hard to become over the past two years. But somehow she hadn't made the connection. She had no idea that I'd ruined her life. And that had given me an opportunity I never would have had otherwise.

I leaned forward, brushing a curl from her cheek, wanting to climb into the bed and hold her, to tell her it wasn't really my fault, I hadn't known what would happen. But the truth was I hadn't stopped to think. I'd been selfish. And as much as I wished I could distance myself from the blame, the thing I'd wanted to hide from myself as much as from her was that if it hadn't been for me, she never would have chosen to turn to a surrogate. Elise and I were more alike than she would ever know. She reminded me of the woman I had once been. But she would never see that. I could never let slip the secret of who I really was. Because if she found out, it would destroy the both of us.

TWENTY-ONE

The phone was ringing, and I smacked my hand against it, cancelling the call, my eyes struggling to open as I focused on the crack between the curtains, bright sunshine pouring in through the gap, making me certain it was late in the day. After I'd got home in the early hours of the morning, I'd realised I was exhausted. My calves had swollen up and my head had been spinning with the desperate need for sleep. I'd downed a glass of tap water, crawled into bed and for the first time in weeks slept without disturbance. I was so tired that neither my back pain nor the wriggling of the baby had woken me.

I frowned, suddenly worried that something was wrong with her – that the reason I hadn't woken was because she'd stopped moving. Pressing my hand to the firm lump I recognised as her bum, I jostled gently, holding my breath as I waited. When she didn't move, I poked harder and was rewarded with an angry kick. Slowly, she stretched out her legs, her feet lodging beneath my ribs as she began to wriggle, and I was so relieved I didn't even mind the discomfort for once.

'Morning, sweetie,' I said, running my hand over what I

thought was her back. 'That was a good sleep.' I stood slowly, determined to have a decent breakfast and take care of both of us much better today. It wasn't okay to stay up half the night and skimp on meals when my body was her only source of safety and sustenance. Stretching my arms high above my head, I heard the pop and click of my spine, and looked down to see that thankfully my calves had returned to their normal size after some much-needed rest.

My phone had fallen onto the carpet, and I bent, careful not to squash the baby, and scooped it up to see who had called and woken me. My heart sank when I saw Nina's name on the screen. I hadn't yet summoned the courage to tell her I wouldn't be coming to France to have the baby, but I knew I wouldn't be able to avoid the issue much longer. The pair of them weren't likely to just drop it if they didn't hear from me.

As if she could feel my resilience waning, the phone began to ring again, and despite my reluctance, I found myself answering it, walking over to open the curtains as I did. 'Hi, Nina,' I said, trying to keep the irritation from my tone.

'Hi, darling, did you sleep well?' she asked, then continued without waiting for an answer. 'My phone tells me that any minute now...' She broke off as my doorbell rang loudly. 'Ha! Right on time.'

'What? Who's at my door?'

'Go and answer it!' she said urgently.

I wanted to ignore it, to climb back into bed and pretend I hadn't answered her call, but it was too late for that now. With a feeling of trepidation, I padded slowly down the hall, unlocking the front door and opening it slowly. A courier stood on the threshold, and I felt relief that at least it wasn't Will, ready to frogmarch me across the English Channel. He passed me a thick envelope, asking me to sign for it before turning and heading back to his van.

'It's a letter,' I said, closing the door and tucking the phone between my ear and my shoulder as I made my way to the living room.

'Open it, open it!'

I sighed, dread beginning to churn in the pit of my belly. 'Hold on.' I put the phone down on the coffee table and ripped the seal of the envelope without enthusiasm. The cardboard folder inside slipped into my palm, and I flipped it open, seeing the Eurostar ticket to Paris, the printout of the hotel reservation for one night. At the bottom of the stack of paper was a second train ticket from Paris to Nice. I swallowed, pursing my lips as I saw that the date on the Eurostar ticket was tomorrow.

'We knew you'd feel guilty about accepting the tickets from us – you're always so uptight about taking our money – so we wanted to organise it before you could tell us no. Isn't it great? It's all sorted! You got Will's message yesterday, right?'

'I did.' My reply was flat.

'Sorry if he was a bit snappy – we've both been tired. But we've got everything ready for you here. Your room looks out over the sea, and there's a spa down the road where they do pregnancy massage, so I've booked us both in. I know I don't have the aches and pains like you, but still, I thought it would be a nice experience to share. And Will told you he's spoken to the obstetrician over here? It's all very modern and clean, and you can have a proper meal afterwards – none of that NHS crap they feed you over there. And the best part is that we've booked an adjoining room so we can be with you the whole time. We've explained the situation and they're happy for us to take the baby in our room straight after the birth so she can be monitored for twenty-four hours, and then of course you'll get the highest standard of care until you're ready to be discharged – in your own private space. Honestly, it's perfect, Maya. I don't know why we didn't think of it before.'

'This is... very thoughtful of you both,' I managed, my teeth gritting together as I tried to stay calm. The fact that the pair of them thought they could go behind my back and organise every-thing without so much as consulting me made my blood boil with rage, a flood of emotions I'd suppressed – rejected – for years suddenly rearing up, refusing to be damped down. 'But I wish you'd waited to speak to me first. I appreciate the offer, but I'm not coming to France.'

'Don't be silly! I told Will you'd baulk at the luxury, but I won't hear another word of protest from you. It's nothing you don't deserve.'

'It's not that,' I said, thinking that this whole plan was nothing to do with treating me, and everything to do with their need to control the situation and have it all their way. 'I *want* to stay here. I'm so close to my due date and I don't want to travel anywhere. And,' I added, unable to keep from responding to her judgemental comment, 'there's nothing wrong with the local hospital. No, I won't get five-star food, but the midwives are world class and I know them all. They've supported me since the start of my pregnancy, and I want to stay where I feel comfortable.'

'I notice you say *your* due date, *your* pregnancy. Are you forgetting she's not your baby, Maya?'

'Of course not – I know that,' I replied. 'But it *is* my birth. And I want to have the baby here. I'm sorry it's not what you wanted to hear, but I won't change my mind. Maybe you can get your money back on these tickets if you're quick.' My voice was quiet, but my words were unusually firm.

Nina was silent for a moment. When she spoke again, the light-hearted tone of excitement had vanished. Instead, she sounded cold. I could picture her narrowed eyes, her pinched cheeks.

'May I just remind you that you signed a contract, Maya.

You agreed to do everything in your power to enable myself and Will to have daily visits so we could bond with our baby.' She emphasised the *our*, and it sent a wave of fury through my veins that she could pretend I was nothing to do with it, just an irritating addition they couldn't wait to dispose of. 'You don't get to just say *no thanks*. You made a commitment to us, and we expect you to see it through. Perhaps we should get our lawyer to give you a call and remind you of the obligations you need to fulfil.'

I gripped the tickets in my hand, crumpling them into a ball, trying to stay calm as I replied. 'The contract said I would let you visit, not that I would have to pack up when I was nine months pregnant and travel by train for the best part of a day so you could see me. And I'm pretty sure it didn't say anything about you getting to dictate where or how I give birth.' I tried to recall what the small print *had* stated, but the whole thing had been a blur. 'I'm sorry, Nina, but this won't be happening. I'm not fit to travel.'

'You might want to check that contract again.' Her voice sounded dangerous, and I felt a chill creep down my spine. 'You made promises, Maya, and I don't think you're being fair if you try and back out now. It's too late for that. We have the right to spend time bonding with our daughter.'

I shrank back against the sofa, her tone making me feel suddenly afraid. Was she right? Did I have to go, even if I didn't want to? What had I agreed to? The thought of arriving there, being under her control, unable to leave whenever I wished, made my skin crawl. It felt like a trap.

'I'll give you today to adjust to the new plan and consider your options. I'd hate to have to force your hand. Let's keep things friendly, shall we?' She gave a tinkling laugh and hung up.

I opened my fist, letting the crumpled tickets fall to the carpet. Nina and Will might turn very nasty if I broke my long-standing habit of jumping through their hoops. They'd begun to believe that they owned me. That they could command me. And, I thought, pressing my hand to my belly, feeling the baby stretch and kick, if I let them down now, I didn't know what they might be capable of.

TWENTY-TWO

Then

The couple's living room was beautiful, and I hated it. Sitting on their plush wide armchair in the bay window, overlooking the manicured driveway with the two matching Range Rovers parked side by side; taking in the expensive art hung on the walls, the clean, polished parquet flooring – it reminded me of everything I'd given up... everything I'd lost over the past year.

I tried not to think of the family who'd collected the keys to my house, moving in to replace my memories with their own far happier ones. I couldn't bear to remember the first day I'd walked through the front door, knowing I'd earned that home, that I'd worked every waking hour so that I could live there. Giving it up had been devastating.

I had no right to feel resentful of any of it – I was here because of my own bad choices, my own mistakes – but sometimes I found it impossible not to feel sorry for myself. The life I'd loved was gone. The self-made business, the luxurious home... the possibility of what might be. There was nothing but emptiness now. I needed to feel something good, something real and raw and positive.

These were nice, caring people, I reminded myself. People who needed me, and who I could help. And in doing so, I could begin to let go of the self-hatred I'd worn like an anchor around my neck for such a long time now. It felt like much longer than twelve months. I'd been so alone. A shell of the confident career woman I'd thought of myself as. I had only seen my parents once over the past year, and though my expectations of their visit had been low, it had still hurt to see the way they looked at me, as if I were worthless. They didn't have the option of showing off my successes to their rich, snobby friends any more, and in their eyes, that made me a waste of their precious time. They hadn't even lifted the phone to call or send a message in more than six months.

I'd never been one for self-pity, feeling frustrated with those people who seemed to wallow in their own misfortune, but it had become more and more difficult not to sink into the abyss and lose myself for ever. I had to claw my way back out now. I couldn't go on like this.

'So,' the woman, Nina, was saying, 'I can't believe I'm saying this, but we've spoken about it at great length, and Will agrees with me, don't you, darling?' She patted the smartly dressed man's knee.

'I certainly do,' he said, smiling.

'We want you to be our surrogate!' Nina announced.

I felt my eyes widen and realised I'd been preparing myself for a no. They were choosing me... It felt somehow frightening, suddenly no longer just an idea but a reality.

'We've spoken to so many women,' she went on, 'but you stood out above all of them as being someone we could really see ourselves connecting with.'

I nodded, wondering if a part of that might be the boarding

SAM VICKERY

school accent we shared. If it made them more comfortable that I was one of their type – though in my case, the accent was the only thing that remained from that privileged life.

'And your willingness to donate an egg, work with a sperm donor,' Will added. 'I'm sure you know how hard it's been for us. Nina has grieved the loss of her womb, and we were prepared to need help in order to have children, but discovering my infertility has made things so much harder. It means the world to us that you're willing to be so generous in helping us to create a family. It's everything we've ever wanted.'

I nodded, overwhelmed by their praise, feeling like a fake, a fraud. It had been a long time since I'd had a kind word directed my way, and their focus on me felt intoxicating, addictive. I wanted them to keep talking, to remind me of all the reasons I deserved to feel good about myself. It was the very thing that had planted the seed of the idea in the first place. That desire to feel cherished, worshipped by this couple, needed so desperately. Taking this path would give me a purpose – a reason to keep living.

'It's an honour,' I said breathlessly, smiling at both of them. 'It means everything to me that you trust me enough to choose me.'

Nina reached to the shelf beside her, then slid a wedge of paperwork across the coffee table towards me. 'I took the liberty of having a contract drawn up, to protect us all... It's nothing outside the ordinary,' she added quickly.

I reached for the pen in her outstretched hand, scanning to see where I needed to sign, then scribbled my signature, jotted down the date and handed the stack of papers back. Nina looked at Will, her eyes sparkling as she seemed to suppress a smile, and I caught a triumphant expression flash across his face before he gave a nod. 'Well, that's that then. I'll send you a copy in the post,' he said. 'For your records.'

I nodded, distracted by the notion that in just a few weeks, I could be pregnant. That I might begin to feel like a human being again, rather than walking through my days like a ghost, drifting on the breeze, wishing to escape the hell that had become my world. Everything was about to change.

TWENTY-THREE

ELISE

Now

'Iced tea?' Julia offered as she walked across the huge beige rug towards the counter, where a jug was already waiting. She poured herself a tall glass and I nodded.

'Sure, thanks.' I eased my feet out of my loafers, curling them beneath me on the armchair, my gaze roaming over her garden, anxious about the possibility of seeing Ben out there. His car had been missing when I'd arrived, and though I'd told myself I didn't care, I'd found I was relieved that I wouldn't have to see him.

Since our encounter the other day, I'd been sick with guilt, berating myself for giving in to the heat of the moment. And yet despite the certainty that I'd crossed a line, I hadn't been able to stop thinking about him. It had been a shock to realise my body could still respond that way to a man. That it remembered instinctively how to move, what to do. It had been something I'd been sure would never happen for me again, a part of me that I'd long since locked away in a box, with no intention of ever opening it. Now, I wondered if that wouldn't have been for the best. It only complicated things between me and Julia. Jeopardised all the plans I'd made for my future. So what if I was waking up soaked in sweat having dreamed about him? It had been a stupid thing to do.

A part of me couldn't help but think of the last man I'd gone to bed with. The way I'd trusted him, believed that he would be the person I'd grow old with, have a family with... the moment I'd realised how wrong I'd been to give my heart to him, only to have it crushed. I was better off alone. I wouldn't make the mistake of falling in love again. I'd been burned too badly once before.

I swallowed back a ball of emotion, blinking away the image of a face that had seared into my mind's eye, then reminded myself to smile as Julia passed me the drink. She took a sip of her own, sinking down into her chair. She'd been warmer when I'd arrived this morning, less tense, and I hoped that her night away had helped. I'd already made up my mind that I wasn't going to go in all guns blazing about the secrets she'd kept from me, the appointments she'd conveniently forgotten to schedule in her calendar so I could keep track of them.

Laura's reminder at the group that Julia would be tired, stressed, *hormonal* had been pivotal in changing my attitude. I should have thought of it myself, should have known how drained she was right now. While I was thinking of what I wanted, I'd neglected to remember that she was growing a whole person inside her body. Of course she wasn't at her best right now. And if I wanted to keep things cordial between us, coming in with accusations and throwing my own emotions at her feet would only serve to facilitate the opposite of what I hoped to achieve.

'I'm sorry I couldn't stop and chat when I ran into you the other day outside the café,' Julia said, offering a smile.

I blinked, unable to hide my surprise at her apologising to

me. I couldn't recall her ever saying sorry before. 'Uh, that's fine,' I replied, leaning over to put my drink on the cork coaster.

'Was that the new friend you were telling me about? The woman you were with?'

I nodded. 'Maya, yes. She's really lovely.'

'And pregnant.'

'Yep.'

'You never mentioned that.'

Her eyes were trained on mine, a question behind the statement that I knew she expected me to provide an answer to.

I shrugged. 'I don't think we spoke about her much at all, did we?'

'Not much,' she conceded. 'But it's an important detail to miss out. How do you feel about it?'

I sighed. Julia knew more than most how I felt about being near pregnant women. It was something I'd confided in her – the pain I'd felt at seeing a round, thriving bump, the way I'd literally had to walk out of pubs and cafés on seeing a woman lowering herself slowly into a chair, a protective hand pressed against her belly. I'd got off a train three stops early once because I'd seen a woman cradling her newborn and it had felt like a literal knife to the heart that her arms were so full while mine were so very empty. It had been unbearable for me to witness, reminding me of what I would never have, the loss something I hadn't been able to come to terms with.

Julia had voiced her concern that I might not cope coming here as her bump grew, but that was different. As much as I wished it could have been me carrying the baby nestled in her womb, I knew that in the end, this time *I* would get to be that mother holding the swaddled bundle against my chest. And that had made it tolerable.

'Sometimes I feel scared,' I heard myself admit, though I'd promised I wasn't going to burden her with that, wasn't going to rock the boat and make her feel she had to put a shield between us. 'I know I'm being silly. But being a mother... it feels like the only path that makes sense for me. And I feel like if I lose...' I glanced down at my lap, not wanting to tell her all my doubts, but needing to say more now I'd started. 'If it didn't happen... if something meant that I didn't get to—' I broke off, my throat thick with emotion, blinking back tears.

Julia waited, a tiny line appearing between her neatly plucked brows, and I wiped a tear away, giving a shaky sigh, feeling the sob fighting to escape my chest. 'It means so much to me.'

'You've never been so open with me about your feelings before,' she said softly.

I looked back out of the window, watching the oak tree on the far side of the garden, the golden-brown leaves dropping one by one as the tree relinquished its hold on them. One caught on the breeze, tumbling and spinning through the air. Every time it grazed the grass below, it was buffeted by yet another gust, carried off in another direction, tumbling over and over. I felt like I was watching the story of my life play out, understanding just how it felt to be thrown in this direction and that. 'I don't find it easy,' I admitted, my voice uncharacteristically quiet now that we were discussing something of depth.

'I know. You've been through such a lot, Elise. Of course your past is going to have an impact on you. But just because you have fears doesn't mean they're any sort of prediction of what your future looks like. You need to stop picturing the worst-case scenario and just see the black-and-white reality in front of you.' She patted her belly, and I looked at her, seeing her features soften, the brisk, no-nonsense woman replaced for the moment by someone who looked like they really empathised with me. It made me feel a sudden warmth towards her, followed by a wave of guilt at the secrets I had, the things I'd never be able to tell her. It was easier to bear when she was being cold with me.

'I understand how strongly you feel about being a mother, Elise, how hard the last few years have been for you. You've made some choices that...' She paused, seeming to search for the right words, and I wondered if she'd been about to make a remark that would have come across as judgemental. 'That haven't served you well,' she continued smoothly. 'But I know that nothing is more important to you than family.'

I nodded, unable to find the words to respond.

Julia put down her glass. 'So, this Maya, what's she like?'

'Sweet, caring, a little intense... I don't think she has many friends. She seems a bit overkeen, but I don't mind. At least I know she likes me. She's the one who seems to initiate every meet-up. I'm not sure she really believes in herself... she seems to have some issues with self-doubt,' I said, thinking of the little comments she'd made, the way she sometimes looked awkward when Will and Nina were brought up, as if she was second-guessing her choice to give them the baby. It wasn't something to go into half committed. I felt protective over her somehow, over all the women at the group, in fact, though some – Lauren, for instance – didn't seem to appreciate it.

'Well, I'm glad you've found her.'

I looked at my watch. 'I should make a move, let you get on.' I hadn't heard Ben pull up outside yet, but I didn't want to risk being here when he did. I wasn't sure how good I would be at hiding the truth, if my expression would betray me.

Julia stood, walking me to the door, and as we reached it, I leaned in, wrapping her in a tight hug. She stiffened, then patted my shoulder, something hugely out of her comfort zone. I appreciated the effort it would have cost her. I pulled back, pressing my hand briefly to her belly, trying to convey my love to the baby cocooned inside. 'Thanks for today. It's been reas-suring. I hope you'll have a chance to lie down for a bit now?'

'I'm not sure,' she said, stepping back.

'Make time.' I smiled. 'I don't want you burning yourself out. Rest. Without feeling guilty for once.'

She gave a little laugh and nodded. 'That's probably good advice. See you soon, Elise.'

I walked out, seeing only Julia's car on the drive, and jogged across the road to mine, climbing in and driving away without hesitation, my heart racing. As I turned the corner, I saw a familiar blue car heading towards me. Ben's face was clear above the steering wheel, and our eyes met for a second. I saw him swerve towards the kerb, pulling over and jumping out, waving for me to stop as I passed him. In the rear-view mirror, I could see his mouth forming my name, his eyes wide as I turned my gaze away and pressed down harder on the accelerator, pretending I hadn't seen him. I gripped the wheel with my sweaty palms and focused on the road ahead.

TWENTY-FOUR

MAYA

'Fuck!'

The pile of papers were spread out on the table in front of me, and I pressed my hands to my face, feeling like an idiot. It had taken me most of the day to locate the box where I'd shoved the yellow envelope containing the contract I'd signed for Nina and Will, and my patience for the task had dissolved almost entirely by the time I'd dug it out of the back of the storage cupboard in the hallway. I'd been exhausted and aching when I'd finally slumped down in the kitchen to read it, but now I was shaking with adrenaline. What the hell had I been thinking signing something like this? I was struggling to recall if I'd even *tried* to read it back then. It didn't seem possible. Surely I would have picked up on what I was agreeing to?

It was embarrassing to think that as someone who'd never approved so much as a purchase order without having my team of lawyers look over it when I'd owned my company, I had signed something so much more impactful without a second thought. Sitting back in my chair now, I reflected on what kind of a state I had to have been in at the time to do something so stupid.

My finger traced the paragraph of small print on the bottom of the third page. I'd given them power of attorney if anything went wrong during the birth. The right to make decisions about my care and the baby's in the event I was incapacitated. Nina and Will had a vested interest in this baby. They had no connection or ties to me. If it came to a choice between saving me or her, I'd in essence given my permission for them to leave me to die.

The thought was horrifying. Was *this* why they were pushing for France? So I could be somewhere I didn't speak the language, couldn't hear the hushed conversations happening over my head while in the throes of labour? Could they really have been so calculating as to prepare for the worst situation before I'd even agreed to the job?

Over the past nine months, there had been numerous occasions when they'd talked about being there in the room for the birth, witnessing the moment their daughter came into the world. I'd stayed silent, letting them think it was a foregone conclusion. But if I'd been having doubts before, this cemented them all the more. I couldn't trust them to have my best interests at heart. Not to leave me for dead and make off with the spoils of my hard work.

As if disgruntled at being thought of as a thing to be traded, the baby kicked, making me gasp, a sharp pain shooting through my cervix, making my whole body tense in pain. I let out a long, slow breath as the unpleasant sensation subsided, patting my belly in apology. I stared at the crumpled pile of tickets I'd tossed into the recycling basket on the floor beside the kitchen door and hugged my belly tighter. I'd been mad to sign over my rights without a thought, but was it too late to claim back some autonomy now? Or would Nina and Will force me to uphold the promises I'd made?

There had been a warning in Nina's tone that had struck fear into me, made me wonder what lengths she was willing to go to in order to have things her way. I stared down at the contract and was hit by the terrifying realisation that in trying to make up for my past, I might have put myself in danger, and I didn't know how to get out of it.

I didn't know why I felt so self-conscious as I walked through the wide double doors to the university library, but I couldn't help glancing over my shoulder, feeling watched, as though at any moment Nina and Will would pop out from behind a pillar and confront me, demand to know what I was doing here. It was silly. They were still safely out of the way in France, and besides, even if they *could* see me now, they'd have no idea what I'd come for. I was only half sure myself. I cringed at the thought of having to borrow the book, wondering what the librarian would think of me, resenting the fact that I no longer had the disposable income I'd once taken for granted to buy it outright and have it discreetly delivered to my home. Or better yet, have a fucking internet connection so I could just google my answers.

When I'd moved into the flat, I'd had no money to spare for such luxuries, and though being a surrogate had eased my financial worries somewhat, I'd grown so used to being cut off from the world of social media and news streams that I'd yet to change that. It was only now that I was realising what an inconvenience I'd created for myself. But as embarrassed and jumpy as I was, I needed to push on and find some answers.

I'd blindly signed that contract. I'd felt so detached, so desperate to make the right choice, that I'd let them guide me down the path they wanted me to take. But looking over it after Nina's outburst, it had been as if I'd seen the insanity of what I'd agreed to for the first time. The daily in-person visits. The consent for them to touch my belly, seemingly whenever they felt the urge. If they'd known in advance how their family situation would pan out, I had no doubt there would have been a section about accompanying them abroad if required – and judging by Nina's furious reaction at my refusal to drop everything and go, I would have bet good money on their regret that it hadn't been included. I wondered if they were talking to their lawyers at this very moment.

My relationship with the couple was nothing like I'd envisioned. I'd seen the way the other surrogates in the group were treated like family members by their intended parents. Taken care of, loved, included but never commanded. It had started out like that for us too. But it seemed that the more I tried to assert myself, the more the mask dropped. Now they treated me like an employee, someone they'd assigned a job to, making it clear they were less than pleased with my performance. It was my own fault. I'd bent over too much, too often, showed them that they could treat me with cool disregard for my needs and still get what they wanted from me. They thought I was a pushover, and it couldn't go on. I wanted to restore some boundaries to the dynamic between us, but before I brought it up, I needed to know my rights. Surely it couldn't be possible to have a contract of this nature, where I couldn't withdraw consent at any time. These were my human rights, weren't they? I just needed to have it laid out in writing to prove my case when I told them how I wanted things to change. It might only be a couple more weeks, but I didn't want any nasty surprises when it came to the birth.

I took a breath, picturing the conversation I would have to have when they came back. How Nina would look at me when I told her I didn't want to be touched without her asking first. How her eyes would narrow and her lips purse like she'd sucked on a lemon. She would no doubt paste on a too-sweet smile, her eyes boring into mine as she agreed – what sane person wouldn't agree? – but would she mean it? Would she stick to it? Or, I thought, fear seeping through me, would she take my request as a sign that I might be changing my mind, and become all the more intense in the build-up to the birth?

I walked up the wide staircase towards the law section and began scanning the thick-spined tomes, opening them one by one to read the contents list. Finding one that looked promising, I flipped through it, skim-reading the section on surrogacy law in the UK. There was a table beside the shelves, two young women who looked like students sitting side by side, their notepads open in front of them as they talked, their voices not quite as quiet as they should have been in the fusty space. I paused as I heard the word 'surrogate', my ears pricking as I tried to concentrate on the words on the page.

'Yeah, I saw a video online last week of a surrogate seeing the baby she'd carried for the first time since the birth. The baby was like a month old, but when he heard her voice, he just sort of froze... It was like he knew something was wrong, like he'd suddenly realised what he'd lost.'

The other woman put down her pen. 'Of course he's going to remember her voice. He probably just thought, hey, I know you!'

The first woman shook her head. 'Honestly, it broke my heart.'

'I get it. Most women would feel the same. It takes someone really special to have the strength to do something like that. But imagine the joy she's given that couple. The feeling of creating a family. It's the most beautiful gift.'

I listened, feeling guilty for a moment that I'd stopped remembering the end result, the reason I'd gone into this in the first place. To give Will and Nina a chance at a family of their own. But what she said next felt like a bucket of iced water had been thrown in my face.

'That's just it though. A baby isn't a gift! Not some inani-mate object to give away because you're feeling generous. It's a tiny human who's being passed to strangers because they feel entitled to have a baby. It's fucking selfish.'

'What does it matter, if the baby is loved?'

'As an adoptee, I can tell you, it matters. My mum had no choice. My biological dad died before I was born. I think they planned to get married, but it didn't happen in time. My birth mum was from a very religious family, who threatened to disown her when they found out she was pregnant. They were from a tiny village in rural India, and my mum had the choice of going away to have me in secret before relinquishing me to a good family, or being ostracised and on the streets where anything could have happened to us.'

'I never knew that,' her friend said gently.

The young woman shrugged. 'I get why she made the choice she did, I really do. But it means I'll never truly understand my roots. I've experienced this feeling, this wrongness all my life... It's hard to explain unless you've lived it. I went out to meet her, my birth mum, a few years back, but our worlds were so far apart, we couldn't really connect on a deeper level. If I'd grown up with her, it would have been so different. I would have belonged there.' She sighed, and I felt the weight of her emotions as if they were my own.

'*She* didn't have a choice,' the woman continued. 'But where adoption is a last resort, sometimes the only sensible option, surrogacy seems to be the new trend for women who feel like they can circumnavigate the hard stuff and get the end result. Why can't they carry their own babies? It feels to me like they just want to take the easy way out, and I find that hard to stomach.'

I slid the book into my bag, unable to listen to another word of their conversation. Wrapping my pashmina around me to hide my belly, my heart racing a hundred miles an hour, I turned and rushed out of the building, wishing I'd never stopped to listen.

TWENTY-FIVE

I hadn't met Harry and Jo until long after their mother had died, and I'd never met their father, but, I thought now, looking at the photographs strewn across my living-room floor, they must have been a beautiful couple. Their children certainly were. I'd always thought it. Harry's features were dark, where Jo's were light, but rather than competing, they complemented one another.

I looked up as the doorbell rang, half wondering if it was another unwelcome delivery, but remained sitting on the carpet, having no intention of getting up to answer it. I wasn't expecting anyone and had yet to even get dressed.

I picked up a photo of the three of us in a pub garden, flipping it over to see the date written on the back. It was from the year we met, back when everything had felt like a dream, Harry sweeping me off my feet, Jo becoming the friend I'd always longed for and never found. It was the first time I'd really connected with people, been wholeheartedly accepted and loved, and their presence in my life had meant the world to me. At the time, I'd never considered that it might be too good to last. In truth, some part of me had reasoned that it was the final piece of the puzzle. That all my hard work, my striving to get where I wanted to be had finally paid off and Harry was just one of my rewards. The cherry on top of every other prize I had earned. If I'd been the person I was now, would I have looked deeper? Past the expensive suits, the fancy dinners and parties? Would I have seen the truth he'd hidden so well?

I turned the photo back over, seeing the way his arm was wrapped around my waist, secure and confident. My smile was wide, *real*, and Jo, beautiful Jo, was leaning back on the wooden pub bench, a glass of white wine in one hand, a cigarette in the other, her mouth open in the laughter that had always come so easily to her. I wondered if she laughed so freely any more. I couldn't remember the last time I'd let myself go that way.

I let the photograph flutter to the ground as the bell rang again, and rubbed the heels of my hands into my tired, blood-shot eyes. They itched with exhaustion, but I couldn't sleep. The Braxton Hicks had picked up again just after midnight, waking me not long after I'd managed to fall asleep. They'd gone on for several hours, and I'd tried to drift back off when they finally died down, but I hadn't been able to stop thinking about that call from Jo. I'd had three more missed calls from an unknown number since I'd blocked her the other day, and it had occurred to me that she might be trying another way. But why would she be attempting to get in touch now, after all this time? The idea that there might be something wrong with her had spun over and over in my head to the point where, as dawn broke, I'd wondered if I wasn't making another monumental mistake in not talking to her.

But I didn't *want* to speak to her, let alone see her. I couldn't bear to think of the things she'd feel compelled to tell me about Harry. What good would it do for any of us to reopen old wounds?

The incessant ringing at the door was setting my nerves on edge, and I used my hands to push myself up onto my knees on the carpet, gathering the photographs in a messy pile and shoving them back inside the envelope. I didn't know why I'd even kept them. I should have burned them a long time ago. Looking at them hadn't helped at all.

I stood slowly, sighing as the bell rang again, this time a long-drawn-out trill that made me want to rip the plug from the wall. Tucking the photographs beneath a pile of bills on the mantelpiece, I rubbed my face and went to answer it, dreading the idea it might be yet another unsolicited package from Nina and Will. This time there would be no accompanying call – my phone was switched off, and I intended to keep it that way until I'd decided what to say to them. *And* what to do about Jo.

Resigned, I made my way down the hall, dizziness making white stars burst across my vision, using one hand to steady myself on the wall as I moved slowly to the front door before flinging it open to see who had disturbed my privacy.

'Maya! You're okay!'

I blinked, confused to see Nina standing there, an expensive-looking suitcase at her feet, her dark eyeliner smudged and her usually shining brown bob looking mussed.

I stared at her, feeling suddenly wide awake. Had she come to try and force my hand, escort me to the train station against my will?

'Nina, what are you doing here?' I saw a flash of doubt cross her expression and realised my tone had sounded rude, but I couldn't hide my shock – the bolt of fear at seeing her here had been instant.

She recovered, smiling widely. 'Dad's all sorted. He moved into a care home yesterday, and my mum has taken on a housekeeper. Will's stayed behind to finalise a few bits and pieces, but he'll fly back in a couple of days to join us. I could tell you weren't keen on the idea of coming to France,' she added, seeming to gloss over her threats, her anger. 'I was worried I'd miss the birth, so here I am.' She pressed her hands to my belly, a familiarity she'd been in the habit of since I'd told her I was pregnant, only this time, I tensed, feeling affronted that she hadn't even asked permission to touch me. 'How's my darling girl been? Still kicking like mad?'

She lowered herself to her haunches, her hands still on my bump, and I was suddenly hyper aware that I was braless, dressed in a ropy old nightie and wearing underwear that was in need of a change. I hadn't had the energy to shower for a couple of days, and having her step into my personal space made me want to physically restrain her. I didn't trust her any more.

I stepped back, wrapping my arms protectively around myself to create a barrier, and saw the look that crossed her features, something that was more annoyance than embarrassment at her lack of tact.

'She's fine,' I answered. 'She's very comfortable in there. I'm sure nothing will happen for a week or so.' I was determined not to tell her about the contractions I'd been having last night. I still didn't want her anywhere near me at the birth – not after what she'd said to me. Was she just going to pretend it hadn't happened?

I waited for her to speak, and when she didn't, I sighed. I didn't have the energy for another confrontation right now, and if she was going to make light of the situation, I would play along. 'You really didn't have to rush back without Will.' I crossed one bare foot over the other.

She followed the movement. 'Your ankles are a little swollen. Has the midwife checked your blood pressure? You know pre-eclampsia is something to watch out for at this stage.'

I pressed my lips together, too tired to come up with a response that wouldn't sound snarky.

'Well,' she continued brightly, clapping her manicured hands together and straightening up, 'let's get inside. I'll put the kettle on and you can catch me up on everything.'

I gave a short nod, unable to summon the energy to argue,

and trailed after her into the living room, slumping down on the sofa. 'There's not much to say. She's growing well. My iron levels are fine. Nothing new to report.'

'Oh, but she'll have been missing my voice,' she called from the kitchen and I heard the kettle spring to life, the chink of mugs being filled. 'You know how important it is for her to hear me. I bet she's been wondering where her mummy's gone.'

I set my jaw, glad she couldn't see my expression. These little comments had been a part of our communication from the very start, so why were they bothering me so much now?

She came back into the room carrying two steaming mugs. 'That's why I thought it would be a good idea for me to stay with you until the birth,' she continued, handing me a cup of weak tea that looked akin to dishwater. A subtle hint about my caffeine intake, no doubt. She looked around the room, seeing the walls in need of painting, the frayed, threadbare carpet that looked decades old.

'You want to stay here?' I asked incredulously. 'But there's no space. I don't have a second bedroom.'

'I know, silly. I can sleep here,' she said, gesturing to the sofa as she plonked herself down next to me. 'Or I can bunk in with you so the baby can hear me when we sleep, listen to my breathing, you know? It could be fun – like a girlie sleepover.'

I stared at her, seeing the expectation on her face.

'No.' I shook my head.

She put her mug on the coffee table and shuffled along the sofa, pressing her hands to my belly again, trapping me against the cushions. 'Look, Maya, I know you must be tired. Let me take care of you. I'm a decent cook. And I can be here so you won't feel afraid when the time comes. I couldn't bear for you to go into labour all by yourself. What if it happens too quickly for you to call someone? I can help.'

I took a deep breath before I spoke, careful to moderate my tone. 'It's a lovely idea, Nina, and I appreciate the kind offer,' I said, sure that she was only thinking of herself. 'But this flat is tiny enough as it is, and I need my space right now. You go back to your place and we can do the regular visits like we did before you left for France. But I'm sorry, you can't stay here.'

She opened her mouth as if to argue, just as the baby gave a series of hard kicks. Nina squealed. 'Hi, my darling! Yes, yes, it's Mummy! I'm back! Did you miss me?' She pressed her face to my belly, cooing, and it took all my willpower not to shove her to the ground.

'Okay, Maya,' she said, finally sitting back up. 'If that's what you think best. But I'm home now, and I'm available twenty-four-seven if you change your mind. Anything you need, it's yours.'

'That's... very kind of you.'

'It's the least I can do. You're growing my baby.'

She lowered her head back to my bump, crooning a nursery rhyme, and I stared up at the ceiling, pretending I was anywhere else.

TWENTY-SIX

'I really need to get to bed,' I said, walking into the kitchen, where Nina was refilling the kettle for what felt like the hundredth time, wondering how many ways I could put it before she might listen to what I was saying. It was nine at night, and she'd spent the whole day in my flat, insisting on making me lunch – an awful green soup she'd said would nourish the baby and build my strength for the birth. Then there had been the hour-long video call to Will so he could chat to his 'little princess'. I'd tried to make my excuses ten minutes in, after he'd said a frosty hello to me then began strumming on his guitar while singing some awful ballad to the baby. I'd closed my eyes, hoping he'd finish playing and excuse himself. When he'd finally put the guitar down, I had thought I could leave him to chat to Nina while I slipped away, but no such luck.

Nina had gripped my wrist, holding me beside her on the sofa, talking nineteen to the dozen about how much it meant that we were all together again, how Will had been so generous to stay in France so she could come back to be here with me. She was doing a far better job than her husband at hiding her disappointment about my refusal to come to France. Will's disposition was chilly at best, so I knew Nina had been honest with him about our taut conversation on the phone the other day. It felt more authentic, at least, to see something real from him. Nina's reaction, on the other hand, was making me feel tense.

After he'd eventually ended the call and I'd tried to cajole Nina out, she'd unzipped her suitcase on the living-room carpet and painstakingly shown me all the things she'd bought during her trip in preparation for the new arrival.

I'd had to force a smile to my lips as she showed me piles of powder-pink baby clothes, little frilly skirts that looked impractical and itchy, hairbands with garish flowers attached. Something reared up inside me, wanting to yell that this wasn't some doll to play dress-up with; it was a child who needed love, comfort, a proper parent. Nina was acting like the baby was an exciting new accessory as she flicked through photographs on her phone of the expensive pram she'd bought, the fancy hand-carved cot being delivered from Nice next week.

The effort of holding my tongue had drained me of all my energy, all my tact. The Braxton Hicks had started up again just after lunch, and I'd had to sit through the contractions, uncomfortable and aching as I forced myself to pretend they weren't happening. I wanted her to leave. Wanted to be free to stretch out on my own sofa, to moan and hold my belly and do whatever the hell my body needed without her eagle eyes watching, calculating my every move.

She looked at me now, her expression questioning, and I wondered if she'd noticed the way I'd pressed my hand to the top of my bump, the wince I'd failed to hide. I couldn't be sure if the pains were getting worse, or if they just felt that way because I was so exhausted from her visit. She stepped towards me, her finger pointing to my belly. 'Was that a contraction?' Her tone was excited, her eyes suddenly bright, and I shook my head.

'No. Just heartburn.'

'Oh.' Her disappointment was palpable. 'Are you sure?'

I nodded. 'It happens all the time now. I just need to find an antacid and get to bed,' I said pointedly. 'I don't have much energy these days, and I need my rest.'

'Well, I did say you should have a nap earlier, didn't I?'

It was true, she'd practically tried to force me into the bedroom, but I'd refused, not wanting to have her here while I slept. Even having her prepare food and drink for me had been anxiety-inducing. I didn't trust her, I realised. Didn't want her doing these things, getting so close. I didn't feel safe. I stared at her, hoping the silence would become awkward enough that she would run out of excuses to stay. My words certainly didn't seem to be having the desired effect on her. Was she hoping that if she was pig-headed enough, I'd give in and let her stay? If these contractions kept on, they were going to become impossible to hide, and I couldn't have her here then. She'd love nothing more than to take over.

My mind went to the contract, the lawyer I'd called after my stressful trip to the library yesterday. I'd realised the book I'd come home with was written in jargon that went completely over my head, so had bitten the bullet and contacted a local solicitor who specialised in family law. He'd been reassuring, but still, it was frightening to realise how much they'd hidden from me, how much of my liberty they'd tried to rob me of in my vulnerable state. And I had just handed it over as if I didn't even care. Back then, I probably hadn't. I'd spent so many months wishing I could just go to sleep and never wake up. That it could all be over, the pain, the guilt... If they'd told me their plans, I might still have signed the contract. But now something had changed. And I knew exactly what it was – it was *her*. Somehow, from within me, this tiny being was giving me a strength I'd forgotten I was capable of. She was waking me from what felt like a century of numbness, making me feel emotions I'd squashed for too long.

Brazenly ignoring my cue to leave, Nina turned back to the counter. I assumed she was going to continue making the peppermint tea, but instead she pulled open the drawer in front of her.

'No, don't look in there!' I exclaimed reflexively.

'Oh, calm down, I'm not interested in your private things. I'm looking for that antacid. For your... *heartburn*,' she said, dragging out the last word as if she knew I was lying to her.

I strode forward, intending to close the drawer myself, but she made a little sound, and I knew it was too late. Slowly, she reached into the drawer, lifting out the envelope containing the contract, and the sheet of paper I'd written my notes on during the call yesterday. 'Morgan's Solicitors?' she read from the top of the sheet. 'You've been speaking to a lawyer? About this?' She waved the contract in her hand. 'Why?' Her eyes had become cold, hard little stones in her face as she stared at me, but for once, I wasn't going to let her win.

I stared back, squaring my shoulders. I'd thought about bringing up the call earlier but decided to wait until the paper-work revoking power of attorney arrived in the post. I didn't want her to try and change my mind before it was all sorted. 'Yes, I spoke to a solicitor. I thought it prudent after...' I paused, not wanting to say *after your threats*. 'We seemed to have some crossed wires about what to expect going forward, and I wanted to make sure I hadn't agreed to anything I wasn't comfortable with.'

'Meaning?' Her tone had never been more chilling. The kettle came to the boil on the counter behind her and she half turned towards it, absently splashing water into the waiting mugs. When she lowered it back to its stand, I noticed with a flutter of butterflies in my gut that her fingers remained tightly curled around the handle.

It felt impossible to explain that I didn't want her to come here without invitation any more. Unfair of me even, knowing what it meant to her. But she wasn't respecting my boundaries; even tonight, when I'd all but thrown her out, she was pointedly ignoring my wishes in favour of her own desire to stay.

'The lawyer said the contract won't hold up. There are things I've signed over to you that are my human rights. Things I'm entitled to change my mind about,' I added, thinking of the conversations we'd had early on, with me giving them all sorts of permissions, telling them my door was always open. *That* had to change. The lawyer had laughed when I'd told him the terms I'd agreed to, explaining that in UK law there was no such thing as a binding surrogacy contract and that Will and Nina had clearly been relying on my ignorance of that fact to scare me into complying. He'd said that whatever I might have signed, they had no rights over my body... nor the baby, for that matter. It had left me stunned to think that after all we'd been through, as far as the law was concerned, this baby was mine.

'So you've changed your mind? Is that it? After everything, you're going to try and pull out now?'

I shook my head, seeing the direction her thoughts were taking, the way her cheeks had flushed red, her upper lip trembling. My gaze darted to her fist, still clenched white-knuckled around the kettle of boiling water, and I took a step back. 'No, Nina, you misunderstand me,' I said, realising she thought I'd decided not to give up the baby.

'Don't you fucking dare! Don't say another word!' she yelled, her hand releasing the kettle and slamming down on the counter with enough force to make me jump.

'Nina, I—'

'No! You aren't going to do this to me, do you understand? I've waited too long, wanted this too much for you to back out now.' She stepped forward, and I bit my lip as another contraction built in the base of my spine, radiating out and gripping my belly in a vicelike hold. I couldn't speak as she met my wide-eyed stare with her own furious gaze.

'You are going to see this through, Maya, or you'll regret the day you ever walked into my life. Do you hear me?'

She stepped closer still, her breath hot against my skin. I was sure she'd see the way my bump had tensed, know what I was trying to hide. She was fizzing with anger, and for a second I thought she might slap me.

Instead, she pressed both hands to my belly, closing her eyes. 'You'll be with me soon, darling,' she whispered. Then she opened them again, staring right into mine. 'Mummy won't ever let you down,' she finished. She waited, as if expecting me to respond, and when I didn't, she turned and walked away. I heard the scrape of her wheeled suitcase on the cheap laminate, then the slam of the door as she left.

I leaned back against the fridge and wondered what I had done, my eyes closing as the image of Elise's face burned brightly in my mind. I couldn't help but wonder where she was right now, what she might be doing. And as I pictured the woman I'd vowed to make my friend, I was hit with an absolute certainty that no matter what, I *had* to keep going, even if it broke me to do it. I had no choice but to give this baby up.

TWENTY-SEVEN

ELISE

It had been three days since I'd last seen Julia. I'd thought we'd left things on a better note, broken through the tension and communicated in a way that for once in our relationship had felt almost healthy. I'd been sure that things would be easier, and yet, as I reread the message I'd sent her, still unread, ignored, I couldn't suppress the fear in my gut that something was wrong. Really, really wrong.

I'd called. I'd emailed. I'd done everything short of turning up on her doorstep – something I knew she wouldn't take kindly to – and still there had been no reply. I thought I'd made it clear how her going non-contact like this impacted me. I thought she understood how much fear was involved on my part. Was she really so selfish? I'd tried everything to find out what was going on... well, nearly everything. There was still the elephant in the room I hadn't been willing to consider before now.

After I'd driven past him the other day, Ben had sent me a message asking to meet up to talk. I *could* call him, ask him to tell me what was going on with Julia and the baby. For all I knew, she could be in hospital right now. Something terrible could have happened to one or both of them. It was so unfair

that she was treating me like my part in all this was of no conse-
quence. It might have been *her* body, *her* choice, but it was *my*
baby she was carrying! I deserved to know the truth.

A toxic series of thoughts had been circling in my mind over
and over, a horrible trickle of dread I'd tried and failed to ignore.
What if she gave birth to him without my being aware and
couldn't stop herself from falling head over heels in love the
moment she held him in her arms? What if she decided to keep
him? Would she even bother to tell me; would she cut me out of
her life and pretend I didn't exist?

As much as I wanted to believe it was impossible, it was
something she'd threatened once before. I remembered the
conversation well. The way she'd looked at me like she was so
much better than me, told me she couldn't do it any more,
couldn't help me, wouldn't try. In the end, it hadn't been
entirely her choice to take back what she'd said and apologise to
me, and I'd seen the glowering resentment she'd felt. But we'd
come a long way since then. There was a level of trust between
us now that had taken time, effort to build. But it was fragile,
liable to crumble at the slightest provocation. And if she'd found
out what I'd done with her husband, if he'd let it slip in a
moment of guilt, it would rip apart those fragile lifelines,
destroying everything.

I picked up my phone, scrolling, my finger hovering above
Ben's name, wondering what to do. If she was with him, if she
saw my name flashing up on her husband's phone, it would
open the floodgates to an argument that might change everything. But I couldn't cope with the not knowing. I had to see
her, had to make sure she was okay, that the baby wasn't in
danger of ending up with the wrong mother. Had to find out
once and for all that she wasn't going to let me down, because
the uncertainty was killing me.

Making up my mind, heedless of the fact that it was almost
ten at night and Julia was going to flip at my turning up on her

doorstep, I grabbed my car keys and headed out into the dark. If she was planning on turning her back on me now, I would do everything in my power to convince her not to.

The light was on in the front window, and the sight of it gave me a momentary reprieve of comfort. It dissipated in seconds. If they were home, what reason would she have to ignore my calls? I felt my hackles rise as I walked slowly across the road towards their house and paused in the darkness of the driveway, unable to see beyond the drawn curtains, trepidation and doubt mingling in my gut. There was a big part of me that wanted to get back in the car, go home, stick my head in the sand and suppress every doubt vying for space in my mind. But a stronger part, fuelled by a sickening fear, propelled me forward. I was here now. And I *wasn't* being dramatic. My calls had gone unanswered for three days – I had to find out why.

I pricked my ears, my finger hovering over the bell, and when I pushed down, waiting for the reverberation to fade away, I was relieved not to hear the sound of a baby's cry. There was that small reassurance at least.

I brushed my long curls back from my face and looked down at my feet, realising that in my hurry, I'd come out in mismatched wellington boots. I couldn't even recall putting them on. I'd forgotten a jumper too. Goose pimples rose on my bare arms, the frilled capped sleeves of my top insubstantial against the bracing night air.

The door swung open and Ben stood there, his eyes widening in horror. 'Elise!' he hissed, moving forward, his hand clamping around the top of my arm as if he would force me back from his doorstep. It suddenly occurred to me that he might think I was here to confess to Julia what we'd done. That he thought our little mistake had been enough to send me into a spiral that would force me out at this time of night to declare my love for him. Didn't he realise this wasn't about him? None of it was. It was about Julia. The baby!

I was about to say as much when she appeared in the hallway behind him. The sight of her still round belly sent a rush of relief through me, and I felt Ben release his grip, stepping back in one swift motion as if the touch of my skin had burned him.

She walked forward, moving in front of him and shooing him away as if he were a naughty puppy. I offered a shaky smile, but it wasn't returned. Her mouth was pinched, her eyes hard little rocks as she appraised me, taking in the dishevelled hair, the inappropriate outfit. 'What are you doing here, Elise?' Her tone was cold, and her frame blocked the door, an unspoken sign that there would be no invitation to come in for a friendly chat. Not that I'd been expecting anything of the sort.

'I... I was worried. You didn't answer my calls, and I thought maybe you and the baby... I thought something might have been wrong.'

'As you can see, I'm fine.'

'But... You can't just ignore my calls. You *have* to speak to me. You can't pretend I don't exist – it isn't fair! You promised you wouldn't do this to me again. You made a commitment.'

'And I have fulfilled my commitment,' she said, her voice turning dangerous. 'I have done exactly what I promised to do. But you cannot turn up at my house just because you feel you're not getting enough attention. It doesn't work like that. You don't have a right to my personal life, Elise. I don't have to return your calls if it's not convenient. I have a family, a life outside of you. I don't owe you any more than what we've agreed to.' She jutted out her chin, her arms folded tight over her breasts. An angry red blotch was creeping up her neck. 'And,' she went on, 'if you ever turn up here like this again, I'll cut all ties without hesitation. Do you understand me? You're lucky I don't do it now. I'd be well within my rights!'

I blinked, tears springing to my eyes as I looked to Ben for support and found his gaze trained on his feet, unwilling to stand up for me even when she was so clearly in the wrong. 'I'm sorry you feel I was overstepping,' I said, my words coming out shaky and raw. 'I just... I wanted to check... to know the baby is okay.' I reached forward, intending to touch her, needing to feel the strength of my son's kicks, to take a scrap of reassurance she was never going to offer.

She slapped my hand away, her face morphing into a mask of pure disgust. 'I knew this was a mistake. I just knew it. Go home, Elise.'

She slammed the door in my face before I could say another word, and I gripped the wall, the world spinning out of control as I realised that everything I had wanted was about to be stolen from me, and there was nothing I could do to stop it.

TWENTY-EIGHT

MAYA

I dialled the number for my voicemail, stepping into the doorway of a closed-down pet shop to let a man with a guide dog pass. I felt as though I was on the run from the police. Nina's sudden departure last night, her refusal to listen to my explanation had made me more anxious than ever. I didn't know what she might do next, but I was sure it wouldn't be good. I'd been so scared that my waters would break right there in front of her on my kitchen floor and she'd seize control of the whole situation. Thankfully, I'd been spared that, and after a long soak in the bath and a cup of herbal tea, my contractions had stalled. I was grateful for the extra time to think everything through. My head was spinning with everything I needed to consider.

Despite the respite from the Braxton Hicks, I'd slept badly, plagued by nightmares of Will holding me by the wrists while Nina, bearing a jagged rusty knife, cut the baby from my body, the newborn's echoey cries growing distant as she disappeared down an endlessly long, dark corridor, walking away with her prize. I'd awoken shaking, limbs numb, nausea swirling in my belly, and seen a text she'd sent at just gone 7 a.m. No mention whatsoever of our row last night. Just declaring that she was coming to take me to the farmers' market at nine – that the walk and good food was just what I needed, and she wanted to make sure the baby got a healthy breakfast. The baby again. Never me. I couldn't imagine how she thought she could gloss over the way we'd left things last night without so much as an apology for the way she'd spoken to me.

I hadn't stopped to think as I'd hurried to dress and leave the flat before eight, hastily locking the door while glancing nervously over my shoulder, half expecting her to turn up early. I'd shovelled half a packet of oatcakes down in the car, temporarily taming the nausea, and driven in the opposite direction to the farmers' market, to the next town. She'd called every ten minutes since half past eight, and now it was nearly midday.

I tucked myself further into the doorway, listening to the tinny announcement that I had fourteen voicemails, and was overcome with guilt. It wasn't her fault that she was excited and seemed not to remember I was a person in my own right. I'd been terrible at setting boundaries with her and Will – had never once spoken up about how they made me feel like a walking incubator. And no matter how much I resented it, I had brought this punishment on my own shoulders. I *deserved* it. That was what I needed to remember. I was having this baby for them because it was my only chance to even out the terrible consequences I had brought about with my own actions. *My* feelings shouldn't have mattered – and up until recently, I'd done a pretty good job of squashing them down. So why now were they exploding like fireworks inside me? Why had I suddenly developed this protective, possessive desire to disappear somewhere they would never find me and wipe out all the good I'd built up this past nine months? I *couldn't* change my mind. I had to go through with it.

I closed my eyes, listening to the panic in Nina's voice as she told me she'd called all the local hospitals and nobody would tell her a thing. I knew I should phone her back. Instead I found myself navigating to Elise's number, pressing down, holding my breath as I waited for her to answer, hoping she wasn't having one of her tech-free days.

'Maya! Hi, how are you?' she answered, the sound of her voice bringing me comfort, calming my nerves.

'I'm okay. I'm just out in town and I'm exhausted. Wondered if you might want to pop down and join me for lunch at the Red Lion?'

She hesitated for a moment, and I bit my lip, wondering if I was coming across as too needy again. She cleared her throat and I prepared myself for rejection. 'Uh, yeah, why not?' she said at last. 'Everything okay? You sound out of breath.'

'Just the baby compressing my lungs. I'll be fine once I sit down,' I said, pressing my hand firmly into the cramp that was tearing across my belly.

'Right. Well, I can be there in about fifteen minutes. Meet you there?'

'Great.' I hung up, seeing that there had been another call from Nina. Making up my mind, I sent a quick text.

Hi Nina, so sorry, my phone was switched to aeroplane. Just saw your messages. I'm out with a friend. All's well with the baby. Come over this evening and we can have dinner and talk. Maya x

I shoved the phone back in my bag, walking with slow, painful steps in the direction of the pub. Reaching it, I flopped down on the bench outside, sweat pouring down the back of my neck, and unzipped my jacket, leaning back to stretch out my aching bump.

'Oh my God!'

I looked up at the sound of the husky, familiar voice, and my heart dropped as I saw the tousled blonde curls, the bright red lipstick on a mouth that was openly gaping at my belly. *Jo.*

She strode across the patio from the door she'd come out of, stopping in front of me with a malicious glint in her bright blue eyes. 'Well *now* I see why you've been avoiding my calls,' she said, folding her arms across her green denim jacket. 'Harry's barely cold in the ground and you've wasted no time in moving on, have you? I can't believe you would do this, Maya!'

I stared at her. 'What did you say?' I whispered, leaning forward, my mouth turning dry.

'Don't you think you owed him more that this? I thought we were a team. Closer than family. But you hung him out to dry, and then when he did exactly what you *knew* he would do, you cut him off, and now he's dead!' Her anger had turned to something far more terrifying, a raw emotion I'd never seen in all the years we'd been friends. I couldn't breathe as I stared at her, watching the tears as they began streaming down her face, smudging her black mascara beneath her eyes. 'Don't you feel any remorse at all?' she whispered. 'You just went and got yourself a replacement and pretended like none of it ever happened, is that it?'

'I... I don't understand...' There was a ringing in my ears, and some part of my mind registered the warm trickle of liquid running down the back of my calf was my waters having broken, but I couldn't move. 'Harry isn't dead,' I said slowly, the words tacky against my tongue. 'He's in prison.'

She opened her mouth, then pressed a hand to her perfectly painted lips. 'You really don't know? Surely you saw the news? You must have!'

She waited, and I shook my head. 'No. I didn't follow the story. I didn't want to know... I couldn't read it, couldn't bear to think of it. I got rid of social media. I haven't watched the news since... since...' I shook my head, unable to process what she was saying. 'What happened?' I asked, unable to picture the man I'd lived with, planned a life with, no longer on this planet. The idea was too painful to contemplate.

Jo gave an ugly laugh, and I recoiled, unable to recognise the woman who'd been my first real friend. She had never looked at me with such contempt, such hatred as she was doing right now. I'd known that whatever love there had been between us had evaporated the moment I kicked Harry out, but I'd never thought it would come to this between us.

'He never went to prison. Never even made it to court,' she said. She dropped her head to her hands, pressing her fingers into her eye sockets. When she glanced up again, she looked so broken I almost wanted to reach for her. 'I can't believe after all the two of you went through, you didn't care enough to even keep tabs on him. He made a *mistake*, Maya. He wasn't in his right mind.'

I opened my mouth to argue, but it would have been cruel, I realised, squeezing the edge of the bench, pain and shock vying for my attention as they chased through my nervous system. For her to describe what had happened as a mistake went beyond the blinkers of sisterly love. Even now, she couldn't see him as anything other than a victim we'd failed to save.

'I thought you would come to the funeral. I waited for hours, Maya. It was dark when they made me leave the crematorium. I needed you there. I fucking needed you, and so did Harry.' She looked away and pulled a pack of cigarettes from a gold, fifties-style case inside her handbag, lighting one and inhaling deeply.

I recalled the way I'd slowly begun to shut down in the weeks after it all happened. I'd barely been able to take care of my basic needs, sometimes just moving from the bed to the sofa, ignoring the work that was mounting up, the phone, the door, not even turning on the television for company. I'd had to cut my hair short in the end after it matted so badly from neglect. I'd lost two stone; the thought of eating making my stomach turn. Looking back now, I could see I'd been catatonic, trapped in disbelief, my desperate desire to turn back the clock my sole focus.

Jo turned to face me, her expression hard once again, though the effect was marred by the streaks of black running through her foundation, the tip of her nose still pink from crying. 'I hope you're a better mother to that poor baby than you were a friend... a *fiancé*. If I'd had any idea *this* was what you'd been up to, I'd never have bothered trying to get in touch. I can see it was a waste of my time.' She shook her head, taking another drag on her cigarette, blowing the cloud of smoke to the side. 'He always was too good for you, Maya.' She spun, walking across the street, her stilettoes clicking on the cobbles, and I watched her go, too stunned to move.

Harry dead? It couldn't be true. The last time I'd seen him... spoken to him, when he'd told me... I didn't let myself finish the thought. All this time, I'd believed he was in prison. I knew I would never forgive him. Knew there was no hope for us as a couple. But I'd hoped he was surviving the experience. That he was getting help, the support he needed, making amends, just as I had been trying to do. And maybe some small part of me had thought I might see him again one day, one last time. Just to look into his eyes and find the man I'd loved all those years ago, before it all turned so sour. But now – now I'd discovered he'd been dead for almost two years. I couldn't believe it.

I needed to go. Find a fucking internet connection some-where and give in to the one thing I'd refused to let myself do since we parted ways. I had to search his name. Read the awful details of what happened that night, and find out how his life had ended without my ever having realised.

I stood so suddenly I saw white pinpricks in my vision and felt myself swaying forward, my hands groping blindly in front of me. Strong fingers wrapped around mine, steadying me, the grip unwavering as I waited for the dizziness to pass. Blinking, my eyes slowly focused on Elise's smiling face. I'd forgotten I'd invited her to meet me here. She looked down, seeing the wet patch spreading across my skirt, and I bit my lip, letting out a gasp as a hot tsunami of pain radiated across my abdomen.

'Looks like we're not going to have time for lunch after all. Let's get you in my car and we can go and have this baby,' she said, guiding me across the car park, her grasp on my elbow reassuringly steady.

I managed a weak smile, wrapping my hand over the top of hers as she helped me into the passenger seat. I let her lean over me, strapping the seat belt in place, and felt a surge of relief. Thank goodness she'd come. I didn't know how I would have coped without her. Looking up Harry was going to have to wait until this baby was born.

TWENTY-NINE

Then

I strode up the street towards my house, teeth gritted in rage, my heels clicking against the concrete. I'd been at the office since seven this morning, had had a day of challenges of the unsatisfactory kind – a major retailer was trying to get a wholesale deal, and their offer was frankly disrespectful, and though I was perfectly aware that it was just business, nothing personal, I couldn't help but feel that the buyer was taking me for a ride because he saw me as a silly girl who'd made a little face cream, not the CEO of my own company.

I hated the meetings I walked into where I knew in an instant what I was up against. The preconceived notion that I was just playing at this, not someone to be taken seriously. It wasn't even that I had an issue proving them wrong. It was just the exhausting fact that I had to keep doing it, time and again.

I'd had a series of draining back-and-forth calls after the meeting, finally getting the buyer to agree to the original – and fair – price we'd provisionally agreed before he met me. And then to top it all off, while crammed on the train like a sardine because I'd made the mistake of getting on with a group of cyclists who'd blocked me in, preventing me from getting to one of the quieter carriages, an old man sitting on the seat in front of me had flashed me and tried to grab my leg. It was now coming up for 9 p.m., the sun was long gone and once again I'd had barely more than a glimpse of it all day. I loved my job. I really did. But some days, especially on a Friday after the bare minimum of sleep all week, the mounting obstacles I'd had to overcome, I wondered if I could keep going.

I turned in through my front gate, seeing the living-room window cast in darkness, though Harry should have been home ages ago. Maybe he was in the kitchen. I'd been hoping he'd cooked something nice. Something big, I thought, hearing the growl of my stomach as I slid the key into the lock. Or failing that, I hoped at least that he hadn't been...

I refused to let myself finish that thought as I stepped over the threshold, hearing the sound of the TV, volume way too loud, coming from the back of the house. Still no light on, I noted, my stomach tensing, dreading what I might find but longing to be proved wrong. Just this once.

I kicked off my shoes, then walked slowly down the hall and through the double-width door into the kitchen diner, flicking on the light. Harry was sitting in the recliner by the gas fire, his eyes facing the direction of the television and yet glaringly unfocused. There was a familiar smell lingering in the air – burning plastic and pungent chemicals – that turned my stomach and made me grit my teeth as a cocktail of disappointment and anger flared up in my veins.

He turned his face towards me, red-rimmed eyes finding mine, his mouth pinched, tense. My gaze followed his hand, his fingernails scratching up and down his arm, the bare skin already pink and raw, highlighting that he'd been doing it a while. Which meant the high had worn off some time ago and he was already twitching, looking around for the next hit. I wondered how many times he'd given in today. It was never just once.

The effect of the drugs was powerful. I'd heard him describe it to Jo as a 'thousand orgasms rolled into one', but just like an orgasm, it only lasted a short while. And unlike the natural high from sex, when *this* high wore off, he was left a shaking wreck of a man, unable to focus on anything but getting back to that state of euphoria again. It had become all-consuming. He was wasting his life. And mine.

I felt my heart plummet. While I'd been out since dawn, working my arse off, he'd been here wasting away, smoking a drug that would destroy him in the end. He didn't even *try* to hide it any more. Didn't bother to put on a front.

I'd had no idea when we first started dating five years ago that he would ever consider touching something as potent – or as dangerous – as crack. He'd been a perfect gentleman. He'd taken me to expensive restaurants, pulled out my chair. He'd been funny too, telling stories that rendered me breathless, my eyes streaming as he got to the punchline. We'd bonded over our miserable boarding-school experiences, and the memories only people who'd been sent away at such a young age could understand. The pranks we'd played on teachers. The way we'd bent the rules as teens. He'd gone midnight skinny-dipping in the creek with his friends and some girls from the neighbouring school every summer, creeping back drunk and sopping wet before the sun rose. I'd never snuck out past lights-out, too worried about the consequences of being expelled, my parents' reaction, but I'd pushed boundaries whenever I thought I could get away with it.

I'd wanted to marry him. To start a family with him. The thought of the father he would be to our children had made me certain he was everything I'd ever wanted, and more. But at some point, his love for the drug overtook his feelings for me, I discovered the secret he'd managed to conceal for so long, and in a matter of a few short months, everything had started to fall apart.

He'd been rising in the world of banking, with an expectation that he would reach the top, and yet he'd missed out on the promotion that had been earmarked for him because he couldn't hold it together in the interview. He lost his job entirely a few months later, and when I discovered he'd squandered his savings on his addiction, it just seemed expected that I'd cover the bills and the mortgage with my salary. And because I loved him, believed that I could make this blight on our otherwise perfect life go away, I did it. I told myself he just needed rest. He had taken on too much. This was only temporary. I made excuses for his behaviour over and over again, and it had entirely the opposite impact from what I'd wished for.

After the secret was out and he saw that he hadn't lost me, he stopped trying to hide the fact that he'd been using. And for a long time, I turned a blind eye, too panicked at what it would mean for my future if I couldn't fix him. I loved him too much. Loved the dream of what we could have. But no matter what I said, how hard I begged, the promises he swore to me in the midst of our tears, he always went back to it.

Two weeks ago, we'd had the biggest row yet, and I'd issued an ultimatum: cut it off cold turkey, or lose me for good. He'd sworn it was done, finished, and yet here he was, once again unable to live up to his vows. Was he banking on the fact that I loved him too much to leave? Or did he simply not care any more?

As I stared at him now, I realised that something had just died inside me. The dream of what we might have been, the future we could have shared – if only he'd wanted it enough. Harry's wasn't a story of tragedy. He had lovely, nurturing parents, had grown up in a tight-knit village where he'd been happy and popular and, unlike me, had enjoyed boarding school, with frequent visits from his parents during his time there. They'd been at every sports day, every award ceremony, cheering him on, and he'd spent every summer with them at home. He was the first to admit he had nothing weighing on his heart, no deep-seated pain he needed to numb. No excuse for wasting his potential like this. He'd simply been offered a pipe at a party, taken it like an idiot and got so hooked on the feeling that nothing could even come close. Not even me. Staring at him now, it was as if a light had been switched on, illuminating the state of my life, the aspirations I'd been struggling to grip hold of fluttering out of reach. If I let him stay, I would never have the life I wanted. Never be happy. This was fruitless.

'Hello, Harry,' I said, keeping my tone neutral as I glanced at the cold, dark oven, the hob annoyingly clear of pans.

'Maya,' he drawled, his mouth seeming to work too hard to produce the word.

'I just got a call from your sister,' I said, the lie coming easily as I dropped my bag on the table. 'She wants you to go round. Said she's got a problem with her boiler.'

His head dipped slowly, his bloodshot eyes rising to meet mine. 'Jo? She wants me to go now?' he asked, the words tacky on his dry lips. He was doing that thing he always did, staring into space as if he was frozen, catatonic.

I nodded. 'Now.'

I saw a flash of a question in his eyes, no doubt wondering why I wasn't tearing into him about finding him like this, as I usually would.

I walked over to the fridge, ignoring him as I pulled out the ingredients to make dinner. The anger that had flared so brightly on seeing him had fizzled out, and I was surprised to realise I felt absolutely nothing. Just a dull, numb awareness that this was over. As if the love I'd had for him had just been carried off on the wind, the heart that had beaten for him suddenly encased in ice.

From the corner of my eye, I saw him rise to his feet, his legs unsteady, and then, seeming to take the gift of my silence, he left, the door closing in his wake. I waited a few minutes, then walked to my bag and took out my phone to call the locksmith. I'd gone back and forth for too long, making excuses, delaying what I needed to do, but now it was time to put an end to this mess, once and for all.

THIRTY

ELISE

Now

The labour ward was packed, red-faced midwives rushing from one room to the next, the gut-wrenching screams of women rising in a cacophony of shared agony. Maya's eyes were wide with terror as she was wheeled down the busy corridor, couples sitting on plastic seats along the walls, clearly not quite ready to be given a room yet not safe enough to travel back home. Maya, however, seemed to be having a rapid first labour. We'd barely made it a few minutes from the pub when she'd begun writhing in the passenger seat, unable to stay put, begging me to hurry. By the time we'd arrived at the ward, she'd been screaming.

As I'd tried to explain to the woman at the desk that she needed help, she'd fallen to her knees, thrown up on the reception floor and been promptly deposited on a trolley. Now, her hand wrapped tight around mine as we were shown into a delivery room, I wondered what she expected me to do. What was *appropriate* for me to offer to do? Should I stay? I barely knew the woman, and yet I could tell she saw me as a friend.

She rolled onto her knees, crying out as the midwife stood by waiting to examine her.

'Maya,' I said gently. 'Is there someone you want me to call?'

I watched her face as the contraction died away. Her expression remained blank, and I wondered if she, like me, was thinking of Nina, Will, the couple who had been waiting for this moment for nine agonisingly long months, both of them in the same vulnerable position as me. My thoughts flashed to Julia, the way she'd slammed the door in my face last night, creating a whirlpool of terror I'd yet to fight my way free from, and for a moment I hoped Maya would show me that these situations could turn out right in the end. That all the fears, the conflicts were simply bumps in the road, and that when it came down to it, the calls would be made, the people who'd been the reason for the life being brought into the world would be the first to know.

'Maya?' I repeated.

'No...' She shook her head, face flushed, her hand finding mine again. '*You* stay... Please, Elise, I need you here with me. You're the only one I can trust.'

I opened my mouth to remind her of the woman who would be waiting by a phone somewhere, but another contraction gripped her, and she made a noise that sounded like a wounded animal. The midwife, a white-haired woman with a warm, trustworthy face, paused as she waited for it to pass. 'Are you happy for me to examine you now, sweetheart?'

'Be quick!' Maya gasped.

The midwife nodded. 'In and out in a jiffy,' she promised, her tone a touch too sing-songy. She slid her gloved fingers inside Maya, and I tried not to look, not to imagine how it would feel to be on the cusp of bringing a brand-new person into the world.

I looked at Maya's face, seeing pure, undistilled fear, and

whispered, 'You're okay... I'm going to stay right here with you. I won't leave – I promise.'

She gave a nod, and the midwife, frowning ever so slightly now, pressed a stethoscope to her belly, her lips moving as she counted under her breath. She looked up, and her expression in that fleeting moment told me something was wrong. Possibly *very* wrong. 'I'll just be one moment,' she announced, striding out of the door without a backward glance.

'What's happening?' Maya groaned.

'I... I don't know. I'm sure it's nothing,' I lied as the door burst back open and a woman dressed in smart olive-green slacks and a navy shirt came in with the midwife.

'Hello, Maya. My name's Rosie Harwood. I'm a consultant obstetrician. Do you mind if I have a little look at you?'

I swallowed, a pulse of trepidation beating in my ears. She spoke so calmly, and yet her movements were quick, efficient, and I could see she was wasting no time, already washing and drying her hands, approaching the bed. Maya made a noise that Rosie took for consent, and the consultant repeated the same examinations the midwife had done just moments before.

'Right then – no, stay where you are, Maya; you don't need to move,' she said, coming to stand beside me so she could look her in the eye.

Maya gripped my hand tighter, and I felt the tender spot on the base of my thumb where I knew she'd pressed a bruise.

The doctor's tone was clear and confident as she spoke. 'Bit of a change of plan, I'm afraid. This little one is having some difficulties with her heart rate, and I think she needs to hurry up and come and meet her mummy. So we're going to nip down to theatre and get her out.'

Maya shook her head. 'But I can't have a C-section. I planned a natural birth!'

'I don't think she's read your plan,' Rosie said gently. 'Babies tend not to play by the rules. Look, we don't have an awful lot of time. I'll have one of my team come and discuss the details with you, and they'll take you to theatre in a few minutes. I'm going to go ahead and scrub up. I'll see you down there, okay?'

Maya nodded. 'Okay,' she whispered.

The midwife strapped a Lycra band around Maya's middle, and we saw the line appear on the monitor she'd placed on the end of the trolley. A piercing alarm sounded every few seconds, indicating a problem.

'I'm going to mute it,' she said, 'but I won't take my eyes off it. I'll stay with you and make sure the baby is well taken care of – you don't need to worry about a thing, sweetheart.' She reminded me of a kindly grandmother – the kind from story-books, not real life.

'Can my friend come with me?' Maya asked, and I nodded without waiting for a reply.

'I'm coming. I won't leave you by yourself.'

She breathed a sigh of relief, but the midwife shook her head. 'I'm so sorry, but since you haven't had time to have an epidural, they'll need to do the C-section under general anaesthetic. The doctor will explain everything to you, but they don't allow visitors when they do a general. Too many people in the room.'

'I won't be conscious?' Maya's voice was shrill with panic. She suddenly gripped her side, pressing her face into the pillow, her voice muffled. 'Oh no, another one—'

She broke off, and I held my breath, watching the line on the monitor dip dangerously low. Finally the contraction ebbed away and the baby's heart rate recovered.

I shook myself, remembering it wasn't me lying there, wasn't my baby holding on by a thread. I pressed my lips together, not sure I had it in me to be here, to face the possibility that one of them might not survive this, and yet I couldn't just go.

'You're going to be fine,' I managed, my own tone overly bright now. Was this why they all spoke like they were high?

Because they were trying to convince themselves just as much as the labouring woman? 'You don't have a choice.'

She nodded as a couple of porters and a nurse bearing a clipboard came into the room.

'Hello, Maya,' the nurse said. 'I'm the ward sister, Michelle. I'm going to help you do the consent form on the way down. The anaesthetist is going to meet us there. Ready, Morag?'

The kindly midwife nodded. 'All set.'

'Give the baby to Elise!' Maya cried. 'I don't want my daughter to be alone. Please, promise me you'll bring her to Elise the moment she's born, while you wait for me to wake up.'

'I'm writing it down right now,' the nurse said. 'We'll give her the once-over and then we'll come and hand her over to Elise. You just wait here, my darling,' she added to me as the porter began wheeling the bed away.

Maya's hand gripped hold of mine, unable to let go, and I reluctantly extricated myself from her, taking a step back.

'I... Yes, okay,' I stuttered. 'I'll wait here,' I repeated feeling slow and dumb.

I heard Maya break into another agonised scream as she was rushed back down the hall we'd come through, with one thought playing on repeat in my mind. She'd called the baby *her* daughter. And with those two tiny words, I understood everything. She had no intention of going through with her promise to Nina and Will. It was what I'd suspected from the first day I met her.

THIRTY-ONE

The room looked so much bigger without the bed in it, wires dangling loosely from sockets where monitors had been detached in a hurry. I lowered myself onto a chair, then stood almost immediately, nervous energy fizzing through my veins, the screams of the women in neighbouring rooms making it impossible to forget where I was.

I walked to the open door, intending to close it, create a barrier between me and the world out there, glancing momentarily down the corridor in the direction they'd taken Maya, wondering if it was already happening. If she was lying on some table, unconscious as they cut her baby from her body. The thought made my head spin, and I realised I hadn't eaten yet today, the lunch I'd planned to wolf down at the pub having dropped off my radar the moment I'd seen Maya sitting outside looking ready to collapse.

I stepped quietly out of the room, spotting a waiting area with a couple of vending machines, making my way past the women in varying stages of early labour. I keyed in the code for a black coffee, and then turned to look at the second machine. It was filled with crisps and chocolate – no real food. My stomach tightened, and I knew there was no point – I'd never be able to swallow any of it in the state I was in.

I grasped the coffee, turning to head back to the room, and froze as a familiar voice echoed towards me. Stepping back to edge between the vending machines, I watched, concealed and wide-eyed as Julia, supported by two midwives, walked slowly along the corridor. She stopped, doubling over, a pained groan rumbling from somewhere deep inside her, and it took all my willpower not to drop the coffee and rush to her side.

It was happening! She was about to birth my son. And if it weren't for Maya, I would never have known. She straightened up and the two midwives helped her walk into the room opposite the one Maya had been allocated. Casting around, I could see no sign of Ben. Where the hell was he?

Head down, I walked back to the empty room, unsure what to do next. She didn't want me anywhere near her. She'd made that as clear as day. If I went in that room now, it wouldn't surprise me if she overreacted entirely. Called the police or some such nonsense.

Holding my cup in one hand, I dragged a padded chair over beside the door, leaving it ajar so I could hear what was going on. I sat down and took a sip of coffee. The flavour was like mud, but it was strong, and I hoped the caffeine would give me a little clarity. This whole day felt like a dream. Too surreal to accept as my reality.

The door to Julia's room opened, and I pricked my ears as in the reflection of the window I saw one of the midwives beckoning to another who was coming out of a bay.

'Can you call her husband again?' she whispered urgently. 'She's begging for him to come. She said they had a row and she's refusing to consent to the section without seeing him first.'

'Can she wait?' the other midwife asked in a low voice.

'Not much longer. She's been in labour since half past ten last night and we're coming up for fifteen hours now. She's still only at three centimetres and the baby's breech. She's had a bleed too. This baby needs to come, and soon. Mum doesn't seem to realise the severity of the situation, though of course I'm trying to make her see sense.'

'You need to be blunt. Do you want me to come in and talk to her?' the other midwife offered.

'No, I already called the consultant. She's coming down now.'

'I hope she can convince her. You know we lost that mum last week. She was adamant she wouldn't go for a section because her cousin had managed a home birth so she thought she should be able to do the same. She'd had a placental abruption! By the time she finally consented, it was too late. The baby survived, but the mum had a massive haemorrhage. I won't forget the look on that poor dad's face when he had to leave on his own with his newborn daughter.'

'I know... it should never have happened. I'm sure she'll agree once her husband turns up, but she doesn't want to go down to theatre alone.' There was the sound of a heavy sigh, and I felt myself holding my own breath in anticipation. 'Try him again. I'm sure whatever happened, once he realises she's in labour, he'll come, and all will be forgiven.'

I heard retreating footsteps and let out a long breath, dropping my head to my hands. Did Julia not realise how precarious the situation was? How easily the little life she carried could be snuffed out? What the hell was she thinking in delaying the section? She and Ben must have argued as soon as I left last night. *Shit.* What did that mean? Had Ben defended me? Had he let slip what we'd done? I couldn't imagine any other reason for them to fall out so badly that he would leave and not even check his phone. Had *I* caused this? I never wanted them to lose each other. I thought it would bring them closer.

I was terrified of what might be happening behind that closed door. Was my son okay? Would he make it?

I stood up, a rush of energy sweeping through me, wanting nothing more than to run in there and demand she stop being so stubborn, but it would only make things worse. Julia hated to feel like she wasn't in control. And I was the last person she'd listen to. Instead, I paced back and forth across the lino, needing to move, to do something, *anything*!

I let my mind wander back to a time when I'd been in love, besotted with a man who had stood by me through good times and bad. Any time we'd hit a bump in the road, it had made us stronger as a couple. In the end, it had been the tough times that had made us – that was what it meant to work on a marriage. I'd thought Julia and Ben would have each other even through the darkest of experiences. But without that net for her to fall back on, it was a whole different story.

I chewed the inside of my cheek, feeling sick, the coffee turning sour on my tongue, debating whether I should call Ben myself. Tell him to come, to lie and say whatever was necessary to save his marriage. To put all the blame on me and tell her that I'd pursued him relentlessly. That it had been *me* who'd initiated everything. That he'd tried to turn me down but I'd refused to stop trying. I wanted him to make it all right. To do whatever it took to get her to save my baby. She would believe him. Thinking of me as the evil woman who'd seduced her husband would be only too simple for her.

I looked at my phone, debating with myself, then shook my head, putting it back in my pocket. Julia wasn't an idiot. She would consent. Once the consultant spoke to her, she'd agree to go down to theatre. She would *have* to.

There was a flurry of activity outside the door, and with an uncomfortable sense of déjà vu, I watched a different doctor head into Julia's room, the porters hovering nearby for the go-ahead, the nurse with that familiar blue clipboard. I craned my head around the door frame, the passing minutes lasting an eternity, finally seeing the trolley wheeled out, Julia lying on her side, her eyes screwed tightly shut, her face red and sweating. She was whisked down the hall, and as I watched her go, my imagination ran wild with all the things that could go wrong in the next hour. My baby *had* to survive. Even if it meant Julia couldn't.

It felt like barely any time had passed when the door was pushed open and Morag, the smiley midwife, entered, pushing a wheeled plastic bassinet in front of her. 'A resounding success. And a very loud baby girl. She's already given us all a good telling-off,' she said, grinning as she parked the cot in front of me. 'I've just given her a bottle and she took the lot. There's another one there in case you need it – I'm afraid Mummy is going to be a little while.'

'Is she okay?' I asked, unable to take my eyes from the tiny baby wrapped in a cream blanket in the centre of the bassinet.

'Still sleeping. But I'm sure she'll come round in her own good time. Her body's had a bit of a shock. She's lucky to have you here. There are a couple of nappies in the cupboard over there, and when I get a moment, I'll bring you some cotton wool and water. But I have to get on now – I've another mum about to go into transition and two more in active labour. No rest for the wicked, eh? You'll be all right?'

'Yes, you go. We'll be fine.'

She nodded gratefully, and I pushed the door closed behind her, looking down at the perfect little girl sleeping soundly. Her eyelashes were blonde, like fairy wings, but her hair was the thing I couldn't take my eyes off. A mass of ringlets, as ginger as my own. I let out a choked sob, unable to believe what I was seeing. Maya was brunette, her hair fine and pin-straight. Which had to mean that the sperm donor she'd used must have been the one to give her baby this head of red curls.

Slowly, though I knew I was playing a dangerous game with

myself, I scooped her up, her head nuzzling beneath my chin, her body curling into my own. The feeling of a baby in my arms – a perfect little girl who looked just like me – was too much. I felt the tears begin to stream down my face as the floodgates to everything I had lost burst open. Was *this* the karma I'd been waiting for all these years? I breathed in the smell of her head and knew it had to be.

Time passed without meaning as I stood in the empty room, my thoughts tumbling over one another, the sound of the baby breathing a slow rhythm. My heart, however, was racing. She wriggled against me and I blinked, pulling myself together, shaking the pins and needles from my feet.

I moved slowly to the door, leaning my head against the wall out of sight as I listened to the midwives at the nurses' station beyond. Hurried conversations about dilation, pain relief, complications. It sounded like one of the mothers had gone into labour early, and the midwives were busy preparing incubators, calling down to the neonatal ward to warn them of the imminent arrival. It was a wonder they managed to keep calm under the fraught circumstances. I heard an exclamation and peeked my head round to watch as a couple of porters wheeled in a trolley, accompanied by a stern-looking nurse.

'Oh! What are you doing here?' the ward sister asked, sounding anything but pleased to see them. 'I told them not to send you back up yet – we don't have anyone to do the handover!'

They continued towards us, and I held my breath as I saw Julia lying on the bed. She was propped up with several pillows, her short dark hair matted to her pale face. In her arms was a small wrapped bundle, and from my position behind the door, I could hear the soft gurgles he made as she fed him from her bare breast. Envy shot through me like fire, and I had to steady myself to stop from rushing out there and demanding she take her hands off my baby.

'I was told to bring her back now,' the nurse said stiffly. 'The handover won't take a minute. The surgery went smoothly, baby cried right away, Apgar of nine, and as you can see, he's having a good feed. Mum's had an epidural and we've placed a catheter, which I'll leave for you to remove once she's up and about.'

'Yes, yes, you don't have to state the obvious,' the sister replied curtly.

The nurse opened her mouth to respond, but Julia interrupted.

'Is my husband here? Did he come?' Her voice was filled with hope, more vulnerable than I'd ever heard before.

The sister softened her tone as she answered. 'I'm sorry, love, we haven't yet managed to get hold of him. We've left several messages, so I'm sure he'll be along soon. Millie!' she called, and I watched as she waved over a stressed-looking young girl who wore the student midwife uniform. There was a poster on the wall explaining that light blue tunics were for students, dark blue for the ward sister. 'Take Julia and her lovely son into the room she was in before and get her settled. Morag will come and see you once she's finished with her other lady and then we'll see about moving you up to postnatal. When I called up there for the last mummy, they were struggling to find beds. It's the busiest I've seen it in months!'

She bustled off, and the porters wheeled Julia into the room. The student midwife followed them, disappearing inside.

A few minutes later, she emerged, spotting the sister back at the desk. 'I've done their obs. They're both looking fine. Mum's absolutely exhausted after that long labour, so I've settled the baby in the bassinet for now and she's going to try and rest. Could barely keep her eyes open, poor thing.'

'I'm not surprised,' the sister replied wryly. 'Imagine going through all that and your husband not even showing his face.

What kind of man turns off his phone when his wife is nine months gone, I ask you?' She gave a tut and strode off again, heading into one of the rooms at the far end of the corridor. The student picked up a thermometer and went in the other direction, heading into the packed bay.

The baby stirred in my arms, and I pressed a kiss to her forehead then placed her gently back into the cot, covering her with the soft cream blanket, a smile pulling at my lips as I looked at her rosebud mouth. I counted to two hundred before slowly pushing the door open and crossing the corridor, wheeling the plastic cot containing the precious cargo ahead of me. Pressing down on the handle to Julia's room, I took one last look left and right to make sure I hadn't been noticed, then stepped into the dimly lit room and closed the door behind me.

Julia was fast asleep already, her head tilted towards me, her mouth open, little snores escaping her lips. Leaving the baby girl in her cot beside the door, I moved slowly, purposefully across to Julia's bedside, where the boy I'd waited nine long months to meet was sleeping. I looked down at his face – rosy cheeks, dark fluffy hair like a baby bird, wrinkled pink hands folded under a tiny chin. He was an angel. Everything I'd dreamed he would be and more.

Behind me, the baby girl made a little squeak and I quickly glanced at Julia, hoping she wouldn't wake, wouldn't catch me here. I had little time, but I didn't need much. I had planned this moment for so long, there was no need to stop and consider a thing. I'd expected it to be much more difficult – I'd prepared for that – but today was a gift. It was as if someone out there was helping me, giving me more than I'd asked for, showing me what I deserved. I knew what I had to do.

With slow, gentle movements, I bent over the cot, scooping the baby boy into my arms and carrying him with quiet footsteps across the room, placing him down beside the little girl. Wishing I had time to admire the perfect pair, to dream of the siblings they would become, the joy they would bring me, the hole they would finally mend in the fabric of my soul, I tucked the blanket around the pair of them, pushed open the door and, without a backward glance, wheeled the cot down the corridor, out of the ward, through the hospital. I felt as though I didn't breathe until I was out in the open air.

And from that point forward, everything was simple.

THIRTY-TWO

MAYA

Someone was screaming. It felt as if it was half a dream, half a disorientating echo spinning just out of my reach. I dragged open my sticky eyelids, my mouth dry and crusted, an ache in my throat and a dull pressure in my abdomen. A heady, nauseating feeling of not quite being in control was engulfing me, and I blinked against the light, finding myself alone in the labour room. I was awake – if a little groggy – but the screaming hadn't stopped. The sound of it was raw, desperate, and instinctively I knew this wasn't just another labouring woman. I pressed my hands to my ears, unable to bear it.

There was no sign of Elise or the baby. I wondered how long I must have slept. If she'd taken my daughter for a walk while she waited.

My daughter.

The word was forbidden, and yet it felt so natural. I hadn't even seen her face, but I knew – I think I'd known for quite some time – I would keep her. Hearing the strained instructions as the doctors tried to contain their panic, believing that she might not survive the birth, had cemented everything in place. I couldn't pretend otherwise now. Nina and Will would try to convince me to change my mind, and when I refused, they would try to scare me with the contract. They'd try every trick in their arsenal to manipulate me into handing her over. I knew it with every fibre of my being. I wouldn't even be shocked if they offered me money at this point. They weren't beyond buying a baby if it got them the result they desired. But this time I wasn't going to be a pushover, agreeing to keep the peace, giving *their* wants more priority than the needs of my baby – myself. No, this time I was prepared to fight for her. And I had no doubt I would win. It was going to be messy, unpleasant, but I didn't care. She was mine. She'd grown in my womb. It was *my* DNA that made up her cells, not theirs! She had drifted off to sleep to the sound of my heartbeat. I'd felt her first kicks and sung to her in the dead of night when the two of us were alone, and I didn't have to pretend I was okay with the awful promise I'd made. My heart on a platter. My soul in payment for a crime I never committed.

I could see now that I had taken Harry's reckless stupidity, the terrible thing he'd done, and, as had always been my habit, placed the blame squarely on my own shoulders. Only this time, it hadn't been him selling the television or forgetting to pay the gas bill. It had been something so much worse. I'd allowed my guilt, that awful sense of responsibility I felt for his actions, to nearly force me into making the biggest mistake of my life. Thank God I'd realised before it was too late. She was *my* fucking baby, and no matter what contract I'd signed, what promises I'd made, nothing was going to change that. I had been weak for too long. I'd let Will and Nina treat me like they owned me, under some misguided belief that I was atoning for my past, but I couldn't do it. I would find another way.

I dropped my hands from my ears, noticing a cannula dangling loosely from the crook of my elbow, and frowned as I realised that the screaming had become louder still. Had something horrible happened? A stillbirth maybe. The cries made goose pimples rise on my arms, taking my thoughts down a dark path I wanted more than anything to avoid. I craved the ability to squash it, shut it out, unable to cope with the emotions it brought to the surface.

Feeling shaky, presumably a side effect of the anaesthetic, I tried circling my ankles, finding they moved just fine. There was a wide bandage across my belly, and though it was numb right now, I wasn't stupid enough to move fast, the thought of dislodging the stitches enough to make me cautious. There were barriers on both sides of the hospital bed, and I eased my way cautiously towards the foot of the mattress, wincing as I lowered my bare feet to the ground, holding on to the bedrail as I tested putting my weight on them. A tugging sensation in my uterus made bile rise to my throat as starbursts exploded in my vision.

Slowly, I stood, taking a tentative step across the room. There was a dreamlike quality to my thoughts as I pulled open the door and stepped into the corridor. They'd given me something for the pain, something strong. I could taste chemicals on the back of my tongue. There were no longer hordes of couples waiting on the plastic seating. Instead, there was a cold, desolate feel to the ward, no sound coming from any room except the one directly across from my own. Further up the corridor, a group of midwives and two uniformed police officers were huddled together discussing something. They didn't look my way as I crossed the hall and pushed open the door, stepping into the room. The screams were almost unbearable from here.

The blinds were closed, but a lamp glowed bright above the bed, where a woman sat propped up, eyes screwed tightly shut, mouth open in a relentless stream of agony. I gasped, stepping closer, realising I recognised her. It was Elise's sister. What was her name? Julie? Julia? She must have gone into labour too. I pinched the bridge of my nose as a wave of nausea pulled at my gut. I needed to sit down. Holding on to the wall, I swallowed and said, 'What's wrong?'

The screaming stopped abruptly and her eyes flashed open, seeing me. 'You have to help me! I need to get a wheelchair. I have to get out of this bed!' she said, her voice urgent, her words coming too fast. Her face was plastered in sweat and her eyes were dilated, terrified. I wondered if her delirious state was a side effect of the drugs they'd given her.

'I'll call a nurse,' I offered, gesturing towards the door behind me. The buzzer lay on her lap and I could see she'd already pressed it. They must not have heard.

'No! They aren't helping! You don't understand. I have to go – she's taken him! They've fucked up my epidural and I can't walk. God knows what could happen before I get on my feet!' She broke off, her eyes narrowing as she looked at my face.

Confusion and pain were swirling incessantly round my mind, making it impossible to concentrate on her tirade. I couldn't stand up any more. I lurched forward, reaching a chair at her bedside and slumping into it. Looking down at my hospital gown, I could see a patch of red spreading across the fabric, and realised I must have split my stitches open.

'You!' Julia exclaimed. 'You're Elise's friend. They said she came here with you! I heard them talking. Did you have something to do with this?' She gave an agonised cry, throwing her head back, then began pressing frantically on the call button again.

I took a steeling breath, pressing a hand to my wound. 'I'm Maya, yes. We met in town, remember? Elise is here too. She helped me. What drugs did they give you, Julia? You're having a reaction to them, I think.' I glanced at her body, covered by a sheet, and wondered if something had happened. 'Have you had your baby?' I asked gently.

Her eyes widened, filling with tears. 'You don't *know*?' She shook her head as if she couldn't believe what she was hearing. 'She's taken him! Elise has taken my baby. They said she's taken yours too! You should be out there searching for them, helping! That's what I'd be doing if I could get out of this fucking bed!'

A needle of fear pricked at the back of my neck, but I brushed it away. 'You're confused, Julia,' I said gently. 'I *told* the nurse to give my baby to Elise to look after. And if she saw you here sleeping with the little fella in his cot, she would have taken him too. I'm sure she thought you wouldn't mind. They'll be down at the café or something; she won't just take him home without giving you a chance to say goodbye. Besides, she still has to bring my little one back to me.'

'Say goodbye?' Julia's face turned white. 'Why would I say goodbye to my own son?' She was gripping the sheet in her fists, leaning forward as much as she was able as she waited for me to reply.

I felt sorry for her, knowing how close I'd come to being in her position, how I'd been on the verge of giving away my baby too. But if Julia had changed her mind, that was a conversation she needed to have with Elise. I didn't want any part in it. 'Look, being a surrogate was never going to be without its challenges. But you and Elise are family. You'll work this out. You just need to come up with some boundaries. I'm sure she'll be back soon with both the babies and you two can have a proper chat.'

'Surrogate? *Family?*'

I sighed, rising to my feet. She needed a doctor. And by the look of the blood soaking through my gown, I could do with one too. 'I'm going to give her a call now and ask her to come back up. You and your sister need to talk.'

Her hand shot out, grabbing me by the wrist. 'Elise is my *patient*, Maya. I'm a psychiatrist.'

'What? No, she...'

She took a deep breath, as if holding on to her self-control with every fibre of her being. 'I need you to tell me exactly what she told you and what you know about her.' Her voice was calm, and something about the way she spoke with such clarity made me lower myself back in the chair.

I gave a shrug, not knowing where to start, struggling to decide what she wanted me to say. I was trying to work out if she was having some kind of hallucination. It seemed like a sensible idea to try and play along until help arrived.

'We met at a surrogacy support group a couple of weeks ago. She didn't tell us much about you – she made sure to only share her side of the experience with the group. Said she wanted to meet others going through the same thing. I know there have been some difficulties between you, how you communicate differently, how best to navigate things, but she loves you and is so grateful to you. You remember we met you in town outside the café last week? You were with your husband. You spoke about the baby,' I said, though I suddenly remembered how off Julia had been that day, how Elise had been trying and failing to get the answers she wanted from her. I'd felt sorry for her, being left out of the important appointments, shoved to one side. 'She's your *sister*,' I repeated, hearing the shrillness of my own words, the panic beginning to seep through them at the thought that Julia might be telling the truth. I didn't want to think what that might mean.

I had left my own daughter in Elise's care, hadn't even questioned my decision, because I knew who she *really* was, knew her secrets and had believed that she was more than capable of looking after a baby. I'd trusted her to protect my daughter as if she was her own. I couldn't have been wrong about her, could I? The moment I'd seen her walk into the community hall, I'd been sure of the reason that had brought her there. Her journey to motherhood had come to this, having to use a surrogate, because of *me*. I knew exactly what it meant to her, because what the rest of the group weren't aware of was the fact that Elise had lost her first baby. And though she didn't realise it, the blame for that lay solely at my feet.

Julia pressed her hands to her mouth and then vomited all over her lap. A moment later, she began to scream again, and this time I couldn't contain my own terror.

THIRTY-THREE

JULIA

Then

Setting the jug of iced water on the counter beside the plastic glasses that looked at first glance almost like the real thing, I nodded to myself, noting that everything was in order. I never kept anything in my home office that could be used as a weapon. It had been a rule I'd made for myself years ago, but these past few weeks I'd become fastidious about checking I hadn't left anything lying around, even changing the wire on my oil-filled radiator to a shorter one that couldn't be easily wrapped round a neck. I hated that I had to think of these things so often when I should be basking in the enjoyment of my pregnancy, but I'd been put in an impossible position and had no choice but to ride it out – for now.

I puffed up the cushions on the two armchairs, then moved to open a window, glancing across the lawn towards the house as the fresh air blew away the faint smell of damp. I couldn't see him from here, but I knew my husband was in the kitchen preparing dinner for our children, getting them to do their homework. When Ben had suggested moving from my office in

town to the old artist's studio at the bottom of the garden left
behind by the previous owner, I'd been reluctant. At the time,
he'd told me he was fed up of me coming home from work every
day to vent about how stressed I was. In the tower block where
I'd worked alongside several other colleagues, my boss, Edwin,
had developed an increasingly claustrophobic habit of turning
up multiple times a day to check on me. He never did anything
I could report, always staying just the right side of professional,
but that didn't stop me feeling uncomfortable every time he
stepped into my office and closed the door.

He was older than me by a couple of decades, his manner
condescending, and had a habit of looming just that little bit too
close, his eye contact unwavering as he berated me for some
imagined mistake while simultaneously undressing me with his
eyes. I'd felt at his mercy, never knowing when he might
stride in.

My contract had a loophole where I was able to take on
private clients alongside my contracted work, and I'd been
trying to build up my patient list, hoping that in time I might be
able to leave entirely and start my own practice. It was a slow
process and I wasn't yet ready to jump ship, but I'd cut my
hours in the office, and now I had more freedom in where I
worked. Edwin hadn't been happy about it, but HR had signed
off my request to set up a home office for both my private cases
and the work I was assigned by him. Having this space, knowing
it was entirely mine, had reignited my enjoyment of coming to
work each day, and on top of that, since finding out that baby
number three would be joining us soon, it had enabled me to
pop into the house between clients to have a quick nap when
the occasion called for it.

Up until now, all my patients had been fairly simple cases.
My private client list was made up of ordinary people going
through tough times: depression, job loss, anxiety. People in
need of coping strategies and a listening ear. The contracted

patients I took on tended to have a different set of problems, but I enjoyed the work with them equally. I was often referred people coming out of prison who needed a bit of extra support to rejoin society: drug addicts, sex workers, those who'd had a rough start in life and who needed help finding their self-worth and getting on the right path. In both avenues, it had been a job I'd found fulfilling and rewarding, and I had every intention of continuing with it after taking a break to have my baby.

I was good at what I did, and confident every time I sat down opposite a patient that I could help them change their lives for the better. But I couldn't pretend I wasn't nervous today. The patient coming this evening wasn't one I wanted to see again, and that had been hard for me to admit. Unlike anyone I'd ever worked with before, she hadn't been sent to prison for petty theft or drug dealing. She was a woman whose story I'd read in the papers two years previously. I still remembered it well. There had been a photo splashed across the front page that had caused uproar in the school playground, parents furious that their little ones had seen it, many of them having nightmares for weeks afterwards.

The picture had been taken by a witness at the scene of the crime – a woman holding a huge knife, emerging from the door to a block of flats, her face and white dress drenched in claret, her mouth stretched in a wide smile as she looked straight at the camera. It had given me chills to see the lack of remorse, the sheer elation in her expression. There had been something in the way she'd walked out of that building with her head held high, blood splattered across her pale skin, that had made me afraid – and I was *never* usually afraid. I was a professional. I'd taken every course offered, had a master's in clinical psychology, and prided myself on being able to see past any crime to the scared or hurting human being beneath. But despite knowing her reasons, her motive, I couldn't erase that photograph from my mind. Couldn't help but judge her... fear her.

When Edwin had sent me the email with her details, I'd tried to refuse, made up an excuse about being snowed under with too much work already. But he'd insisted that as the best-qualified psychiatrist on the team, I was the perfect fit to help this woman.

It was a condition of her parole that she see me twice a week. She'd been given an early release, just two years into a seven-year sentence, and I couldn't help but question if whoever had made that call had been in their right mind. Because the truth was, despite outward appearances, there was something about her that made my skin crawl. The way she'd looked at me when she first walked into my office, the overly friendly way she'd asked about my pregnancy, my due date, the way she called me by my first name and made sure to use it just that little bit too often; how she touched my belly even after I told her to back off. I was sure that to anyone else she'd seem warm, confident, *affectionate* even. But I saw right through her.

I sometimes wondered if she'd been so broken by what had happened to her that she'd lost the part of herself that helped her see the difference between right and wrong. It would make sense that she had been badly damaged by what she'd been through, the things she'd had to witness. And I knew if it had been me in her shoes, I would have been broken-hearted too. But I wouldn't have taken the law into my own hands. I would never have done what she did. And maybe that was because she was already unstable before any of it happened. I would never know for sure.

We were six sessions in and I knew no more about her now than I did when she first came. She gave me nothing. If I mentioned the past, the people she had lost, she pretended I hadn't spoken and looked out of the window towards the house, making me regret ever giving up my tiny office in the anony-mous tower block in town. I hated that she knew where I lived.

More than that, I hated that I'd seen Ben waiting to catch

her on the drive, infatuated by her looks, wanting to chat as she left her sessions, though I'd asked him a thousand times to respect the boundaries I needed to keep between home and work. In a hormonal rage, I'd committed the cardinal sin of telling him about her crime, hoping he'd see how ridiculous he was being thinking he was indulging in a harmless flirtation with her. He thought I was jealous, uptight, said he was only being friendly, but I just wanted him to see that she was a damaged woman with an evil streak he should be cautious of.

His flirtatious nature had always been a bone of contention in our marriage, though I trusted that it never went further than a bit of banter and some lingering looks. He'd been popular in school and uni, and never quite got over the loss of female attention after we got married, still needing to know he was desirable, wanted by every woman he encountered. He'd always been too touchy-feely for my liking with my female friends, but it was inappropriate with my clients, and in the case of Elise, it was downright dangerous.

I was sure he had stopped talking to her after I'd broken her confidentiality and told him her secret, and for a while I'd thought I could get past my discomfort until the baby arrived, but after she had begun turning up outside my GP surgery and appearing at my midwife appointments, and I'd realised she'd somehow hacked into my personal calendar on my computer, I'd blown up at her, telling her she'd gone too far and I wouldn't see her again.

I'd tried to pass her off to another member of the team, telling Edwin I didn't want to keep working with her, that she was becoming obsessed with me, stalking me, but he'd thought I was making it up. He'd made a lot of noise about my maternity leave, hinting heavily that if I wasn't up to the work now, maybe I wouldn't have the stamina on my return to keep up with the other doctors. Maybe there wouldn't be any work coming my way. So I'd shut my mouth, reminding myself it was just a little while longer.

I sighed, looking at the clock, hoping she wouldn't turn up so I could call her parole officer and have her put back in prison where she belonged. What did that say about me? I should want to help her. If *I* couldn't, who else could? It was my job to make sure she was fit to be a part of society, and I would never forgive myself if I didn't at least try.

I placed a hand on my belly and reminded myself I only had a few more weeks until my son was born, and then I could take a nice long maternity leave – a little while longer and then Elise would no longer be my problem.

THIRTY-FOUR

MAYA

Now

The room was spinning, my thoughts in disarray, distorting the sound of Julia's screams in my ears and making my breath come in short, sharp bursts. Whatever they had given her was making her delusional. She was hallucinating. She *had* to be. The alternative was that my baby was in the hands of someone Julia didn't trust. Someone potentially dangerous. I looked down at the spreading blood on my hospital gown, feeling detached from it, as if it were someone else sitting in this chair. Someone else's baby who was unaccounted for.

The door burst open and Morag and another midwife rushed in, accompanied by two men in suits who I guessed by their grim expressions and confident strides were senior police.

'Oh God, Maya! You're awake,' Morag cried when she saw me sitting in the chair beside the bed.

The other midwife rushed to help Julia, whipping the soiled sheets from her lap and unfolding a blanket from the end of the mattress to drape over her bare legs.

Morag lowered herself to her haunches in front of me.

'What on earth are you doing in here? I'm sorry nobody was there to explain what's happened to you, love. We've been so busy clearing the ward – all the patients have been taken upstairs. Someone has been checking on you every ten minutes, but you told us you wanted to sleep. You just kept waking up and then drifting right back off. I wish you'd pressed the call button – I was listening for it.' She looked slightly put out that I'd dared to leave my room. 'Oh! You're bleeding!'

'I'm fine,' I insisted, glancing behind her to where the two suited men stood, averting their eyes from my dishevelled appearance.

'You need to get back to bed and we can have the doctor look at your incision. You shouldn't be up without support just yet.'

'Where's my baby?' The words were barely more than a whisper, and I realised I was afraid to say them out loud, unsure if I was ready to hear the answer.

Morag and the other midwife shared a look as Julia let out a moan that sounded almost animal.

'I don't know what's happening,' I continued. 'Julia seems to think my friend has left the ward, but she's not making any sense. Why would she do that? Where are Elise and my daughter?'

Morag's eyes were wide, as if she was unsure how to answer what I knew to be a simple question. A question she *should* have been able to answer. I felt sweat pool in the palms of my hands as she stared at me then rose to her feet.

'I... I'm going to get the doctor. I can't let you sit here bleeding like this.' She rushed out of the room, and the second midwife muttered something about getting Julia some fresh water before following her out.

'Have you found her? Is there any news?' Julia's voice was frantic, desperate, as she looked at the two men.

'Mrs Clarkson.' One of the police officers stepped towards

her. He nodded in my direction. 'Miss Fion. I'm DCI Ronson, and this is my colleague DS Browning. We have everyone at our disposal searching for the suspect and your babies. We will do everything we can. Mrs Clarkson, I know you've already spoken with PC Green, but I need you to tell me everything you can. How long had you been sleeping before you noticed your son was missing?'

'It was about half an hour. She couldn't have got that far in thirty minutes, could she?'

'No. She couldn't. But can you tell me—'

'Stop! Shut the fuck up, will you!'

Three faces turned to look at me as I launched myself up from the chair, standing breathlessly before them, my hand pressed to my belly. 'I don't understand what's going on! Why are the police searching for Elise? Why would you cause such a scene because your sister's gone off for a wander with our babies? Why is everyone acting like something terrible is happening? Explain it to me! Because I don't fucking understand!'

'For Christ's sake, Maya!' Julia exclaimed. 'I *told* you. Elise Williams is not my sister. She's my *patient*. She's a murderer! She's been coming to sessions with me since she was released from prison a few months ago. I told them she was a liability, but nobody listened. She made out she was a victim. A grieving woman who'd made one stupid mistake. She fooled everyone – *you* included, it would seem.'

She pressed her hands to her eyes, then yanked the blanket from her legs, slapping at them, trying to get them to move, though they lay like stone against the mattress, still paralysed by the epidural. Eventually, she looked up, her cheeks flushed, her eyes desperate. 'She's not the person she led you to believe, Maya. She's a dangerous woman who has clearly been spinning lies to you about our relationship, and now she's disappeared with both of our babies.'

She shook her head, her eyes turning wet. 'I was confused when I woke up. I thought the midwife must have taken him off for a test or something – I was angry that they hadn't thought to ask my permission. But when the midwife came in, I realised nobody knew where he was. They were all trying to work it out, talking about who was on the ward, and then I heard them say Maya and Elise... and I remembered meeting you. I knew in that moment that something bad had happened—' She broke off with a sob. 'I knew it the instant they said her name. They told me your baby was missing too... Do you get it now?' she cried. 'This isn't your new best friend taking the babies for a nice walk so you can get some rest. This is a convicted murderer... it's kidnap!'

She turned to DCI Ronson. 'Maya said Elise told her I was going to be her surrogate. I'm not sure if she's deranged enough to have convinced herself of it, or if she just used that story to get close to another pregnant woman, but she's been planning this. It wasn't some whim. She told Maya I was carrying my baby for *her*!' She slapped her leg again, leaving a bright red mark. 'For fuck's sake! Move!' she screamed, raking at her bare thighs with her fingernails. She looked back to the police, her eyes half mad with panic. 'Please, just go... You have to find her. You have to get those babies back!'

My legs felt like jelly as I shook my head, trying to absorb the words, the news that my baby girl was in the arms of a murderer. That Elise wasn't the friend I'd thought she was.

'No,' I whispered. 'No!' A tremor ran the entire length of my body and I suddenly understood Julia's unrelenting compulsion to scream. I could feel the terror radiating through me, the urge to run, to go after her, find her.

Bending forward, I gripped the bedrail for support. 'Did she take her car? There must be footage! CCTV! Did you go to her house?'

Ronson gave a nod. 'The place on Broadwell Street? Yes –

empty. All her stuff's there, coffee cup still in the sink. The back door was unlocked. There's no indication that she intended to leave. If, like you say, she believes this surrogacy story she's been telling people, if she's suffering from some kind of psychosis, it's possible that sometime soon she'll take the babies back to her home, where she feels safe. She won't be thinking straight, won't consider that she's going to be picked up as she won't believe she's done anything wrong.'

I pictured the big house, the beautiful garden room, the huge picture windows. The night I'd let myself in, creeping through the place like some criminal, thinking she was the victim of my mistakes. An innocent, grieving woman who'd lost her baby girl and needed support, comfort. I had been so sure that *I* was the bad guy, never doubting that Elise was someone I could trust. I'd explicitly told the midwife to give my newborn daughter to her. What had I done?

The door opened again and I looked up, expecting to see the doctor. Instead, the man who entered made my mouth drop open.

'*You!*' I cried, suddenly seeing an explanation for all this mess. One that made far more sense to my frazzled mind. 'This is *your* doing! You've put her up to it. Where is she? Where are the babies?'

The man stopped in his tracks, glancing over his shoulder as if I might be addressing someone else. He looked back to me, and I glared at him. 'I'm sorry...' he said, his brow dipping in confusion. 'I don't think we've met, have we?'

I took in his preppy collar, the handsome, clean-cut face, recalling the look of resigned fear in Elise's expression when she'd opened her front door to find him there. The text message she'd got that had wiped the smile from her face that first session at the group; the way she never mentioned her personal life...

'You might not know me,' I said through gritted teeth, 'but I know who *you* are! I know she's afraid of you. I know that you control her and cow her and she's too frightened of you to fully break ties. She told me there were people who wanted to stop her,' I went on, a thought pricking at the back of my mind though I refused to let it break through. I pointed a bloodstained finger at him, noting as I did that it was shaking. 'This man has been in a relationship with Elise! And I believe he's the person pulling at the strings. If anyone knows where she is, it's him! I wouldn't be surprised if he's taken them somewhere, locked the poor woman up!'

The man let out a shocked laugh and shook his head. 'Has someone called the doctor about that bleeding?' he asked, turning to the detectives.

One of them went to the door, and I heard voices and realised they were talking about me.

The man turned his dark eyes on me again. 'Look,' he said, his voice softer than I expected, 'I know you've been through a shock. But you have it wrong. My name's Nick Pratt. I'm Elise's parole officer.'

'And,' Julia added, 'she wasn't lying about people wanting to stop her. If Nick or I had heard even a whiff of the word surrogacy, we would have put a stop to it all. We would have put her right back in prison where she belongs and none of this would be happening now!'

'Parole officer?' I repeated. My strength gave out and I collapsed back down into the chair.

Nick turned to Julia and the two detectives. 'When I met with her at her house last week, I got the feeling she was hiding something. Her tag came off three weeks ago, and she seemed a little too smug about the fact that I couldn't keep tabs on her any more. She's been turning her phone off for long periods of time, no doubt worried I'd find out where she was going, what she was up to. Something like this would have taken planning,' he added grimly. 'She seemed secretive, but with nothing concrete to report, all I could do was wait and watch.'

'Tag?' I asked weakly.

'When she was granted early release, one of the conditions was that she wear a tag and have a curfew for the first three months. And she stuck to it like clockwork, never broke it once. She hated it – not that she would ever have admitted to being bothered. She never gave away a thing about what she was feeling.'

I suddenly recalled a comment she'd made during lunch last week, something I'd brushed off as melancholy due to the changing seasons or impatience for the baby to be born. Later, after she'd left, I'd replayed it over and over, wondering if it had been a cry for help, if she was asking me to get her away from the man I'd seen.

She'd been looking down at her coffee and said, 'You know, sometimes I feel like a dog that's been chained up in a kennel. I run and run in circles, never getting any further than I was when I started. I long to break the chain... snap it in half and sprint until my legs burn, until I'm finally free.' She had looked up, meeting my concerned gaze, but before I could ask if she was okay, she'd got up to fetch us both a slice of carrot cake, and when she'd come back to the table, she'd changed the subject. I'd felt like it wasn't the time to pry, but now I wished I had.

The detectives asked Julia a few more questions, throwing one or two my way, though I could barely formulate basic answers. 'We met a few weeks ago at the community centre. At a surrogacy group... No, I haven't informed the intended parents of the situation – I only just found out myself, and besides, my situation has changed. I'm keeping the baby.' The shame I felt at having to admit I'd nearly given her away voluntarily burned across my face, and seeming to sense I was reaching my limit, the detectives made empty promises to report back soon and left. Nick made to follow them.

'Wait!' I cried. 'Just tell me one thing. If this is all true... if Elise really is a murderer, who did she kill?'

He looked at Julia, who seemed to have retreated into herself in a self-protective bubble. 'I'm surprised you didn't recognise her. It was a massive case, all over the news. Two years ago, a man broke into a family home in an armed burglary, looking for money to fund his drug habit. He ran into the male occupant and shot him in the back... only, the man he shot was holding a baby... The bullet travelled right through both of them and they were pronounced dead at the scene.'

The air seemed to have been sucked from the room. I shook my head, my heart thumping erratically. 'But,' I choked out, 'the man who did that... he went to trial... he was caught! He went to prison!'

Then the sudden memory of Jo in the pub car park in the moments before I'd gone into labour, telling me Harry never made it as far as a trial, hit me like a bucket of iced water to the face. I'd been about to go home and google the case when Elise had arrived. With everything that had happened since, I'd forgotten about that conversation.

'Surely...' I whispered, the puzzle pieces slotting together to form a sickening conclusion in my mind. 'No...' I pressed my hands to my mouth, terrified of what Nick was about to tell me.

He shrugged. 'He was caught, yes. Arrested and charged. But his lawyer managed to negotiate bail on the condition he attend Narcotics Anonymous and seek treatment for his habit while awaiting sentencing. It was clear that he was going down for a long time, and the judge happened to have lost a son to heroin and was obviously influenced by that when he granted bail. The shooter's name was Harry Meyers.'

I pressed my lips together, wanting to deny everything Nick had said. I'd known what Harry had done to Elise. After I'd thrown him out, he'd surfed sofas for two weeks, calling me daily with increasingly desperate threats, telling me he couldn't cope, wouldn't survive without me, didn't know what he might be capable of. He said I was his only hope. His sister would take him in, fuss over him – offering to run him a bath or make him some soup – but she wouldn't fund his habit. She'd never given him a penny towards it, and he knew it was the one thing she wouldn't budge on. I had to do the same. Show some backbone for once. So I'd washed my hands of him... told him to pull himself together and grow the fuck up, then I'd cut him off.

That phone call, when I'd heard those awful words – 'You drove me to this, Maya. Remember that. They would be alive if you hadn't done what you did' – had haunted my every waking breath for two years. I'd seen Harry's face plastered across the news in the days that followed, including a shot of the two of us together, lifted from his social media, my face on the front page, sharing in his shame for the whole world to see. I'd read the story of the family destroyed by the crack addict and known that he was right – that if I'd been a better person, got him help, done things differently, that poor woman would still have her husband, her four-month-old daughter.

I had convinced myself that I could make up for it by becoming a surrogate, giving away my own child – the child I'd wanted for so long – to a woman far more deserving than I could ever be. I'd thrown myself into the task of restoring my karma, squashing down any doubt, obliterating my own feelings, knowing it was my fault, my selfish behaviour that had created this situation.

When Elise had walked into the surrogacy group, I'd been sure she'd take one look at me and tell everyone my role in her misery. But by some miracle, she hadn't recognised me. And that had given me the opportunity to get close to her, to make it my mission to somehow make amends. Ensure that whatever had happened, she was able to move on. I would support her any way I could.

I'd blamed myself for her needing to go down the surrogacy

route, knowing I was the reason her daughter was dead. I'd assumed she'd fallen into an abusive relationship with Nick in her despair over losing the man she *really* wanted. The husband my selfish addict of an ex had stolen from her. Back then, after hearing that Harry had been arrested and charged, I'd cut myself off from the world, avoided the news entirely, unable to stand it, to bear the thought of what people would be saying, picking apart the lives of the power couple we'd portrayed ourselves to be, racked with humiliation and self-loathing. I'd put my head in the sand and pretended it hadn't happened. But it seemed that in blocking the case from my consciousness, I'd missed the most important piece of the story.

And in doing so, I'd made the biggest mistake of my life.

THIRTY-FIVE
ELISE

Then

There was a storm raging outside, fat raindrops pelting down, making me wince as I thought of the bucket Mitch had placed under the leak in the loft, having been stood up by one roofer after another. We would have to call round again on Monday and get someone in to fix it before the whole thing came crashing down.

I flipped the lid of the toothpaste, splodging it onto my toothbrush and crossing to the open bathroom window to watch as lightning flashed overhead, making the world come alive despite the late hour. I loved the night. Loved being safe and cosy in the home Mitch and I had created, though admittedly it still needed a lot of work – and money – before it reached its full potential. Thunder rumbled in a deafening drumroll, and I rinsed off the toothbrush, splashed some water on my face and closed the window.

I padded down the dark hallway, hoping I hadn't left anything out to trip over, not wanting to switch on a light and

wake them. Pushing open the bedroom door, I saw that Mitch
had left the red-tinted night light on, casting a soft glow over the
room. Pausing in the doorway, I smiled at the sight of my
husband fast asleep, our new baby daughter, Luna, curled into
his side, her little fist wrapped tight around his thumb, his
strong arm forming a protective barrier around the precious
bundle. We'd got into this lovely habit in the past few weeks
after I said I was missing having two hands free to get anything
done. Mitch had begun taking Luna up to bed after her feed,
and I had stayed up to paint, the freedom intoxicating, the
process meditative as I concentrated on the canvas in front of
me, a moment to refill my cup, explore my creativity.

I'd taken to motherhood as if I was born for it, Luna filling
my days and giving me a sense of purpose I felt I'd been
searching for ever since I could remember. And though I valued
my alone time now more than ever, after a couple of hours, I felt
myself craving her company, her closeness, wanting to smell her
sweet milky skin, breathe her in and have her warm against my
chest. I couldn't wait to climb into bed beside Mitch and have
my baby back in my arms. There was no joy that compared to
slotting into the gap and drifting off to sleep beside the two
people I loved most in the world.

Tiptoeing over to my dressing table, I took off my earrings,
dropping them in the antique mahogany jewellery box, then
unlatched my necklace, swearing under my breath as I realised
it was tangled in my hair. I worked at the clasp with my fingertips, embedding it deeper, then jumped as a deep laugh
sounded behind me. Turning with an expression of mock
annoyance, I saw Mitch watching me, his eyes open, sparkling.

'You want me to get the scissors again?' he offered.

I wrinkled my nose. 'This bloody hair. I don't know why I
ever think I can get away with wearing jewellery. Between
Luna starting to grab everything in sight, and my curls swal-

lowing everything that comes within a metre radius, it's a lost cause. I thought hair was supposed to thin out after pregnancy!'

'I've no idea. But it's beautiful. Although I'm sure you'd look just as gorgeous bald. Shall I grab the clippers instead?' he joked.

Luna stirred, and he lifted her effortlessly to his chest, easing himself up from the mattress and walking over to me. He pressed a kiss to the top of my head. 'Be right back with the tool-kit. Second time this month, right?' He winked and disappeared, cooing to the baby as he walked, though I knew she'd stay mostly asleep at this time of night.

I sighed, giving up on the job of untangling the delicate chain from my locks.

When the sound of breaking glass echoed from somewhere nearby, I stood from the dresser, heading to the window, wondering if the noise had come from next door – the elderly lady who lived there was forever forgetting to close the door to her porch, and in this wind, it would be swinging off its hinges. The noise of the thunder and rain was deafening as I opened the bedroom window to peer outside, and it was hard to tell what had smashed, but it was gone midnight now. Whatever it was would still be broken come morning; I wasn't about to head out into the storm to investigate.

I shut the window and fiddled again with my necklace, trying to work the tangled hair loose. Going to the open bedroom door, I looked down the long hallway to where the light shone from under the bathroom door, wondering what was taking Mitch so long. He must have decided to change Luna's nappy while he was up looking for the scissors. I was about to climb under the covers to wait for them when I remembered I'd taken the scissors into the spare room last week when I was wrapping a birthday present for him.

Padding back down the corridor, I called out as I passed the bathroom, 'Don't worry if you can't find the scissors; I think I know where they are.'

I heard a muffled reply from behind the door and grinned, knowing Luna would no doubt be wriggling like a wind-up toy as he tried to multitask. My breasts tingled and I hoped they'd hurry up so I could get into bed and feed her.

The top drawer to the desk where I kept all my stationery and art supplies was fit to burst, and I rummaged through it, trying to find the rusty old scissors, wishing I'd remembered to buy a spare pair. I always forgot and then no one could find them when we needed them.

Giving up, I straightened, rubbing my palm over the base of my spine, my back still aching even four months after giving birth. It had been a tough pregnancy and an even tougher birth, and the only thing that had got me through the never-ending pain-filled days was Mitch – his unerring support, the way he'd cared for me so selflessly. He'd cooked every meal, he'd pushed the wheelchair I'd needed when I was in too much pain to walk towards the end. He'd been gentle and sweet and loving, and without him, I knew, it would have been too much to bear. I was so grateful that we'd made it through the other side, even if I still had niggles in my body now and then. We had our family now, and next year, once we'd adopted a dog, we'd be complete. I knew there was no way I would manage a second pregnancy, but I was content – more than content, in fact. I was blissfully happy.

There was a creak in the hallway, and I frowned. I hadn't heard the bathroom door open. Going to the door, I squinted into the darkness, my eyes focusing on the silhouette of a man who was not my husband standing at the far end of the dark corridor, his tall, thin outline illuminated by the red light coming from our bedroom behind him. I suddenly remembered the sound outside, the broken glass. I hadn't even considered it could be someone breaking in. I was too busy thinking of sleep, my warm bed, my stupid necklace.

Before I could speak, the bathroom door opened and Mitch stepped out, his head down as he turned towards the bedroom.

'Mitch, no! Wait!' I cried, and he spun to face me with a quizzical raise of the eyebrow, our baby nestled against his bare chest. I opened my mouth to warn him, but my words were drowned out by a bang that sounded too loud, too close. Mitch's mouth went slack, and I saw the horror on his face as a deep red rose bloomed on the back of Luna's white babygro, a short, sharp cry bursting free from her tiny chest. And then silence. I stepped forward, my hand outstretched, a scream bubbling from somewhere deep inside me. Then, as if in slow motion, as if I might have a chance to stop it if only I knew how, my husband stumbled and fell forward, taking my daughter with him.

The man was a coward. He had run after he'd fired the gun into my husband's back. As I fell to the floor, tried to breathe life back into the corpses of my baby girl and my soulmate, not caring if he shot me too, he'd turned and fled – but not quickly enough. Someone had heard the gunshot, called the police. He'd been found hyperventilating, his head between his knees as he sat on a park bench, the gun tossed to the far end of the wooden seat as if he couldn't bear to touch it again. A week later, he'd released a statement saying that he was sorry. That he hadn't meant for the gun to go off, he'd never realised there was a baby... that he'd undo it all if he could. But it was far too late for apologies. Words were nothing. They couldn't bring them back, couldn't change the unbearable fact that I would never be able to erase the memory of how it had felt to hold my daughter as she bled out – that everything that had mattered to me was gone.

The first few days afterwards had been pandemonium, reporters knocking on the door, waiting outside the house to get a photo of the tragically grieving wife and mother, pointing out tactlessly that I was no longer either of those things. A widow, they'd called me, and it had struck me that there would never be a word that could sum up all that I'd lost. Broken didn't come close.

One of the neighbours had brought a stew over, though I couldn't bring myself to eat it, and my parents had called from New Zealand or Australia – wherever it was they were currently travelling through. I could never keep up. They didn't offer to come back to support me. To be honest, I hadn't expected them to. They'd made it clear that as far as they were concerned, once I turned eighteen, they'd finished raising me and I was on my own. I hadn't seen them face to face in years and I'd ended the call as soon as I could, unable to tolerate their empty platitudes, the surface-deep sympathy coated with an anxious undercurrent that I might ask for more than they were willing to offer. I wouldn't give them the satisfaction of thinking I needed them.

It was after the drama had died down and the newspaper reporters had moved on to the next tragedy that it had really begun to sink in. I was alone... back to where I'd been before I met Mitch, my days endlessly long, empty. But this time it was different. I might have been grieving, but I wasn't lost, searching for meaning in a void. I had a clear purpose, and I wouldn't rest until I'd found a way to reach my goal. I devoured every update about the man, his arrest, the pathetic reasons and excuses he made for why he'd broken into my home and killed my family. He'd been looking for money for drugs, and his lawyer had already started making statements about his determination to get clean, his repentance for 'the terrible accident', as if it hadn't been all his fault.

Yesterday morning, I'd seen in the news that he'd been granted bail, a decision that was sparking anger and controversy, being debated widely. People were furious that a man who'd committed a crime like his should get to wait for his court date in the comfort of his own home. It was clear that he'd be going to prison, and for a very long time. Nobody could understand why the judge would make such a reckless choice. But *I* wasn't angry. Far from it.

I stopped on the second-floor landing of the narrow stairwell now, leaning my head back against the wall, the sienna light overhead casting a surreal glow over the space, silent at this time of night save for the sound of my breathing. I felt like I'd been granted an opportunity. If he'd been refused bail, he would have gone straight to prison and I'd have spent the whole of his sentence waiting. I would have served every year, every fucking minute right alongside him, waiting for the moment when he would finally walk free and I could exact my revenge. But this was so much better. I could move forward after tonight, knowing he wasn't breathing the same air, walking around, eating and laughing and living his life while *my* family were gone. Once this was over, I could let go of some of the pain. It was unbearable right now. I'd barely eaten since that night. Barely slept. I couldn't close my eyes without hearing Luna crying for me, the nightmares dragging me back to that moment again and again, the way her eyes had glazed over and I'd known deep in my core that she was gone. I would die from this agony unless I did something to end it. This wasn't a choice – it was survival. Mine over his. I wouldn't allow him to destroy me. This was a new beginning.

There would be consequences for me, I never doubted that, but I had already accepted the price I would pay for tonight. It didn't matter. I didn't care. And once I made it out the other side, perhaps I could find a new purpose, something pure and beautiful. Something I would protect until my dying breath.

I closed my eyes, thinking of Luna, her sweet little smile, how she'd held my finger when I fed her, the way she'd looked so deep into my eyes, I'd felt like she was seeing right to the heart of who I was. She deserved justice. I wasn't a bad person. Any mother would do the same for their child.

The steel knife I'd slid down one side of my leather boot was warm against my skin, and I wrapped my fingers round the handle, easing it out slowly so as not to cut myself. The blade was long – almost beautiful – as the orange light hit the polished metal. It was sharp too – I'd made quite sure of that. I'd ordered it online, not bothering to try and conceal the transaction, using my real name, the bank card I used to buy my groceries. I *wanted* them to know it was me.

There had been a moment of doubt before I'd left to come here when I'd suddenly wondered if I was just hyping myself up for a task I could never see through. If I would hold the weight of the weapon in my hand and feel the bravado seep out of my body, turning to run jelly-legged back home, leaving the bastard to the whims of the jury. But no, I thought, a wry smile pulling at the corners of my lips as I tightened my grip on the handle. That wasn't the case at all.

I began to walk, taking the steps up to the next floor, pausing outside the door I wanted. I glanced over my shoulder, checking I was alone, then, holding the knife under my arm, used the clever little tool from my pocket to unlock the door. It gave a satisfying click and I pushed the handle down, confirming it had worked. The tool had been a gift from my husband after I'd locked myself and Luna out three times in as many weeks in my sleep-deprived post-baby state. He'd put it in a flowerpot in the front garden so I would never have to wait out in the rain again. These days, I always left my back door unlocked, half hoping someone would find it open and come and put an end to my suffering once and for all. At this point, it would have been a mercy.

The thought of Mitch's face, the way he'd left his meeting and driven home without a second thought to unlock our front door, the way he'd loved me more than I'd ever deserved, brought a rush of emotion to my mind, my eyes filling with tears, needing to be with him, wanting more than anything to feel his arms around me, the smell of his skin filling my senses, that safety I'd felt in his presence. But it was impossible.

Anger swiftly washed away the sadness, fuelling me, reminding me of what I was here to do. I took the knife back in my hand, pushed open the door and stepped inside. And for the first time since that terrible night, I felt a burst of excitement take flight inside my belly. I was going to enjoy this.

THIRTY-SIX

MAYA

Now

Panic is like a fire igniting within the deepest part of your body. The heat rushes outwards in tendrils, closing your airways as it burns your throat, clouding your vision, searing through your gut. All sense of reason is destroyed, decimated in the path of its destruction. Nick was looking at me with kind eyes, and I wanted to tear them from his face – I didn't want his sympathy; it only made his words feel more real.

I lurched up from the chair, swaying forward, gripping the bars of Julia's bed for support before spinning on my heel and rushing out of the room as fast as I could manage. I could hear Julia calling my name, but I didn't turn back.

Crossing the hall, I headed to my own room, pausing in the doorway as I took in my surroundings. It seemed like a lifetime ago that I was waking in that bed, warm and hopeful and excited to meet my baby girl. I felt like the world had been ripped from beneath me and the woman standing here now was someone completely different, unrecognisable from the person I'd been before.

My gaze darted around, searching for answers I knew I wouldn't find, pausing as it landed on my handbag slung over the back of a chair. I dashed over to it and yanked open the zip, pouring the contents onto the bed. Dried, crusted blood was flaking from my fingers, but I didn't care. I picked up my phone, holding it tightly. It took me three attempts before I managed to unlock it, and I stared at the screen, hoping desperately to see a message pop up, or a missed call. Something from Elise to make everything okay so I could go back in and tell Julia that she was wrong, that they were on their way back now, that everything had been a silly misunderstanding, blown out of proportion.

There were fifteen missed calls, and my heart thudded with hope as I clicked on them, followed swiftly by disappointment as I saw the call log. Every single one was from Nina. She'd left numerous voicemails too. I listened one by one, pressing delete as I heard her voice, her anger palpable through the phone as she demanded to know where I was, why I wasn't returning her calls. I longed to hear Elise instead, but there was nothing from her.

With shaking fingers, I found her number and called it, pressing the phone hard against my cheek, listening as the automated message told me the mobile phone I was trying to call was switched off. There was no opportunity to leave a voicemail, just a long, dull tone signifying I'd been cut off. I tried again and again, the urge to scream building inside me with every moment, every frustratingly long beep. My breath came in jagged gasps. I was aware of a growing pulse of pain spreading through my belly, the trickle of warm blood running down my thighs. Some distant part of my mind knew I needed help, but I pushed it aside, thinking only of my daughter.

Elizabeth... The name forced its way to the front of my thoughts, and I was suddenly reminded of the grandmother I'd adored as a little girl. I'd stayed with her on weekends every now and then when my parents went on trips. She'd lived in an

old ramshackle farmhouse on a sheep farm, with oil lamps and
open fireplaces, big stone hearths and plenty of cobwebs. She'd
taught me how to bottle-feed the orphan lambs, how to bake
sourdough and how to knit. She'd been such a good storyteller –
funny tales that had taken me away from my reality and trans-
ported me somewhere warm and safe. Those weekends with
Grandma Elizabeth had been the only times in my childhood
I'd felt welcome. Wanted. Like my presence wasn't simply a
nuisance to be tolerated. I had never wanted to go home.

I pressed my hand to my belly, repeating the name out loud.
'Elizabeth,' I whispered. 'I'm going to call you Elizabeth.'

The phone in my hand began to ring, and I answered it,
breathless with anticipation. 'Elise!' I cried.

'It's Nina! Where the hell have you been, Maya? I've been
worried sick!'

I blinked, Nina's voice too close, too real. I didn't know what
to say.

She continued, her voice shrill. 'I've called the hospital over
and over again and they won't tell me a thing! What's going on?
Is the baby okay? Are you in labour? Will's on a flight back as
we speak – where are you? Just tell me and I'll be on my way.'

'No.' The word was forceful, and I heard the stunned
silence that followed. 'I'm sorry, Nina. I can't do that. I've
changed my mind.'

'What?'

'I'm not giving the baby to you... *I'm* her mother. And I'm
keeping her.' I closed my eyes, hoping that I would get that
chance. That Elise would bring her back to me.

'You can't do that! You made a commitment to us, *promises*!
You'd never even have got pregnant if it wasn't for us asking you
to. You signed a fucking contract, Maya!'

I blinked away the spots exploding in front of my eyes, my
legs trembling as I shook my head. 'Fuck your contract and fuck
you! You know as well as I do it means nothing. The law is on

my side. Find someone else to manipulate, because I won't be bought.' I ended the call and threw the phone on the bed, pressing my bloodstained hands to my face.

'Maya...'

I looked up at Morag, who'd appeared in the doorway, a new doctor beside her, and shook my head, eyes wide, unable to fathom how this could have happened, how I'd neglected to consider the possibility that I couldn't trust Elise. We'd been so similar. I'd liked her... she was so much like me. I'd thought she deserved happiness, but I'd never considered she might take mine.

'Maya,' the midwife repeated gently, stepping into the room. 'Let's get you back into bed. Dr Broon is here to have a look at you. I've brought a clean gown.'

She took hold of my arm, and I felt my head spin. It was the drugs. I was hallucinating. Things like this didn't happen in real life! 'What did you give me?' I asked, looking at the doctor, my voice loud, harsh. 'Bring me my baby. I want my baby – now!' I realised it was the first time I'd taken a stand since the night I last spoke to Harry. The first time I'd felt I could fight for something.

'We're doing everything we can,' Dr Broon said, his hand supporting my other elbow as the pair of them guided me back to the bed.

I shook my head as I let them manoeuvre me onto the mattress.

'They'll find her, won't they?' I pleaded, thinking of the CCTV that was everywhere nowadays. The true-life crime programmes where they always tracked down the suspect. There was no way she would be able to hide, not with two babies. They'd trace her somehow.

Morag eased me back against the pillows. 'I'm sure they will, love. There are people out there this very moment looking for her. You need to take care of yourself so that you're in a fit state to look after your baby once she's back in your arms.'

'Can I take a peek at your incision?' Dr Broon asked, waiting for me to nod before going to wash his hands.

He returned, lifting my gown up to just above the dressing, and I heard him putting on some gloves. His words seemed to blur in my mind, my thoughts floating out of reach. With a sense of dread, I tried to catch them, sure that once they drifted too far, I'd lose them for ever. I had a nagging urge to do something, but as I tried to instruct my body to move, my mind fought harder, spinning, drowning. I couldn't stop my eyes from closing, no matter how hard I tried. As I gave in to oblivion, I knew I'd done it again. I'd ruined another life.

THIRTY-SEVEN

I lay unmoving in the lumpy hospital bed, my discharge papers folded beside me on the mattress, my clothes hanging over the back of the chair, ready for me to put on once I could summon the energy to get up. The hospital gown was too thin and the seam was rough against my sensitive skin, but taking it off, leaving without a baby in my arms, felt like a surrender.

Julia had left last night after her epidural had finally worn off, though it was clear from her frequent gasps and moans that she should still be in bed, recovering from her C-section. I'd only been half aware of her coming in to say goodbye, her frantic energy no less dampened by her pain as she told me she was going out to look for her son herself. Her parents had turned up in separate cars to help with the search, and when her dad had come into my room, wrapping an arm around Julia and making a promise that they wouldn't stop until they'd tracked Elise down, I was reminded of the chat I'd had with Elise in the café, where she'd told me that she and her parents weren't close. I tried to remember what her expression had looked like when I'd asked if it was the same for Julia too. Had there been any trace of a lie in her response, some clue I'd missed? I didn't think so. It was baffling to look back and see how easily the deception had slipped from her tongue.

I'd nodded, wanting Julia and her dad to go, to leave me alone, and as I heard their conversation fading down the hall, the routes they were each planning to take, a feeling came over me that they would be unsuccessful. If the police hadn't found her yet, what made Julia think she and her elderly parents stood a chance? Elise wasn't going to go to any of the places she might have discussed during her therapy sessions. She wasn't stupid.

I pressed my hand to my abdomen now, feeling the fresh dressing beneath my gown. The bleeding had turned out to be only superficial, a few of my stitches having snapped open. I hadn't had to return to theatre; instead, the doctor had been able to redo them under local anaesthetic. He'd been gentle and kind, though I was sure from his manner that it was costing him a lot not to chide me, but that only made it worse, knowing he was making a special effort because I was someone to be pitied. Today, the pain wasn't too bad.

I didn't know what to do. Going home, back to that empty, lonely place in the knowledge that my daughter was out there somewhere... I didn't think I could stand it. But I couldn't stay here indefinitely. Besides, I had one more thing to do before I could leave.

As if on cue, my phone beeped, and I read the message from Nina.

We're outside. Just waiting for the nurse to buzz us in.

I closed my eyes briefly, steeling myself for the difficult conversation I knew I was about to have. Pulling myself up to a sitting position, I tucked the discharge papers beneath the blanket, not wanting them to know my plans.

A few minutes later, the door opened and Will came in, Nina close behind. Her eyes scanned the room, and I knew she was looking for evidence of a baby – a cot, a stack of nappies. I saw her frown, her gaze raking over my belly, still swollen but no longer full and round.

'What's going on?' she asked. 'Where is she? Please don't take her from us! We've been out of our minds, Maya. When I got your text to come here, I tried to call, but you didn't answer!' Her tone was accusing, angry, but I realised I wasn't afraid of her any more.

Will put a hand on her shoulder, squeezing as if trying to remind her to stay calm. 'What's happened, Maya?' he said, his eyes meeting mine. 'Is... is the baby okay?'

I took a deep breath, wishing I could have skipped this part, sent the whole story in a text then blocked them – stuck my head in the sand. But that wasn't fair. They'd invested their hopes, their time into this dream, and as much as I regretted letting them take over my life these past nine months, I couldn't shy away from doing this face to face. It was the right thing to do.

'The baby's gone,' I said, my voice oddly flat, devoid of emotion. It was a conscious effort – I didn't want to fall apart in front of these people. They weren't my friends. They saw me only as a means of getting what they wanted. 'Yesterday I was rushed in for an emergency C-section under general anaesthetic, and while I was unconscious, someone I thought was a friend abducted her. She also took another baby from the ward.'

'You can't be serious!' Will exclaimed.

'Oh my God...' Nina swayed against him, her hands going to her mouth, and I continued speaking before they could ask more.

'The police are searching for them at this very moment. They have been since yesterday.'

'Why the hell didn't you call us? We have a right to know!' Will exploded.

I shook my head. 'Actually, you don't. I'm sorry, I know you had your hearts set on this being your baby, but...' I took another breath, locking my fingers, squeezing my palms tightly together, 'As I said when we spoke on the phone, I can't go through with it. I'm going to find her and I'm going to keep her. I know that's not what we agreed, but she's *my* baby. I'm her mother, and I won't hand her over to anyone.' I spoke vehemently, though I was afraid it was too late, that I might never get to hold her, even once.

Nina's mouth dropped open. 'I never thought you really meant it! I assumed you weren't thinking straight, that they'd given you too much pain relief or something. Oh my God...' She stared at me, her eyes wide and afraid. 'This is my fault, isn't it? Because I pushed you? I threatened you. It's my fault. I made you think we aren't good people. But don't you see, it's only because we want her so much! We've invested everything into this dream, and I know we haven't always shown our best side, but we'd be good parents. We'd love her with our whole hearts, we really would.' She walked over to the bed and grabbed my hand. Hers was drenched in sweat, and I could feel the thrum of her pulse beneath the skin. 'Please, Maya, don't be rash about this.'

'Nina's right,' Will said. 'You're flooded with hormones right now; you've been through a lot in the past twenty-four hours. Let's not discuss this now. We all need to focus on doing whatever we can to find the babies and bring them back. Who *is* this woman? Why was she even allowed on the ward?'

I shook my head, his words bouncing off me like snow melting on a windshield. I could see the panic in his eyes, his determination to talk me round, but he was wasting his time. 'I'm only going to say it once more to the both of you,' I said, my voice stronger, more confident than I'd heard it in a long time. It brought back a flicker of a memory of who I used to be. 'The baby is mine. I don't care what you made me sign, what we agreed. She's mine. If I get her back, I won't let her go again. Not ever.'

Nina burst into tears, pressing her hands to her face, and Will stood frozen, shocked, as if he didn't know what to do, how to cope with being denied what he wanted.

Nina looked up, tears streaming down her cheeks. 'I know I handled it all wrong, Maya. And I'm sorry. I made you feel like you were just an incubator, like we were trying to buy you.' She shook her head. 'Desperation can make you become someone you don't even recognise. I could feel you changing your mind weeks ago, I knew it was all falling apart, but I was too afraid to speak up, to ask. I guess I thought that if I held on tighter, it might be okay. If I was always there, always calling or visiting, a reminder of what we agreed, you wouldn't have space to question the plan.' She sucked in a deep breath, wiping roughly at her eyes, then turned and walked over to Will, her arms wrapping around his neck.

'Will you let us know if they find her?' she asked, her voice trembling with emotion. 'We won't visit. We'll give you space. A chance to change your mind. I can't believe someone could just...' She shook her head.

'I'll let you know.'

She nodded, her hand slipping into Will's, guiding him towards the door. 'We'll leave you to rest.'

I watched them go, relieved the conversation was over. I'd thought I was doing the right thing. Somehow it had made sense that in being the reason for Elise losing her daughter, I should give away mine to even the score. But it didn't work like that. I could see now that Elizabeth would have become the victim and I would only have caused more pain, no matter how good my intentions might have been. She belonged with me, her flesh and blood. The mother who had carried her. The only one she knew.

I leaned back against the pillow, and for the first time since I'd heard the news about the abduction, I felt the tears begin to fall.

THIRTY-EIGHT
ELISE

Two weeks later

The sun was streaming through the thin curtains, and I blinked, turning my head to face the dawn glow, stretching my arms above my head, enjoying the pull of my muscles, the crack of my spine. After lying flat on my back all night, I was always achy come morning.

I stifled a yawn with a smile, looking down at the babies, one nestled into each side of my chest, their little bodies still scrunched into the foetal position as they pressed against me. For a day or so after they were born, I'd considered naming them after the two people I missed most, Luna and Mitch. It would have been so special to be able to say those names out loud again, have them become real once more, but after the initial elation of having succeeded had died down and I began to think straight, I changed my mind. As lovely as it would have been, it was too risky. I didn't want anything to link me to that story, ruin a plan that had taken months to conceive, by falling victim to nostalgia in the final stretch. Besides, wasn't this supposed to be a fresh start? A new beginning?

The names I'd chosen in the end were perfect. Nova and Phoenix. Both were a nod to Luna and the astronomical theme her father and I had loved, but I alone would know the connection to the past, take a moment every day to think of the older sister they would have adored. It hurt to imagine how the three of them might have been together. But then, I reasoned, if I'd never lost Luna, I wouldn't have Nova and Phoenix now.

I sighed, thinking of the moment I'd realised this was the only path left to take. It's impossible to explain the agony, the emptiness that comes with being a mother without a baby to hold, a child to nurture. To have been some tiny being's entire world, needed and loved to the point of exhaustion, to have purpose in every moment of the night and day, only for it to all suddenly go up in smoke and to be left in a void of nothingness.

It hadn't taken long for the need to become all-encompassing. I'd been locked in a prison with five hundred women, and all I had wanted was to get pregnant. That craving had fed me, fuelled my every waking moment. I knew nothing could ever replace the love I had for Luna, but another baby, a pure, innocent little person I could focus all my love on, might stop me from ending it all. Because when I wasn't planning, thinking of how I could become pregnant again, those were the far darker ideas that took over. And as much as I'd been tempted to give in to them, I had still held tight to a scrap of hope that there was a better life waiting for me. A second chance for happiness.

In the women's prison, there had been a guard who flirted with me – the only man I ever saw with any regularity during my two years locked up. The way he looked at me, I knew he could be tempted. I could remember the blind need, the lack of logical thought behind any of it; the practicalities of being pregnant in prison, the reactions of those people who held my freedom in their hands hadn't even crossed my mind at the time. It had been stupid in hindsight. I might have had another baby stolen from me had I given birth behind bars.

But in the end, it hadn't mattered. When it had come down to it after months of getting closer, and I finally had the guard alone, locked in a toilet cubicle, the sound of his belt buckle clinking as it hit the tiles, I'd baulked. The smell of his body, the way his fingers kneaded at my breasts, the rough scrape of his beard as he tried to kiss me – it made me sick. I couldn't go through with it, no matter how much I might have wanted the end result. All I could think of was Mitch, the last time we'd made love, the experience the polar opposite of this.

So I'd waited, despite myself. I told the guard I'd report what had happened if he didn't put a good word in for me, and by some miracle, charming the warden, being the good girl, I saved myself from him and got myself released early. Once I was settled back home, mindful of the fact that that disgusting leech Nick Pratt was watching my every move, I found a site on the internet where I could order sperm to be sent in discreet packaging to my house. It was risky, but I knew it was my only option. I was too fragile for a one-night stand with a stranger.

But it didn't work. For four months I injected the stuff into my body, closing my eyes and hoping for it to take hold, trying sample after sample to no avail. Finally I booked myself into a private fertility clinic, using a fake name, telling the doctor I couldn't possibly be infertile as I'd already had a child.

After a series of tests, she called me into her office, sat me down with a grim expression and gave me the unsatisfying diagnosis of 'unexplained secondary infertility'. My first pregnancy had taken a huge toll on my body, and I had known it wouldn't be easy a second time around, but I hadn't realised it would be impossible. The doctor had asked if I'd been stressed lately, explaining the impact that could have, and then brightly announced that at least I had one baby already. Not everyone was so lucky.

It had taken all my strength to walk out of there with my head held high and not slap the chirpy smile from her condescending face. After that, my options had narrowed considerably, and I'd known the only way to succeed in my desperate desire to have another child was going to be a far more difficult road.

I thought back to that first meeting at the surrogacy group, the story I'd felt compelled to share about my sister having donated an egg to my cause. Julia would have hated to hear me saying such personal things to a bunch of strangers, but that was just her way, and I understood her better than she realised. The truth was, she had been more of a sister to me than any other woman in my life, at least since the murder of my family. It had been a surprise to me how quickly I'd been erased from the lives of those people I'd loved and trusted in the wake of what had happened. Friends who had stood by my side at Mitch and Luna's funeral, held my hand, made me dinner, had blocked my number and pretended I didn't exist. Not one of them had visited to break the monotony of my sentence, nor to tell me I'd done the only thing possible given the circumstances. I heard a rumour that people were afraid of me. That my lack of remorse was chilling to them somehow. It wasn't something I could begin to understand. How could I possibly feel the slightest sliver of sorrow for having sought justice for my loved ones? *Of course* I didn't regret what I'd done.

Memories of that night, the way he'd screamed in agony, the look of absolute terror in his eyes as the blade pushed into his pale skin through those skeletal ribs, blood swelling around the shining metal, dripping down to stain the sheets beneath his sweat-coated body, had been a comfort to me when the lights went out and I had nothing but the darkness cocooning me in my cell.

When I'd come home after my time in prison, not one person had called to check up on me, offer a listening ear. Julia had been the one constant since my release, and we even bickered like sisters. I had enjoyed that. It made it feel all the more right that she be the one to repair the missing piece of my life, to give me a tiny slice of herself to carry with me for ever. She might never realise it, but despite the animosity she'd shown towards me, I had a lot of love for her. How could I not when she'd given me so much?

Nova wriggled against me, her little hand opening and closing, searching in sleep, and I slipped my finger into her palm, feeling her grip tighten, comforted by my presence. Taking her hadn't risked my plans, though it hadn't been my intention to do it. I'd thought through the choice in the moments prior to leaving the hospital, going over everything, making sure I wasn't endangering the outcome in bringing her too. She'd slotted in without a glitch.

I had never imagined I'd be able to get onto the labour ward. The fact that both Julia and Maya had been there at the same time, the ease with which it had all unfolded when I'd bargained for a much more complex situation, had made me sure that this was meant to be. That somehow Mitch was watching over me, helping me, knowing it was the only way I could keep going without him and Luna by my side. I'd never been a religious person, never believed in ghosts, spirits, but I couldn't explain how else it had all come together so perfectly. It made me realise just how right I'd been to make this choice.

Phoenix began to stir, and I sighed happily, rubbing my hand across his back until he settled, the smell of Julia long since gone. Both of them smelled like me now. They wore the clothes I had bought months previously, the spare room filled with boxes of them, from tiny babygros to clothes that would fit in five years' time. The nappies I'd had ready and waiting. The bottles had been washed, lined up in the cupboards, and I'd stored enough formula to see me through two years, even with the extra mouth to feed. I'd stocked up on everything I could possibly need, knowing I wouldn't be able to go out and buy anything, that any missed detail could be the end of it all. I'd had the house, a fully furnished old stone cottage in North Wales, lined up before I'd even met Julia. Before I knew I'd be matched with a pregnant therapist. She had fallen into my lap at the perfect time. This had been the first place I'd come once I'd got my tag off, the man who'd rented it to me months before having grudgingly taken in my deliveries, leaving the boxes in the hallway ready for me to unpack and organise.

It had been my cellmate in prison who'd put us in touch, telling me he was a recluse, cut off from society, and just needed someone there to pay the rent so he didn't have to get a job. I'd heard those words and known he was exactly what I needed. Someone who wouldn't see my face on the news. Someone who wouldn't want to get involved in my business. I'd listened to Rebecca tell me about the cottage – a place she described as homely and idyllic, nearly a mile away from the owner's main house – and asked her to put us in touch.

The remainder of the payout from Mitch's life insurance – more than half a million after I'd paid off the mortgage on the family home – had been sitting in my bank account gaining interest the whole time I'd been in prison, and it had been easy enough to withdraw the lot bit by bit once I was no longer being watched by Nick every moment of the day.

I'd split it into bundles and hidden it around the land and property, burying the lion's share under the floorboards of the shed in a locked safe, paying my rent in cash a year upfront just as the landlord preferred. I'd given him an alias, we'd barely crossed paths, and I doubted he'd recognise me if he passed me in the street. My own house would remain empty. I could picture the police swarming through it, ransacking my things. It didn't matter. There was nothing there I cared about. The only thing I'd taken was the plastic box from the garden room filled with photos of me and Mitch, the letters and birthday cards we'd sent each other over the years. Luna's scan pictures. The little things that were irreplaceable. It was stored in the spare room with the babies' things. When they were older, perhaps I'd show them a couple of items from it, but not enough that they would ever guess the full story. I wouldn't burden them with that.

Rebecca, my old cellmate, would have been the only fly in the ointment, having known about my agreement with her friend. I'd spent countless hours thinking about it in the weeks running up to Julia's due date, wondering if the police would question her, if she might give up this address, but in the end, it had resolved itself. She'd committed suicide a week before the babies were born, and the relief I'd felt when I'd heard the news had made me doubt for a moment if I was truly a good person after all.

I eased myself out from between the babies now, sliding down to the bottom of the mattress and standing up, watching as the perfect pair continued to sleep soundly. It had been Julia's own fault that she hadn't got to say goodbye. It hadn't been what I'd initially intended, but I'd realised a while back that she was going to be difficult. When she'd tried to let me go as a client, ignoring the sisterly bond we shared. When she'd judged me for killing the man who'd destroyed my family. I'd known then that she wasn't a proper mother. That she wouldn't have done the same. Would never have sought justice for the death of her child, her husband. She didn't understand love like I did. And that poor baby growing in her womb deserved someone who would risk their freedom to fight for him. Who would step in front of a bullet if it came to it. Julia wasn't that person. She wasn't fit to raise him.

When I'd realised that after a few sessions with her, the thought process that followed was so organic, so simple, I never once questioned it. I was a mother in need of a baby, bursting with love I needed to share, and here was a baby who needed me. The tryst with Ben had brought me no guilt – I knew she didn't love him either – but it had been stupid and I'd regretted it. If she had found out sooner, it would have made things harder.

And Maya... I walked to the bedroom fireplace, sliding a framed photo from a box, lifting its weight in my hands. I hadn't known about our connection, hadn't realised who she was until I saw it on the news in the aftermath of my disappearance. But how serendipitous, that I should take her baby when she'd cost me mine.

Though Nova had never been *her* baby really, had she? Maya had planned to hand her over to some stranger, someone she didn't even like, from what I could tell. What difference did it make that I'd taken her instead? Nova would be loved, cherished, wanted, and wasn't that all that mattered? No, I couldn't bring myself to feel anything for a woman who would give away her own baby like that. Julia and Maya would be fine. They could never have understood what it meant to be a mother – not like I did.

I looked down at the photo in my hands and smiled, seeing Mitch's handsome face, then stretched up to the hook I'd hammered into the wall last night. I'd run out of time before the babies needed feeding, and had fallen asleep before I had a chance to hang it up, but now his warm eyes smiled down on us, and I touched his cheek.

'Welcome home, darling,' I whispered. 'Our little ones will be waking soon. We'll be safe here.'

I almost felt as if I could hear him reply, smell the coffee he'd always brewed so strong in the mornings, mine served black and bitter in the *Red Dwarf* mug he'd gifted me on our fifth anniversary. I pictured the chipped, well-loved mug sitting in my sink back in the home that had once been so happy and wished I'd had the foresight to bring it with me.

I walked over to the window and peeked through the curtains. Beyond the sprawling garden where I planned to keep chickens, grow my own vegetables, there was nothing but rolling green hills and fields as far as the eye could see. We would have to stick close to home from now on, and I had no doubt that it would become more complicated as the babies got older, more curious. But we'd make it work. I'd picked the perfect spot.

A couple of rabbits were chasing each other in the damp, dewy grass, the weak sun glistening on the blades, making me think of crisp Christmas mornings, how I was going to give my babies the most wonderful childhoods, the most blessed lives. I sighed happily, feeling a sense of peace I hadn't known in years as I turned to look at my sweet sleeping babies. Nobody would ever find us here. We were home.

THIRTY-NINE

JULIA

Six months later

I stood at my living-room window, shielded by the net curtains, as I watched the man in overalls replacing the 'For Sale' sign with one that read 'Sold'. I'd imagined that this moment would finally draw something from me, some feeling of loss, heartbreak even, as the reality of selling my family home came to fruition. But with the high-pitched sound of the drill buzzing in my ears, I realised it hadn't materialised. There had been only one emotion consuming me for months now. Nothing else could break past it, nothing had the power to shake the conviction of my simmering anger. At the police's incompetence. At Elise's deception. At the loss I still couldn't bear to accept. And more than all that, at myself for not telling my boss to go fuck himself when I'd had the chance and walking away from a woman I'd known in my heart was dangerous. The moment she'd come into my life, I'd seen it. Feared her.

Reaching into my pocket, I pinched the now bobbled fabric of the tiny vest I kept with me at all times, my thumb and fingers anxiously rubbing at the material. There were already a smattering of tiny holes in the garment, but I couldn't bring myself to stop the habit. Holding it, touching it was the only link I had left to my baby. The one real thing that could convince me that this hadn't all been some awful nightmare.

When I'd gone out to buy the things I needed for him, I'd been conscious of the fact that everything was for the last time. Ben would never agree to another baby – he'd have preferred to stop at two – and with that knowledge at the forefront of my mind, I'd savoured every choice, every blanket and babygro that extra bit more special to me. The vest had been the first thing I'd packed in my hospital bag. I'd folded it lovingly, knowing that the next time I saw it would be on my baby boy.

I slid it from my pocket now, running my finger along the row of tiny bluebirds flying around the oak tree printed across the chest, the image worn and faded now. The moment I'd seen it, I'd broken into a smile. I'd chosen the name Oakley, and though I couldn't bear monogrammed clothing, I loved the subtle nod to his name. Only *I* would know it was there, hidden under his clothing, and it felt like a private joke I could hold close. Only I'd never had the pleasure of dressing him in it for the first time. Never held his little wriggling thighs in my hand as I tried to do up the poppers. Never got to do any of the wonderful 'lasts' I'd been dreaming of, because *she* had taken it all for herself.

I closed my eyes, thinking of the card that had been waiting on my doormat when I'd finally made it home from the hospital. I'd assumed it was from my neighbour who'd seen me the night I went into labour – a 'Congratulations on Your New Arrival', like she'd sent for the previous two babies – and hadn't been able to face opening it. It had been a week later when I'd finally ripped into the envelope. Emblazoned across the front of the card within were the words *Thank you to my sister*, and I'd been confused, given that neither Ben nor I had any siblings. But when I'd opened it, read the message inside, my blood had turned to ice.

To my wonderful sister Julia,

I can never thank you enough for your generosity. Thank you for acting as surrogate for me, for understanding what this means to me. It's been a rocky road, but we made it through. You've given me back my family.

All my love,

E

I'd heard Maya's claim that Elise was telling people this nonsense, but until that moment, I hadn't realised that she'd convinced herself of it too.

The man on the driveway straightened up, drill in hand, and without turning to glance my way headed back to his van and drove away, no doubt on to the next house to put an end to decades of memories, destroying someone else's world. It had been fascinating to discover just how quickly the life I'd thought was secure had crumbled to a pile of dusty rubble, too damaged to repair. Ben's confession, blurted in a moment of vulnerability when he'd finally arrived at the hospital, that he'd slept with the woman who'd abducted our baby. The way the love I'd had for him had evaporated in that exact moment, leaving nothing but the bitter salt of his tears behind. He'd moved out that same day, and it had only occurred to me later that now I would have to endure half the week without my older children with me, handing them over to a man I would hate for the rest of my life.

It had been the final straw, losing them too. I didn't know where my baby boy was, if he was even alive, and the only thing that might have kept me going was them, and yet Ben took them from me time and again, leaving me to rattle round an empty house, consumed by the noise inside my own head, the anxiety inescapable. The house might have been silent, but in the privacy of my mind, there was never peace, not for a moment. I would concoct stories, scenarios that were more violent, more vicious than I'd believed myself capable of. Things that would have frightened me just a few months ago, before I truly understood what it meant to be this broken.

I chewed my lip, glancing towards the clock on the mantelpiece. Maya would be arriving soon. I shouldn't be working, shouldn't be taking on clients – not in this state. But when Ben had given me the ultimatum of letting him move back in or selling up so he could buy a place of his own, I'd known I had no choice. I needed to work. Needed the money, the freedom it gave me. For the most part, I was simply going through the motions, asking the questions I was expected to voice, but I didn't care about any of the people who came to sit on the sofa in my therapy room, their pathetic problems, their inability to see past the inconsequential mess they'd created and pull themselves together. I was numb to them all.

Maya was different though. She'd asked to come and talk to me two weeks after the babies were snatched, and I'd agreed, offering to take her on for free. The lines were blurred over whether it was a working relationship or some sort of tragic friendship, but what I did know back then was that she was the only person who could grasp what I was feeling.

Like me, she hadn't been able to sleep. She'd been pale, full of self-hatred and blame for making such a reckless choice, trusting Elise without ever knowing what she'd done. Together we'd sobbed, screamed, held each other. But as the months had passed, the police offered fewer updates and hope began to fade. And where I had grown more angry, more determined than ever to find my son, Maya had somehow begun to change.

She'd got a new job at a big company. She'd started taking

care of herself again, wearing make-up and new clothes. She'd come to see me and said in her straightforward, quiet voice that she felt like the time had come to let go of the regret, the resentment. That she'd chosen to believe that wherever she was, Elise was taking care of the babies. She'd been a devoted mother to Luna – everyone had said so before she took justice into her own hands – and, Maya reasoned, her grief had made her do something impulsive and rash but motivated by love.

Sitting in my therapy room, her hair freshly highlighted, her lipstick too cheery, too bright, she'd sighed, then said, 'Look, Julia, I know how hard it is to move forward. I've spent years of my life feeling guilty for my part in what happened to Elise, the loss of her husband and baby girl. I wouldn't have chosen this, and there's a part of me that I can't prevent from thinking terrible things, fears I can't stop from bubbling up inside me. But for the most part, I choose to believe that she just desperately needed to be a mother again. And as much as I wanted that for myself too, as much as I dream of my daughter every single night, the scales have been balanced now. Maybe this was how it was supposed to be for me.' Her eyes were gentle as they met mine. 'I'm only sorry you got caught up in it too.' She shook her head. 'But I've let myself be dragged down for too long by guilt, regret... If I'm not careful, I'll destroy myself. I *have* to let this go and move forward, take back some control of my life. It's the only way I can keep my head above water.'

The words had been like a slap in the face. She'd been the one person who could fathom what I was going through. Ben hadn't carried the baby. With the first two, he had looked upon them as objects of entertainment, cute new fixtures in the home for months until he began to feel any real sense of love for them. He reasoned that he hadn't had nine months getting to know our son as I had, couldn't possibly love him at first sight without the influx of birthing hormones I was privilege to. He'd been sad, he'd cried, raged even, but he didn't get it. Not properly.

And now Maya had somehow come over all saintly, and what? Decided to forgive a woman who'd escaped with her baby, her own flesh and blood, because she was tired of feeling down about it? I couldn't even begin to empathise with her.

I caught my reflection in the mirror over the clock. The once shining brunette bob was now grown out, stringy and greasy, my brown eyes rimmed with permanent dark circles, my cheeks hollow and gaunt, lips cracked and peeling. The reflection fed me – it was what I needed to see. I wanted my pain to be scrawled across my face, needed the evidence of the trauma I'd experienced on display for all to see, written in the creases of my features. To shock people when they witnessed what I'd become.

The outside matched the inside now. I would never again be the woman I'd once been – that image-conscious girl who'd strived to have everyone view me as successful, beautiful… good.

At Elise's third session, she'd looked me dead in the eye and said I was judging her. That I thought I was better than her. She was right. I'd been unable to fathom not just what she'd done, but the way she'd gone about it. I think it had been the pleasure she'd taken in the act that made her different from the others. There had been one hundred and eight separate and very deliberate stab wounds recorded on Harry's body during the post-mortem. I'd asked her about that number, and she'd told me the reason with chilling honesty. One for each day of her daughter's life.

She'd broken into his flat while he was sleeping, handcuffed his wrists and ankles to the bed and tortured him for more than two hours, making sure to save the deepest wounds for last. Some were only an inch or two beneath the surface of the skin. Later, the police had found a search on her phone for the major arteries, deducing that she'd made a conscious effort to miss them until the last possible moment, not letting him die until she'd extracted every last ounce of agony from him. *That* was the part that had made me recoil in disgust. Imagining the stomach she'd have needed to stand over him, soaked in his warm blood, the smell of metal filling her nostrils, hearing him beg for his life, the screams as she jabbed him again and again. That awful smile she'd been photographed with as she walked outside, knowing he was dead.

Elise's crime hadn't been a retaliation brought on by a red mist. It was cold, calculated, and that made her more dangerous, more terrifying than anyone I'd ever met.

She told me I was living in a different world to her, and though I'd given no response, I'd secretly agreed. I had come from a close-knit family who up until recently had still got together for Sunday lunch every week. I'd been a prefect at school. Never got a bad grade, never missed a homework deadline. Never cheated on a boyfriend or taken more than my fair share at the dinner table. I'd been a golden child, thriving on praise, loving the attention that being good brought me. I'd told tales on my friends when they broke the rules and reasoned that it was their own fault in the first place for doing the wrong thing. To me, the world was black and white, right and wrong, and the lines down the middle were uncrossable.

Somehow Elise had seen all this the moment she looked at me. She had judged me too, and in doing so had realised I could never understand what she'd chosen to do to Harry. Was *that* why she'd targeted me? To punish me? To make me finally open my eyes to a world I'd always been protected from? To absorb her pain, feel it become a part of me, burrowing like mites through the marrow of my bones, leaving me no more than a hollow shell, liable to shatter at any moment? Or had it been because she thought I was an easy target? Believed that I would never come after her the way she had Harry?

I stared into my glassy-eyed reflection and wondered if she could have fathomed the monumental mistake she was making.

Because the truth was, she was right. I *had* lived a sheltered life. Hadn't been able to put myself in her shoes, understand how she could do something so grotesque and derive pleasure from it. But now things were different.

I heard Maya's car pull up on the driveway but didn't turn my head. Fury fizzed through my veins, pulsing relentlessly through my body, fuelling me. It never abated. I never grew tired. I had to keep going. I had no doubt I would find her – I wouldn't stop until I did.

I had three private detectives searching for her, and when I finally tracked down my son, what she'd done to Harry would seem like a fucking warm-up compared to what I had planned. I would make her regret the day she'd ever set foot in my office. The moment she'd ever thought she could take my son, *my* baby, and pass him off as her own. And when that time came, I thought, a smile spreading across my taut features, the reflection morphing into a clown mask, the expression false and unnatural on my sallow skin – when I had my son safely out of her grasp, I was going to let her be the first to see the monster she'd created.

And I was going to enjoy it.

A LETTER FROM SAM

I want to say a huge thank you for choosing to read *The Perfect Baby*. If you enjoyed it, and want to keep up to date with all my latest releases, just sign up at the following link. Your email address will never be shared, and you can unsubscribe at any time

www.bookouture.com/sam-vickery

I hope you enjoyed reading *The Perfect Baby* as much as I enjoyed writing it. If you did, I would be very grateful if you could leave a review. I'd love to hear what you think, and it makes such a difference in helping new readers to discover one of my books for the first time.

I always welcome hearing from my readers – you can get in touch at www.samvickery.com, or find me on my Facebook page.

Until the next time,

Sam

www.samvickery.com

 facebook.com/SamVickeryWrites

ACKNOWLEDGEMENTS

I am extremely grateful to everyone who helped bring this book to completion. So many people work behind the scenes, editing, designing, marketing and working their magic to give each book the best possible publication. I am very lucky to have such talented people who I can trust with my story.

To my wonderful editor, Jennifer Hunt, who is always able to envisage the end product, who writes the most compelling taglines and descriptions, and who always has just the right solution to any problem, I am so grateful to you! Thank you! To my wonderful team of editors and proofreaders, Jane Selley, Lauren Finger and Laura Kincaid, thank you! To Sarah Hardy, for all your hard work getting the book into the right hands and helping it be discovered by new readers, thank you. To Aaron Munday, the fantastic designer who came up with such a creepy and eye-catching cover, thank you. To Billi-Dee Jones for being such a wonderful cheerleader when I needed it, thank you. To the whole team at Bookouture, thank you so much for all that you do. I never stop pinching myself that I get to call myself one of you!

To my wonderful readers, new and old, you mean the world to me. Thank you for continuing to buy and recommend my books.

And lastly, to my family, who have to live with me through insomnia, deadlines, frustrations and excitement, thank you for being you and for letting me do the same.

PUBLISHING TEAM

Turning a manuscript into a book requires the efforts of many people. The publishing team at Bookouture would like to acknowledge everyone who contributed to this publication.

Audio
Alba Proko
Sinead O'Connor
Melissa Tran

Commercial
Lauren Morrissette
Hannah Richmond
Imogen Allport

Cover design
Aaron Munday

Data and analysis
Mark Alder
Mohamed Bussuri

Editorial
Jennifer Hunt
Charlotte Hegley

Copyeditor
Jane Selley

Proofreader
Laura Kincaid

Marketing
Alex Crow
Melanie Price
Occy Carr
Cíara Rosney
Martyna Młynarska

Operations and distribution
Marina Valles
Stephanie Straub
Joe Morris

Production
Hannah Snetsinger
Mandy Kullar
Jen Shannon
Ria Clare

Publicity
Kim Nash
Noelle Holten
Jess Readett
Sarah Hardy

Rights and contracts
Peta Nightingale
Richard King
Saidah Graham